THE PATHWAYS TO THE HEART

A Coming-of-Age Anthology

MANDI ELLSWORTH   PAULA KREMSER
E.B. WHEELER

Rowan Ridge
Press

The Pathways to the Heart, second edition, © 2020 Mandi Ellsworth, Paula Kremser, E.B. Wheeler

First printed published by Cedar Fort Media © 2017

Print ISBN 978-1-7321631-7-1

First printing: July 2020

Published by Rowan Ridge Press, Utah

Cover and interior design © Rowan Ridge Press

Front cover photo: Regency woman in cream dress © KathySG

Back cover photo: Cowboy on the trail at sunset © CustomPhotographyDesigns

❁ Created with Vellum

Regency England

The Courtship Cure

PAULA KREMSER

Mary Worthington stood up to take her leave of Mrs. Morris. Even though Mrs. Morris had been ill, she stood, too, out of respect for Mary's position.

"Don't get up on my account," Mary protested. "You know I can see myself out."

Mrs. Morris ignored her, of course. Most of the time her neighbors seemed to forget that Mary was the sister of the Duke of Cheltenham, but there were always these small reminders that they couldn't completely forget to pay her deference.

The sound of screaming from outside pulled their attention to the door. Up until this point, the visit had been calm. They were just finishing their conversation about the trouble Mrs. Morris had with choke weeds in her garden. Now, seven-year-old John Morris ran into the cottage, bringing the screams inside.

John's yells were sincere cries of pain, and he held up his injured arm for his mother and Mary to see. Mary's stomach dropped at the sight of John's arm dangling at an odd angle. Mrs. Morris, likely still weak from her illness, fainted.

Luckily, Mrs. Morris was near a chair and Mary was standing by her. Mary grabbed Mrs. Morris and directed her fall back into the chair. Mary's arm got stuck behind Mrs. Morris, and it took several tugs before she was finally free. Immediately, she directed her attention to John.

He was holding his obviously broken arm with his other hand and his screaming hadn't abated one bit. John's older brother, Samuel, came in the cottage behind him. Mary raised her voice to be heard over John's screams and asked, "Samuel, what happened to John?"

Samuel looked scared and he visibly swallowed before answering, "He fell off the roof of the cowshed."

Mary raised her eyebrows. "Why was he on the roof of the cowshed?"

Samuel looked at the ground but finally admitted, "He followed me up there."

Mary barely heard him, but really, the reason didn't matter at the moment; John would need a doctor. "Samuel, John's arm is broken. You need to fetch Doctor Milner."

Looking even more worried now, Samuel asked, "But isn't the doctor away?"

Mary was leading John to the window seat, but she stopped and turned around as she remembered. "Oh, yes. I had forgotten that Doctor Milner left. But he said he would get another doctor to come stay while he's away. Run to his house and see if someone is there."

Mary turned back to John and led him gently to the shabby, flat cushions in the window seat. She put a pillow behind him and helped him lie down. She took a close look at his bent arm, and a strange sensation prickled along her scalp. Mary could understand why the sight of it had caused his mother to faint. As gently as she could, she helped him steady his arm against his chest. Once that was done, his cries quieted a bit. It was then that Mrs. Morris revived and opened her eyes.

After fanning herself with her hand several times, she said, "Oh Mary, what happened?"

Mary thought it might have been easier if Mrs. Morris had just stayed unconscious, because she now had two patients to tend to, and when she left John's side, he began to cry in anguish again.

Mrs. Morris stood up, but her color wasn't good, and Mary worried she would just faint again. "Mrs. Morris, I think John's arm is broken."

The woman's eyes widened and she looked unsteady once again.

Mary quickly supported her with a hand under her elbow.

"What should we do?" asked Mrs. Morris.

Keeping her voice calm and reassuring, Mary replied, "I've already sent Samuel for the doctor. There is nothing for you to worry about now. Perhaps you should lie down on your bed. You've been ill, and I'm here to look after John."

Mrs. Morris looked at John's broken arm for a short moment and looked away again quickly. "Yes, if you really don't mind, Mary, I'll take your advice. I'm feeling very dizzy."

Mary found it odd sometimes that her neighbors took her advice so readily, even about things she knew nothing about. This was a situation where being the sister of a duke certainly wasn't going to help her; she'd have to rely on her own abilities.

Mrs. Morris left the room, and Mary moved over to John's side once more and studied his arm. Honestly, if Doctor Milner hadn't found a replacement for while he was away, it could be many hours before a doctor could be fetched, and she couldn't just leave John's poor arm like that. She had seen a servant with a broken arm once and had seen the splint, so she knew that it needed to heal straight.

Mary thought about it for a moment before jumping up and foraging in Mrs. Morris's kitchen. She found two of Mrs. Morris's longest wooden kitchen utensils and placed them on either side of John's arm.

In her most reassuring voice, she said, "John, you are being so brave."

The tears continued to squeeze out the corners of his eyes and leave trails down to the pillow, belying Mary's words.

She left the utensils in place and pulled the ties off her bonnet as she continued, "I'm just going to steady your arm for a moment. Try to stay as still as possible. It might hurt a bit, but surely not as much as falling off the cowshed."

John screamed louder for a brief moment as Mary adjusted his arm, but he quieted quickly this time, and Mary was relieved to see his arm looking quite straight again. She wrapped the ties around his arm as gently as she could and secured them. Once that was done, she distracted John with cool drinks of water, raisins, and stories while they waited for Samuel to return with a doctor.

Doctor Walter Tyndale was all too happy to put down his book at the urgent knocking at the door. When a lad was shown in and explained his purpose, it was just as Walter had hoped. The young man had come to request help for his brother, who had broken his arm.

Walter tried not to smile at the news, pleased as he was for the opportunity to use his skills once more. Walter was a baronet now, no longer a practicing doctor, but when Doctor Milner, the doctor in Aldwickbury, had left for Bath for his own health, he had contacted Walter and asked him to take on the responsibility of caring for the village in his absence. Walter had been happy to. He had called on some of Doctor Milner's patients this week, but so far, none of them had needed him. At last, here was an opportunity to help someone by using his skills.

Walter immediately sent to have his horse saddled and grabbed the few things he would need and put them in his bag. The servant was ready with the horse saddled by the time Walter reached the front gate. After mounting his horse, he reached a hand down for the boy who had come to fetch him and helped him up to sit on the back of his saddle. He asked questions as they went and found the lad reluctant to answer, but Walter was finally able to discover that his younger brother had fallen off a roof.

"How do you know his arm is broken?" Walter asked.

"It was bent sort of strange, sir," the boy replied. "Besides, Mary said it was broken."

"Mary?" Walter questioned.

"She was there helping Mum today."

Walter had assumed from the lad's appearance that the family didn't have servants, but perhaps this was a girl who just came a day or two a week.

The boy directed Walter to his house. After dismounting, he realized there was nowhere to tie up his horse, so he ended up wrapping the reins around a hedge and just hoped his horse would stay put.

As he crossed the threshold into the small cottage, Walter's eyes adjusted to the dim interior. He quickly spotted his patient lying near a window. A young woman with a concerned expression was leaning over the little boy, smoothing his hair back. She stood up and moved out of the way when she noticed Walter.

Moving further into the room, Walter took the recently vacated seat next to the patient. As he leaned over to examine the boy, he was surprised by what he saw. The broken arm had been set with a spoon and a spatula secured to his arm with the floral ties from a bonnet. In wonder, he turned to look at the girl who had stood and moved back when he entered the room.

"Did you set the boy's arm?" he asked incredulously.

She was watching him with her back against the wall and her arms folded. She licked her lips nervously. "I straightened it. Is that what you mean?"

Walter nodded and gestured to the spoon and spatula holding the boy's arm straight, "I've never seen it done quite like this before."

Walter's comment seemed to make her even more anxious and she said, "I wasn't certain that Samuel would be able to find a doctor. If I had known you would arrive so quickly, I would have left the job to you."

Walter wished the job had been left to him, but he couldn't fault her work. "It's fine. I'll just replace your splints with mine."

Walter opened his bag and found the splints that he would use. They were small and made from cedar and had a slight curvature that would allow them to contour to the arm to hold it in place better than the handles of utensils. Walter worked carefully to undo the home-made splints. To his surprise, the young woman came right over to kneel next to him and began very gently helping as well. She took away the homemade splints and then was back at his side while he wrapped the injured arm with gauze.

When he set the new splints next to the boy's arm, she seemed to notice that it was a two-man job and asked, "May I help?"

Walter could do it alone, but it certainly would be easier with an extra pair of hands. "Can you hold the splints steady?"

She nodded and moved her hands into place as he pulled his away. The touch of their hands caused him to lose a bit of focus; her skin was quite warm compared to the little boy's. He pulled the wide leather straps from his case and began securing the splints. It would have been much easier if he hadn't been trying so hard to avoid contact again.

While they worked, Walter stole glances at the young woman who had taken care of his patient before he could arrive. He was quickly realizing his assumptions about this girl being a servant were probably not quite accurate. She spoke well, and as he really looked at her for the first time, he noticed that while her dress didn't look new, the material was quality. Her features were beyond what one normally came across. Her skin was smooth perfection and her brown hair shown even in the dim cottage. A few messy curls hung over her shoulder with a few more framing her face. He couldn't quite catch the color of her eyes in the dim cottage, but he could tell they were accentuated with a look of concern as she watched his patient squirming. Finally, the splints were secured and Walter was happy with the result.

The boy looked over at her and asked pitifully, "Mary, can I have another drink of water?"

"Of course, John," she replied with affection in her voice.

It was clear to Walter now that the girl must be a kind neighbor or relative. Her family was probably better off than the Morrises, but far below his own social standing, especially since he had been awarded his baronetcy. Still, he was intrigued by her capability for one so young. He was curious about who she was and how she was related to the Morrises. Walter helped John sit up gently and fitted him for the sling that he had brought with him. Finished with his patient now and hoping to find out more about Mary, he started up another conversation.

"So, are you in charge of these boys, then?"

She started back in surprise at his question and even pointed to herself and asked, "Me? No, I'm not in charge of these boys."

Even though she was surprised by his question, he didn't think she seemed offended, but still he apologized. "I'm sorry, I just assumed you must be minding the boys since I haven't seen their parents."

"Oh, er, Mr. Morris is out working, I suppose." Walter thought she looked a little uncomfortable at reporting the whereabouts of the Morrises to him, as if she wasn't sure she had the authority. "And Mrs. Morris, well, she fainted when she saw John's arm. I don't think she typically would have fainted, but she's just recovered from being ill all week and is still regaining her strength."

"Mrs. Morris has been ill?" Walter asked, trying not to feel put out that she had recovered without any help from him, while he had sat around Doctor Milner's empty house all week wishing he could be useful.

"She's had a fever and complained of quite a severe headache, but I've been here to see her every day."

So that's why he hadn't been called, Walter realized. "Perhaps I should check on her now, since I'm here." He hated that he sounded like he was asking for her permission. He should have phrased it differently.

She looked a bit hesitant, as if she didn't want to turn her patient over to his care. "I'll see if she'd like that." She went to a back room but came back almost immediately and reported, "Mrs. Morris is asleep. I think she was feeling better this morning and tried to do too much and has worn herself out."

Walter would probably have given the same diagnosis if he'd been given the chance. Doctor Milner hadn't warned him about a girl named Mary who seemed to be his unofficial apprentice. "I'll check on her tomorrow when I come back to see how John here is doing," Walter said, making it definitive this time, rather than asking for her permission. "Are there any other patients that you've been seeing to that might need my care?" Walter hoped that didn't sound as petulant as he felt.

She thought for a moment, looking completely unsuspicious that he was annoyed with her, then said, "Mr. Dunfee has a hacking cough that just won't go away. Dr. Milner recommended cold yarrow tea several times a day before he left. When I saw Mr. Dunfee on Monday, he thought it was helping a bit."

"I wonder why he recommended cold tea. It would surely loosen his cough better if the tea was hot."

Walter had just been musing to himself, but Mary answered anyway. "I suggested the same thing to Mr. Dunfee when I visited him yesterday," she said. Walter could hear the satisfaction in her voice that their opinions had coincided. "And I brought him honey, too, because I think it helps as well, don't you?"

Of course, both those things would help. Walter had one or two other remedies that could help with hacking cough, but this girl had already used the first recommendations he would have given.

Walter couldn't keep himself from saying, "Dr. Milner never mentioned he had an apprentice."

Mary looked at him for a long moment before comprehending his meaning. "Oh, you mean me?"

Walter just nodded.

"I'm not Dr. Milner's apprentice," she exclaimed.

"You seem to have several patients in your care and even a well-trained physician couldn't have set John's arm better with what you had on hand."

"You really think I did a good job?" she asked, looking as though she was holding back a smile.

Walter hadn't meant it as a compliment as much as a complaint. He had been so bored in this tiny village with no one needing him. Seeing her delight at being praised, he dropped his defensive tone a bit when he added, "Certainly. Setting a broken bone requires strong nerves and presence of mind. I've seen it done poorly, so I definitely know when it's been done right."

The girl bit her lip shyly at his words, then a brief smiled appeared which she quickly repressed. Finally, she smiled in earnest and it lit up her whole face. Even the room seemed brighter.

Walter couldn't bring himself to complain about her taking all his patients. She looked so pleased to be told she was good at caring for them, as if a compliment was a rare thing. He wondered what her home life was like. She was well-spoken enough that she must be educated, but her accent and tone were the same as the few other people he had met here in the village.

Walter gave John a dose of laudanum to help with the pain. He gave a few instructions to John and his brother Samuel and reminded them that he would be back tomorrow. Mary walked out of the house with him and waited while he pulled his reins from the hedge. Walter asked her for directions to Mr. Dunfee's home, and she pointed as she directed him.

"Follow along the hedge until you go up the second hill: the big one. Vintner Lane will be on the right. It's not marked, but as you look down the lane, you'll see that it curves quickly out of sight to the left, so you'll know you're on Vintner. Then the Dunfees are the second gate you come to. Their gate is rusted and difficult to swing open at the moment, so if you continue about twenty yards past their gate, you'll come to a stile where you can tie your horse and easily step over, then double back."

Walter raised his eyebrows at her detailed description.

He climbed on his horse and set off, but turned back once. He was expecting to see her walking back towards the house, but she just stood by the hedge watching him, as if she were taking note of every detail about him so she could repeat it back later. She didn't look the least concerned to be caught watching him, but Walter quickly turned back around.

The next morning, Mary was up with jittery excitement for the day ahead. The new doctor would be back to check on John Morris, and Mary had decided that she would be at the Morrises when he came.

She usually practiced the pianoforte in the morning, then she would typically read for several hours or paint or embroider. She nearly always visited neighbors in the afternoon and then was home again in time for dinner. A typical schedule wouldn't be possible today. Mary couldn't concentrate on music or reading. She didn't know what time the doctor planned to visit John Morris, and she wouldn't risk missing him. When she woke up this morning, she had recalled his handsome face, and her heart started racing. The expression in his brown eyes when he had looked at her was something she wanted to see again.

After she was dressed and had her hair arranged, she went through the corridor, down the grand staircase, turned and walked to the back of the house, then down the servants stairs to the kitchen to collect a basket of food for her visit to the Morris family. She was about to run out the door when she thought that a picture book from the library would be a useful thing to bring, so John wouldn't be too bored while confined to his bed. She hurried back up the stairs toward the front of the house and walked behind the grand staircase to the library. Unfortunately, the library was where she ran into her brother, Oliver.

Mary was quite startled to see him but managed to nearly hide it as she said, "Oh, hello ... Oliver."

It had always been a little hard for Mary to use her brother's first name. Oliver was twelve years older than her and had already been away at school for several years when she was born. Since their grandfather passed away last year, Oliver had taken over the title of the Duke of Cheltenham. Now she was the only person she knew of who called him Oliver. All the servants referred to him as 'Your Grace,' and that's how Mary thought of him.

"Mary," he acknowledged her. He apparently looked at her long enough to notice her bonnet, because he asked, "Where are you off to so early? I thought you weren't allowed out to socialize." The question was a bit mocking. Oliver had always been critical of how Grandfather had isolated Mary from society.

"I'm visiting John Morris, who broke his arm yesterday," Mary quickly replied.

"I should have assumed it was a charitable visit," he said with a knowing smirk, making Mary feel like she was the one who was receiving charity rather than giving it.

Changing the subject, Mary said, "I didn't even know you were here. Did you arrive last night?"

Oliver had a house in London and more than one estate in the country, but Cheltenham Manor was Oliver's primary holding and the only home Mary had ever known.

"Yes, I arrived quite late. I've been wanting to come out to the country to do some shooting, and there was something I wanted to speak to you about anyway."

"Really?" Mary asked. This was the first time he'd ever come with even half a purpose of seeing her as far as she could recall. Oliver gestured for her to take a seat in front of his desk.

Once she was sitting, he began, "I spoke to my solicitor last week and he brought to my attention that your portion in the funds has done quite well, and you will probably be much sought after. It hadn't really occurred to me before."

Mary took a moment to work out what he was talking about. Finally, she realized that when he said "portion in the funds" he was referring to money.

Feeling startled, she asked, "When you say 'sought after,' do you mean ... for marriage?"

Oliver rolled his eyes, and she wished she had kept her question to herself. "Of course that's what I mean," he replied as if his infinite supply of patience was almost used up. "You should have a come-out ball."

That wasn't what Grandfather had wanted for her.

Putting up her most logical protest, she said, "We can't have a ball; we're still in mourning."

"Grandfather died nearly a year ago."

Mary certainly didn't want to mark the anniversary of his death with a ball. She stared at Oliver for a long moment. She was surprised that he was taking any interest in her at all. If his solicitor hadn't mentioned it, she thought it would have been several more years before he thought to try to marry her off.

Oliver interrupted her thoughts by asking, "Are you eighteen yet?"

"I'll be twenty in June," Mary responded.

"Really?" Oliver seemed genuinely surprised. "I'll have Jensen plan the come-out ball right away. We'll do it at the Mayfair house in London in... two weeks."

"I won't know anyone," Mary protested. "Who will even come?" Though it was less than a half a day's journey, Mary had never even been to London.

Oliver chuckled, and Mary felt ignorant as he replied, "I'm the Duke of Cheltenham and I almost never host a party. Trust me, it will be a crush."

Mary couldn't imagine much pleasure out of a night of meeting endless new people who were really only interested in fawning over her brother. "Oliver, I'm not sure this will work. I've never even learned to dance."

Oliver huffed a sigh of exasperation and muttered under his breath, "What could Grandfather have been thinking?" Then louder he said, "Let's make it three weeks, and I'll hire a dance instructor for you."

"It's not just the dancing," she protested. "I won't know how to talk to anyone."

Mary didn't see this as a fault, but Oliver did. Grandfather had very intentionally shielded Mary from high society, and Mary knew Oliver had always disapproved.

He looked at her shrewdly for a moment as if considering whether or not that was a valid reason. But in the end he discounted it. "You have 50,000 pounds, and you are the sister of a duke." He paused briefly as he looked her up and down as if seeing her for the first time. "And you're not bad looking, I suppose. It shouldn't matter that you are lacking in social graces. With all your other advantages, what you lack will be politely overlooked."

Mary had always been a little intimidated by Oliver, so they didn't interact much. If she thought his opinion was right, she would have quickly agreed to have a come-out ball and already made her escape. She knew that introducing her into society was a bad idea, though.

"But why must I have a come-out ball at all? Can't I just go on as I have always done and live here on my own?"

"That won't work. I'm planning to marry within the year, and it would be easier to set up a bride at Cheltenham Manor without a little sister here. Especially one who insists on being so unsociable."

Mary let out a huff of air at the insult. She socialized plenty, just not with people Oliver approved of. Oliver wasn't paying attention to her. He just continued on, "If Grandfather had had any wits, he would have brought you up a lady and then every eligible gentleman in the aristocracy would be tripping over himself trying to marry you." The very thought made Mary glad that her grandfather had shielded her from such ridiculousness. "The old man is gone now, and I won't have you living in this eccentric way any longer."

Oliver's words seemed final. They were disrespectful, too. Their grandfather may have shunned society in his later years, but he had still been a duke.

After considering the matter for several silent moments, Mary finally decided to just go along with it. It didn't really matter anyway. It would just be one night at a ball, and when Oliver saw how inept she was in society in general and at attracting gentleman in particular, he would give up on the idea of marrying her off to someone in the aristocracy.

"Very well, Oliver."

She stood up to leave and perhaps Oliver sensed that she was just placating him because in parting he said, "You'll have to make a considerable effort over the next few weeks so you don't embarrass both of us. I'm confident that once you come out, you'll have marriage offers, and we will take the best one."

Mary acknowledged his words with a nod of her head and left the room, annoyed that he was so determined to get her married off.

Mary tried to put all thoughts of a come-out ball out of her mind as she walked the two miles over to Aldwickbury. She distracted herself instead by thinking about the new doctor. If he could be at her come-out ball, perhaps she would actually enjoy it. But it wasn't possible. Even though she didn't have much experience in high society, she knew that as the sister of a duke, she wouldn't be allowed to make a match with a country doctor. The thought led to one that she'd never really entertained before: that perhaps Grandfather *had* been wrong to keep her isolated from her peers.

Mary had never heard her grandfather say it in words, but she knew he had always disapproved of the way Oliver had been brought up, and Oliver had always disapproved of the way Mary was brought up. As half-siblings, they had different mothers. Oliver's mother had lived until he was ten, then at her death, he had been sent away to school. Mary's mother had died at her birth and she didn't remember her father; she had been only one when he died. Grandfather had raised her.

As Mary was growing up, she noticed that after Oliver visited, Grandfather's spirits would be low for several days. One time at dinner after a visit from Oliver, her grandfather had said, "Mary, high society is poison for a good soul." Mary had known he was referring to her brother but hadn't known how to respond. "It's always been that way," he had continued. "But the youth today are far worse than when I was a young man. This is why I'm handling your education. I don't want your benevolent nature spoiled by them."

"I'm not benevolent," Mary had protested. At the time she had confused the meanings of benevolent and belligerent.

Grandfather had smiled indulgently at her. "Of course, you are, and to make sure you continue so, tomorrow your maid will take you on a charitable visit to Aldwickbury so you can visit those who are less fortunate."

Mary hadn't cared one way or another about the charity, she had just been excited about the visit. Being brought up as isolated as she was, she was always desperate for people. The next day, she had carried a basket of necessities and walked with her maid into Aldwickbury to meet some of her poor neighbors for the first time. Her maid hadn't been happy to have the assignment and had hurried Mary along. It had instantly become Mary's favorite time of day. She had easily convinced the maid to let her go alone from then on. She loved talking and was finally able to socialize to her heart's content. Sometimes, she could play with other children, but she had loved asking the grown-ups all sorts of questions, too.

The visits to Aldwickbury changed in her early teenage years. She realized the differences between her circumstances and those of the families in the village. She made every effort to make sure that her visits didn't feel like charity, but her consciousness of it made a change that she couldn't undo: she felt like an outsider.

Then Grandfather's death last year had put her on more equal footing with her friends in the village once more. She visited them because she needed their comfort. Even though she always had her basket with her, full of her charitable offerings, she knew she was receiving more than she was giving. The neighbors she visited were her friends now, but these weren't the types of friends who hosted dinner parties or went for rides in the park, so Mary didn't ever see them outside of her visits.

Feeling that she was part of the village was different from actually being part of it, as Oliver's visit this morning so aptly reminded her. She would have to marry someone who was worthy, according to Oliver, of the sister of a duke. This is where Grandfather had made a mistake. She wouldn't fit in with her peers, but if Oliver persisted, she would have to choose a husband from among them.

She would never be allowed to choose someone like the handsome new doctor. But their brief encounter yesterday made her wish she was the sister of a farmer rather than the sister of a duke.

She had noticed right away that his features were perfectly handsome, but more than that, his countenance had been open and pleasing. Her fancy had been really caught when he had looked at her with admiration. He had been impressed with how useful she had been with John and the other neighbors. Each time she had mentioned something else she had done to care for someone, he looked more and more surprised. She wanted to impress him again. She wanted that heady feeling she had experienced when he had looked at her that way, which was the point of her arriving early with the intention of staying at the Morrises house all day if she had to.

When Mrs. Morris let her in, Mary was happy to see that her friend was looking much better today.

"Hello, Mrs. Morris. How is John this morning?" Mary glanced to the window seat, but it was empty.

"He's been quite uncomfortable and didn't sleep well." Mrs. Morris went on to describe the rough night they'd had, and that John had really only been able to fall asleep finally a few short hours ago and was still in his bed.

Mary thought about it and wondered what the new doctor would recommend. After his praise from yesterday, she wished she knew what to do and could attend to John before he arrived.

Mrs. Morris turned the subject to her gratitude as Mary handed over the basket. "Mary, you were so helpful yesterday. I still can't believe I fainted. What would I have done without you?"

Mary smiled more genuinely than she typically did when accepting gratitude. Mrs. Morris really had needed her yesterday. It was wonderful.

"Speaking of helping," she said as she reached into the basket that Mrs. Morris was now holding and pulled out sturdy work gloves. "I brought these with me to help with those choke weeds in your garden."

"I shouldn't let you do that." Mrs. Morris looked worried at the suggestion.

"Of course you should. I'm sure John will need your attention, and you certainly won't have time to weed the garden anytime soon. Besides, I have my own little garden at home that I weed all the time." Mrs. Morris looked at her strangely for a moment. To clarify, Mary added, "It's just a small side garden with flowers. I couldn't take care of all the grounds at Cheltenham Manor on my own." Mary didn't think this next part would go over too well, but she needed Mrs. Morris' help, so she went ahead and said, "You could in turn help me."

"How could I help you?" Mrs. Morris asked, clearly thinking it wasn't possible.

"The new doctor who was here yesterday," she said and Mrs. Morris nodded. "Well, he doesn't know that I am the sister of the Duke of Cheltenham. You and I know how little that means," Mary said in a confiding tone. "But the doctor is an outsider and is unlikely to understand. He let me help him yesterday, and I can't even tell you how much I loved it. I thought I might try to convince him when he comes to check on John to let me tag along on his other visits. If he knows who I am it will ruin my chance."

Mrs. Morris looked at her with a suspicious smile. "You want to go along on his visits because you like visiting patients? Or is it because you fancy the doctor?"

It was both, but Mary wouldn't answer that. "Visiting patients, of course," she replied, hopefully with a straight face.

Mrs. Morris raised her eyebrows and Mary shrugged.

Mrs. Morris' smile became a knowing grin. "You get an awfully dreamy look on your face at the thought of visiting patients."

Mary dropped her arms in an exasperated gesture. How was she so transparent? "You didn't even meet the doctor yesterday. He could be sixty with grey hair growing out of his ears for all you know."

Mary was basically describing Dr. Milner. Before she met Dr. Tyndale, she had assumed all doctors looked like him. Dr. Tyndale, however, was young and didn't have any physical flaws that Mary had spotted. His brown hair was neatly trimmed. From his eyebrows which had risen several times during their conversation yesterday to his perfect grin that she had spotted as he was leaving, he was a pleasure to look at.

"If he is, I'll question your choice in men," Mrs. Morris responded. "You might enjoy visiting patients, but I'd wager this new doctor is the real reason you want to go along."

"Either way, the fact that my brother is a duke will ruin it for me. Could you please just not tell him?"

"Lying doesn't seem like the best way to go about this, Mary," Mrs. Morris said, dropping her teasing tone.

"We won't have to lie," Mary quickly reassured her. "There is no need for introductions because I met Dr. Tyndale yesterday. He knows my name is Mary and that I am your neighbor. Those things are both true. If he asks you anything specifically, I would expect you to tell the truth, of course. But if he doesn't ask, then there's no reason to bring it up."

"You are strange, Mary, you do realize that? If I were the sister of a duke, everyone would know it, and you certainly wouldn't see me pulling weeds out of the garden. I blame your grandfather."

Mary took that as Mrs. Morris' agreement. "I give him all the blame and all the credit for how strange I am. Just help me keep Dr. Tyndale from realizing it, and I'll be so far in your debt, I'll probably still be weeding your garden when I'm sixty with hairy ears."

Walter decided to check on John Morris sooner rather than later the next day. As he trained to become a doctor, Walter had thought that he would have ample opportunity to help people. His short career as a physician had come to an abrupt end when he had been on hand to save the Prince Regent's cousin's life less than a year ago. He had prevented what everyone had thought was certain death, and the Prince Regent had awarded him with a baronetcy as a result.

Walter's social status had been decidedly low as a boy, but then his father had made good money in trade. As a result, Walter had been a late addition to his class at Eton when he was fourteen and then had gone on to Cambridge. He could have chosen a more lucrative career, but a doctor was what he had wanted to be, and his superior education had made it so he could be a good one. Having been educated with future dukes and earls, but always far beneath them, it was strange when his new baronetcy had resulted in him being given a small holding just north of London.

His father couldn't have been more pleased. He had always wanted Walter to live the life of a gentleman and aspire to more. His father had ambitions for Walter that were far beyond what Walter had for himself. With his new baronetcy, he had been admitted to clubs and invited into the society he had always been just on the periphery of. Still, all these months later, it didn't feel like he fit in his new role.

Everyone, especially his father, had assumed the advancement meant he would no longer practice his physician's trade. Walter had assumed the same, of course. He had more responsibilities now, both in society and with his newly acquired property. This was why it was such a gift to be able to help people as a physician once more. It was so satisfying to start his day by checking on a patient, *his* patient.

As he passed the hedge in front of the Morris' cottage, he was startled out of his thoughts by a movement to his left. He jumped back in surprise, and the person who had startled him looked up. It was the same young woman from yesterday, Mary. She was busy pulling weeds from the garden but when she caught sight of him, she quickly stood up.

"Hello," she said. "Are you here to check on John?" When Walter nodded she continued, "I'll come in with you. He was sleeping when I arrived earlier, so I haven't had a chance to ask him how he's doing, but Mrs. Morris said he didn't sleep well in the night."

Walter let himself smile. Maybe she was trying to take over his work as a doctor, but he could see that she also genuinely wanted to be useful. She seemed very chatty and stayed by his side as they crossed the threshold into the cottage.

Mrs. Morris greeted him with a broad smile. "I didn't expect you to be so young, and with such nice ears."

Walter reached up and touched one of his ears. What a strange thing to notice about him. Before he could think of any reply, Mary redirected his attention to John, and Walter walked over to where he was lying for the examination. Walter checked the boy over quickly, trying to disturb his arm as little as possible. The bruising today was significant, but Walter was fairly confident John would have an easy recovery as far as broken bones went. He gave Mrs. Morris more laudanum and instructed her to give John a spoonful at bedtime to help him sleep better but to use it sparingly.

There really was nothing else to do. Walter was about to reluctantly take his leave, when Mrs. Morris said, "Doctor, don't you think Mary is looking a bit peaked?"

He hadn't thought that at all, but he turned his attention to her and looked with more attention now. If she were peaked, she would have been pale and unhealthy looking. He thought she looked the opposite. He couldn't honestly say she was anything but healthy. She was certainly giving Mrs. Morris a strange look.

"Are you unwell?" he asked Mary.

She looked back at him, but before she could answer, Mrs. Morris did. "Her face is flushed and she looks ready to collapse from all the hard work she's been doing. The best thing for her would be a nice walk in the fresh air." Walter couldn't understand what Mrs. Morris was getting at with all the contradictions. He looked at her expectantly for a moment.

Finally, Mrs. Morris said, "She should accompany you to your next patient."

Walter would have liked that, but instead, he admitted, "I don't have another patient to visit."

Mrs. Morris said, "Miss Westerlee is always sick. You should visit her and take Mary with you to show you the way."

Walter turned to Mary and said, "I would be happy to have you come along."

Mary was trying to communicate something to Mrs. Morris with pursed lips and wide eyes. She quickly schooled her expression, and said, "Yes, let's go."

She hurried out the door as if she was trying to let Mrs. Morris have her way before she could say anything else.

This was just the opportunity Walter had wanted, but he could never have orchestrated it so well. He had been thinking a lot about Mary since yesterday. He wanted to get to know her better.

Once they were away from the cottage, Walter said, "In my hurry to look after John yesterday, I don't think we were properly introduced."

Mary glanced at him with a frightened expression in her eyes for a brief instant and then looked down quickly. She blinked several times. He knew she wasn't shy, so Walter quickly realized his mistake. He felt terrible for making her feel like she had breached etiquette. Brought up in this small village, it was unlikely that proper introductions were ever necessary.

"The fault is mine, entirely," he tried to reassure her. "I'm Walter Tyndale," he said, intentionally leaving out his title from his name. When his words went unanswered, he added, "Mrs. Morris called you 'Mary,' didn't she?"

She looked up at him with a quick glance. "Yes. That's right." She almost looked relieved that he had taken the introduction out of her hands. "I'm Mary."

Walter wanted to kick himself. Obviously she didn't know how to do an introduction. Walter wouldn't make her feel uncomfortable again by trying to correct her and ask for her full name. "Well, Miss Mary, it's a pleasure to meet you."

"Nice to meet you too." Her face was partially turned away but Walter thought he could see a pleased smile on her lips and a slight blush on her cheeks.

Walter asked her some questions about this Miss Westerlee they were about to visit and was impressed again by her knowledge.

"Do you often visit patients with Dr. Milner?" he asked.

She shook her head. "I think you must have quite the wrong impression of me. I don't even know Dr. Milner all that well."

"How is it that you know so much about all his patients?"

"I just know the families in the village. If they've been ill, then I stop to see them more often to try to help. Dr. Milner has occasionally been there at the same time as me, but not too often."

That was different from what Walter had expected. He questioned why Mary didn't need to hurry home. She seemed like such a useful girl, he wondered why her family didn't rely on her. Perhaps she was one of a large family that didn't notice her absence as she spent her days visiting her neighbors.

"Do you have an impressive family?" he asked.

Mary's sharp look made him wonder if he had asked the very question she was embarrassed to answer. "My family?" she asked, and Walter just nodded. Her brows were drawn together as she considered his question and finally she responded, "My family is not impressive, actually." He thought he heard her whisper under her breath, "Not to me anyway," but it definitely wasn't meant for him to hear.

He realized she had probably misinterpreted his question. But really, she had given him more information than he had even asked for. An unimpressive family. Even if she had come from an affluent family in the village, Walter's father would still be unimpressed. With his new baronetcy, his father expected him to marry a lady, not a tenant farmer's daughter. Walter wouldn't think about marriage much except that his father had ambitions for him and pressured him constantly to aim high in that regard. It didn't stop his interest in Mary, though.

"Does your family not miss you when you're away from home all day?" he asked.

"No." She paused for a moment as if considering the idea for the first time. She didn't sound sad, but rather factual as she added, "No, I'm certainly not missed."

Walter was surprised that this vibrant girl was not missed. She had lovely brown hair that shown in the sunlight since she was carrying her bonnet, a different one than the one she had used the strings from yesterday to tie John's splints. Her skin was the color of cream, but with a tint of pink as an undertone that accentuated her cheekbones, and her cheekbones, in turn, accentuated her eyes, which he couldn't quite catch the color of. They were either green or blue, but walking side by side as they were, he couldn't get a close enough look to tell. She had a mourning band on her sleeve, and he decided he had been prying already, he might as well ask about it too.

"May I ask why you are in mourning?"

She glanced down at the band on her arm and then her eyes met his gaze, long enough for him to notice that her eyes were green and sad. "My grandfather died last year. It still feels very recent, but it's time to come out of mourning, actually."

"I'm sorry to bring up such a sad subject."

"Actually, I've been thinking about my grandfather a bit already today. I do miss him. I was in his care for as long as I can remember."

Walter added this to the image of her home life he was creating in his mind. Perhaps she was the youngest of a large brood and had been often left in the care of her grandfather while everyone else was busy. "So, the two of you were close then?"

"We were close. I've always been proud of that because he didn't let many people close to him." Walter saw her smile at the fond memory. Then as he watched her face, the smile dropped and was replaced by a concerned look with her eyebrows drawn down. "He had eccentric ideas and I always thought they were right before. But now, I'm not so sure."

"What kind of eccentric ideas?"

"Well, for instance, he didn't like balls and assemblies, so I've never learned how to dance. I didn't care before, but now my brother is pushing me to learn." She made a face at the idea of it. "I wonder if I had learned, if I could have attended some of the local assemblies. Instead, not knowing has kept me rather isolated."

Walter was surprised that she hadn't even attended the local dances. Everyone except servants attended those. "You've missed out on everything? Just because your grandfather didn't like dances?"

"Maybe he didn't care about the dancing one way or another, but it was just people he didn't like," Mary mused.

"Even on our short acquaintance, it's hard to imagine a relative of yours that doesn't like people."

Mary shrugged and smiled. "I know he had his reasons. He was disillusioned at some point and became reclusive, but he never spoke of it, so I don't know the particulars."

"So now he's gone, you're thinking about breaking from his ideas."

"Something like that," she said. "I've never had to worry about impressing anyone here, but my brother cares a lot more about impressing his peers. Now that he's pushing me to be social, I can see that it's going to be uncomfortable for me. If I'm to fit in, I guess I don't have a choice."

Walter could understand that sentiment well enough. It was at a much higher level than she was speaking of. He was a titled gentleman now but didn't feel like he belonged in the high society he found himself now a part of. It was strange to him that for the first time in his life he seemed to have found a person with whom he could converse with as an equal, and he didn't even know exactly where she fit into society.

At least she wasn't a servant. Given the area, her family was most likely farmers. He was disappointed that she wasn't a lady that he could court, but he hadn't expected it anyway. At least there was one advantage of her not being a fine, upper class lady. They could enjoy this walk without a lady's maid or a groom along as a chaperone.

They were in the main part of the village. Mary led him to a door in a long row of houses and knocked.

After Walter heard Mrs. Morris say that Miss Westerlee was always sick, he worried she might be the kind of trying patient who always fancies herself ill. After meeting her, he realized that, this time at least, her complaints were genuine. She was nauseous and within a few minutes of their entering, she needed a bucket. Mary held it for her, and Walter assumed this wasn't the first time Mary had helped Miss Westerlee in such a way. Walter administered the remedies he had with him while Mary rinsed the bucket outside, swept the floor, and brought Miss Westerlee a clean handkerchief. He was realizing more and more the value of an assistant.

Mary was almost too eager to help. When Miss Westerlee was in the middle of asking Mary something about a manor house, Mary interrupted her asking, "Are you about to be sick again?" Then she rushed over with the bucket and put it right up in Miss Westerlee's face, saying, "Don't talk now you poor thing." They had been preparing to depart, but Mary turned to him and said, "I'll stay a bit longer since she's likely to need my help again soon."

Miss Westerlee looked more surprised than sick just then, but Mary was certainly prepared to do whatever was required and then some. It was a good thing, really, because Walter had to go to London tomorrow. He'd rather visit patients with Mary again, but he had promised to meet with his friend Joseph who needed help with his estate. Before meeting Mary, he had been looking forward to a break from his monotonous days in Dr. Milner's house. Now, at least he knew Mary would be there to look after anyone who might need help.

"Perhaps you could check on John for me tomorrow," Walter suggested as he prepared to leave.

"You won't be checking on him? Do you have other patients you're seeing tomorrow?" she asked.

"I have to leave for London in the morning. I'll be back the following day. I'm sure the boy would prefer your ministrations to mine, anyway." He wasn't just saying it to flatter her. He truly thought she was skilled at caring for those in need.

For some reason that he couldn't quite put his finger on, Mary was a bit of an oddity here in this village. She reminded Walter of himself when he had been at Eton. No one had disputed his right to be there, but he had never really fit in. Mary seemed to not quite fit in, either. Although it was different, he couldn't say quite how. It was this sense that she belonged here in this village but was an outsider too that made Walter feel like he understood her.

He was fairly certain that he liked Mary. Far more than he should. Enough that he thought he would probably disregard her social status and pursue her anyway. She's the type of girl he would have pursued if his father hadn't become wealthy and he hadn't become a baronet. He realized that a change in wealth and title hadn't changed his true nature. He needed to decide how he was going to break it to his father. Walter would be staying with his father while he was in London; perhaps he'd tell him about Mary while he was there.

He realized he had been staring at her for far too long. He bid her and Miss Westerlee goodbye and took his leave.

Walter found the management of his property to be one of the few interesting aspects of his elevated lifestyle. His friend from school, Joseph Langford, didn't enjoy it one bit. Walter had been helping Joseph run his estate ever since Joseph's uncle had passed away five years ago. He was meeting Joseph at White's today.

The club was crowded, as usual, but Joseph found him almost as soon as he walked in. "Tyndale, it's good to see you again."

"I'm sure it is," Walter replied. "You know, it would probably be easier if I just met with your steward directly. Skip the middleman." Walter gestured toward Joseph as he said it.

"Haha," Joseph rolled his eyes but smiled too. "I haven't even asked for your advice in months ... well, nearly a month, anyway."

They found an unoccupied table and took a seat to talk about Joseph's massive estate and some of the problems he was having. His steward was a very capable but humble man who didn't trust himself to make a single decision without consulting his employer. Joseph, in turn, was not very capable, and while he could be decisive on small matters, he knew he needed sound advice for big decisions.

After Walter had advised Joseph on rotating crops and a job for a tenant's son who had recently come of age, the friends let their conversation drift to other subjects. While they talked, the door opened, and a man came in. As several patrons noticed the new arrival, conversations around the room grew quiet. It was a momentary thing. The man who had just entered joined a table across the room, and the noise returned to its previous level. Walter's eyes had followed the man, too. He thought he recognized him, but was curious about the reaction of the room to his presence.

Turning back to his friend, he asked, "Is that the Duke of Cheltenham?"

Joseph nodded as he responded, "Yes that's him. Oliver Worthington, the Duke of Cheltenham."

"Why did it go quiet when he came in? I mean, I understand he's a duke and wants to make an entrance, but surely his presence here is common enough?"

"He's been the subject of a lot of talk over the last couple of days. Rumor is he's hosting a come-out ball for his sister in a few weeks."

Walter lost attention for the subject almost immediately. He didn't enjoy attending balls. It was unlikely he'd receive an invitation anyway, and he hadn't even known the duke had a sister.

Before Walter could revert back to their earlier topic, however, Joseph asked him, "Did you know he has a sister?"

Walter just shrugged and said, "I never heard that he did."

"Almost no one has heard of her." Joseph gave Walter a significant look, as if this was the news that had everybody whispering about the duke. "Apparently, she is a much younger half-sister raised at Cheltenham Manor practically in isolation."

"Where is Cheltenham Manor?"

"I don't know. Herefordshire, I think ... or maybe Hertfordshire. I can't remember. Anyway, this sister of his is now to be introduced to society and is supposed to be the belle of the season. She has 50,000 pounds."

It seemed strange that such a girl could go unnoticed by all of society. It must have been quite intentional. "Why is Cheltenham suddenly bringing his sister out of isolation?"

"I think it's because he's pursuing Miss Atthill, along with every other gentleman in town this spring, and he wants to get rid of some of her admirers."

"He's using his sister as bait for all the eligible bachelors just so he can get Miss Atthill without competition?"

Joseph just gave a slight shrug, but he obviously thought it was true.

"So that is what the whispering is about, then."

"Mostly that." Joseph agreed. "Every man hoping to find a wife this season is now considering the unknown Miss Worthington, and Miss Atthill seems to have lost some of her followers. But almost more intriguing are the rumors that Miss Worthington is completely good-natured, totally unspoiled by society, and that she is a rare beauty as well."

Walter allowed himself only a small smile, but it was enough to signal to Joseph that he thought it was all ridiculous.

"You think it's not true?" Joseph asked Walter.

"When something sounds too good to be true, it usually is." The thought of Mary with the wind tangling her hair and loosening her bonnet while walking with him to his next appointment flashed through his mind. Was she too good to be true? He pushed that thought aside and asked, "Besides, where did these rumors originate? If no one has ever seen this girl, or even knew she existed, how is her beauty and her character suddenly known?"

Joseph's eyebrows dropped down as he thought about that. "You know, I didn't think about that."

"The rumors have to come from the Duke of Cheltenham himself." Then he emphasized, "And if he has to tell everyone how lovely his sister is, she's anything but."

"Well, if he's lying, everyone will know it soon enough. The invite list for his sister's come-out ball is apparently quite extensive."

Walter just shrugged again. Perhaps the girl was as wonderful as rumors portrayed her to be, but he seriously doubted it. "Or by then he'll have secured Miss Attwell for himself and it won't matter what his sister is like. So do you plan to pursue this paragon as well?"

Joseph gave a small smile that conveyed his admission, then he asked, "Why aren't you thinking about pursuing her? Wouldn't you like to marry a beautiful girl with 50,000 pounds?"

Walter chuckled a little at the improbability of it. He was part of society, but it seemed to him as if he were just grudgingly admitted. His father had risen from obscurity, and the money that came with his new estate was still quite modest.

"I'll step aside for you, my friend," Walter said magnanimously, but with heavy sarcasm.

"You're a baronet now; there's no reason you can't pursue any lady you choose."

Walter wished that were true, but he knew very well he couldn't. If he chose to pursue Mary from the village, he would be looked down on by everybody and severely disappoint his father. If he chose to pursue the Duke of Cheltenham's sister, he would be laughed to scorn for thinking so high.

Walter knew Joseph knew it too, so he flippantly asked, "Then why should I settle for Cheltenham's sister?"

Joseph smiled, understanding how Walter felt about his situation, but then glancing around the room he said, "I don't have a chance, either. Every single gentleman in London is planning to pursue her. I'm sure it will be nearly impossible to catch her eye. The real reason the room went quiet when the Duke of Cheltenham came in is because most men are plotting to get Miss Worthington for themselves." Leaning slightly closer and lowering his voice, Joseph continued, "Lord Keswick is desperate for money and is planning a full charming assault on her. I overheard Charlie Hampton asking Mark Hayes for help with his plan to get her alone and in a compromising situation so she'll be forced to marry him. And Bonham told me that Leonard Webster has some dirt on the Duke of Cheltenham and plans to blackmail him so he will be the only one with permission to marry his sister."

Walter gently shook his head and sighed, wishing it wasn't so and wishing he was surprised by all the scheming. "Poor Miss Worthington," he said. "No matter how much money she has or how beautiful she is, she doesn't deserve this. And if she really is unspoiled by society, she'll be too naive to catch on until she's already married to one of those scoundrels."

Joseph nodded. "Yes, it's pretty much hopeless for noble fellows like us."

Walter appreciated that Joseph included him as a "noble fellow," but Joseph actually had a chance with Miss Worthington if he could catch her attention. He, however, was unlikely to even catch a glimpse of her from a distance. While he felt sorry for the unknown young lady, he didn't dwell on it. A girl like that would never be attainable for him.

Walter arrived at his father's home on Oxford Street in time for dinner. Their conversation was pleasant, and Walter decided to keep it that way and not tell his father about Mary. He wanted to spend time with her and see if he still liked her as much as he thought he did. If he really pursued her, there would be plenty of time to break the news to his father later.

Walter realized his mistake at breakfast the next morning. He was almost finished and about to leave when a footman brought Walter's father the post. His father's eyes lit up at the sight of one envelope in particular.

"This one is addressed to you, Walter. It's from the Duke of Cheltenham. It looks like an invitation," he said excitedly.

Thanks to his conversation yesterday with Joseph, Walter knew before he opened it that it was an invitation to the duke's sister's come-out ball. He said as much to his father as he pulled the card out and then he added, "I'm surprised my name made it on the invitation list."

"You're going, of course." His father brought his hand down on the table in excitement. "Can you just imagine if you marry the duke's sister?"

Walter let frustration color his laughter. "The Duke of Cheltenham would never let me near his sister. He probably has a secretary who was instructed to send out the invitations, and because I have a title, my name was accidentally included."

"You undervalue yourself, son. Accident or no, you have an invitation and we're going. You have as much a shot with that girl as anyone."

"Why do you want me to marry someone so high above me? I thought when I was awarded my baronetcy that you would be content for life."

"I will be satisfied when you connect our family to one of the fine old families in England."

"You earned a lot of money father. I acquired a title. Can't we leave it to the next generation to connect the Tyndale name with a noble family?" Walter asked, wishing his father didn't put this pressure on him.

"Where is your ambition, son? An opportunity like this doesn't come along every day and I'm not going to let you throw it away."

"Father, I'm not going to bother with this," he said, holding up the invitation. "I'm never going to marry Miss Worthington."

"If you don't try, you certainly won't. I realize it's not likely, but all I'm asking is that you give it your best shot. Perhaps you will be the one she chooses."

Walter thought about Mary back in Aldwickbury, and he already knew who he would choose. "Father, I'll agree to attend this ball on one condition. If I give it my best shot and Miss Worthington doesn't choose me, then you'll give up this idea of me marrying some fine and fancy lady and leave me alone when I choose a wife."

"Do you promise to give it your very best effort? Because I'll agree if you really try."

"Very well, I promise. We'll attend this come-out ball, and I will do everything I can to get Miss Worthington's attention. And when it doesn't work, you'll just have to be satisfied with whomever I choose."

His father reluctantly agreed, and Walter left for Aldwickbury as quickly as he could.

Mary hadn't seen her brother again after their encounter in the library. He had gone back to London before she returned home for dinner. Mary hadn't been at all surprised. His visits to Cheltenham Manor were always brief. This time, however, the effects of his visit were felt after he left. He had written a short note telling Mary that a dance instructor would be coming in two days, and that's exactly what had happened. The man came from London and must have been thrown in a carriage before the sun was up to reach Cheltenham Manor as early as he did.

The lesson was just as disastrous as Mary would have predicted. Her new instructor, Mr. Faucheux, was just as French as his name. He was haughty with disdain at Mary's lack of knowledge. Their lesson was punctured with his questions and exclamations, such as, "Have you never danced the reel?" Or, "A lady who doesn't know how to step allemande? I never heard of such a thing!" And, "You are not even familiar with the cotillion?"

It was a long two hours. Mary gently sighed as Mr. Faucheux touched his fingers to his forehead and closed his eyes. Mary wished he would just teach her one dance, but he had already tried to teach several and she was having trouble keeping track of them all.

"Mr. Faucheux," Mary began in her most reasonable and convincing tone. "I think you must be exhausted from teaching someone so inept as me. How about if we end our lesson for today, and I'll practice on my own for a while to see if I can get better?"

Mr. Faucheux looked up with a spark of hope in his eyes. "You do need practice," he agreed.

"More than anything," Mary replied, although she was starving, too.

With a few vague instructions to be light on her feet and command the attention of the room, he finally left her to work out the steps on her own.

Mary waited only a minute before escaping to the kitchen. She ate bread and butter while she filled a basket for her neighbors and friends and was off on her visits, finally.

Two hours later, Mary's basket was empty and she was feeling optimistic again. She had visited Mr. and Mrs. Dunfee today and they had had kind words to say about Dr. Tyndale. Perhaps she would even get to see him again tomorrow if he was back from London. She was about to walk home, but she was feeling bad about not practicing after she had told Mr. Faucheux that she would, so she stopped in the meadow before she reached the lane and tried a few of the steps. She had paid close attention to the lesson this morning, but Mr. Faucheux had taught her so much, so fast, that she kept confusing everything in her mind.

Mary went through the first few steps of a dance she thought she remembered. Almost immediately, a horse and rider came into view on the lane. Before Mary could stop hopping and drop her arm, she recognized Dr. Tyndale.

As little as Mary knew about society, she was fairly certain that being caught dancing alone in a meadow should be a highly embarrassing moment. She dropped her arm and her gaze, wondering if Dr. Tyndale would be completely appalled by her behavior or only mildly offended.

She realized he had dismounted and lifted her eyes once more, relieved to see that his expression was open, not censorious in the least.

"Are you dancing?" he asked her.

"I'm trying to learn," Mary responded. "But I keep confusing the steps. Have you ever heard of the cotillion?"

"Yes. I've danced it many times," Dr. Tyndale replied.

Mary suddenly wondered if learning this dance wasn't a waste of her time after all.

"Oh, then do you know if the slide step comes before or after you meet in the middle and twist around your partner?"

"It depends on which cotillion you're doing."

"You mean there's more than one?" Mary asked in startled surprise. What if she was learning the wrong one?

Quickly reassuring her, Dr. Tyndale said, "Well, there's only one cotillion in fashion at the moment. Perhaps that's the one you're learning?"

"I really don't know. Can you show it to me and I'll try to remember?"

Dr. Tyndale glanced toward the lane before saying, "I suppose I could do that."

He looked a little self-conscious, but Mary knew everyone in their little village, and they might tease, but no one would care about a little dance instruction in the meadow.

Dr. Tyndale removed his hat and set it on his saddle then came and stood just a few paces from Mary. For several moments he just stood there.

Mary wasn't sure how to put him at ease, but she tried by offering, "Would you like me to count the rhythm for you?"

He met her eyes and the corners of his mouth turned up just a bit. "That's not necessary, I'll just hum the tune."

He did seem more at ease after that. He began promenading, then reversed direction. His voice was clear as he hummed the tune that matched the steps.

Mary didn't recognize the tune, but she was fairly certain that the steps she was watching Dr. Tyndale perform matched the ones Mr. Faucheux had tried to teach her this morning.

Mary spoke over his song. "I think that's the one I'm learning."

She watched him another few moments, then when he stepped to where she imagined the center would be, she stepped in too. Their hands touched as they rotated around each other. His hands were inside his riding gloves, but Mary's hands were bare. She had gloves, of course, she just never thought to wear them. When they stepped back, Mary stopped dancing and closely watched Dr. Tyndale's feet again as he continued.

Mr. Faucheux could take lessons from Dr. Tyndale. He was a superb dancer. It was also much easier to learn the steps with a tune than with Mr. Faucheux's repetitively counting, "One, two, three, four; one, two, three, four."

When Dr. Tyndale finished, Mary asked, "Would you go through it again? I'll try to join in more this time."

He smiled, and Mary was glad to see he didn't look self-conscious anymore.

"Of course," he said.

After their third try, Mary was fairly sure that she knew the steps. After she said as much to Dr. Tyndale, he asked, "So, your brother convinced you to learn to dance?"

"Yes, but I'm still not convinced that I will like it. Learning the steps has been a bit frustrating, although easier with you."

"When is the next assembly?" he asked.

"I don't know," Mary admitted. "A few weeks, I think."

"And do you suppose you'll attend them regularly after that?"

"I'll have to see how this first dance goes before I decide. Mostly, I aim to not embarrass myself too much."

"You're a fine dancer; I'm sure it won't be embarrassing for you at all."

Mary shook her head. "I hope you're right, but if I bump into every other dancer and topple them like domino tiles, everyone will be grateful if I never show up at another dance again."

He smiled at her self-depreciation. "Or perhaps you'll be so amazing, everyone will ask you for lessons."

Mary smiled back and let herself enjoy gazing at Dr. Tyndale's handsome grin through a stretched-out moment. The time passing finally made Mary realize that she would keep the staff waiting if she didn't return home soon for dinner. She tore her gaze away to look for her basket.

"I'd better get home for dinner," she said regretfully.

"You're going this direction?" he asked gesturing up the lane.

Mary nodded, and he fell into step beside her. She was a bit nervous now. She didn't want Dr. Tyndale to walk her home.

She was distracted from her thoughts when Dr. Tyndale asked, "Have there been any patients needing my attention while I was away?"

"I visited John and the Dunfees today, and they seemed to be doing quite well."

"With you here to help, I wonder why Dr. Milner even thought to ask me to come and replace him."

Mary realized he was teasing when she looked up and saw that he was smiling. "Probably he asked you to come so that broken bones could be set with proper instruments instead of kitchen utensils."

"I thought it was very resourceful of you."

"Yes, well," Mary tried not to let another grin overtake her face at the compliment. She quickly told him, "Miss Westerlee was asleep when I called, so I don't know if your remedies from yesterday helped or not."

"Perhaps I'll start by visiting her tomorrow."

They had arrived at the crossing, and Mary stopped walking. She would be turning here and leaving Aldwickbury for home, and she really couldn't let Dr. Tyndale walk with her any further.

She turned to say goodbye. "Thank you for teaching me the Cotillion."

"Do you want me to walk you home?" he offered.

Mary tried to act as though she weren't hiding anything. "Oh, no. It's out of the way, but perhaps I'll see you tomorrow? That is if you'll let me help you with your patients again. I could meet you at Miss Westerlee's home."

"Do you really want to?" Dr. Tyndale asked.

Even though Mary could tell he was teasing and already knew the answer to that question, she still answered with enthusiasm, "Yes, of course, I want to!"

Dr. Tyndale grinned broadly and touched his hat to her as he said, "Until tomorrow, then, Miss Mary."

Mary was just relieved that he hadn't insisted on walking with her further.

Two-and-a-half weeks later, the village of Aldwickbury was as healthy as it had ever been. As an excuse to spend time with Mary, Walter had asked for her help as he visited nearly every home in the parish. He had treated everything from rashes and ingrown toenails to goiters and infected cuts.

Today's visit was something extra.

"Well, Mr. Lund," Walter began after he and Mary had been admitted to the house. "I was thinking after our last visit that you could probably get around much easier with a wooden leg. The amputation site is uneven, but I'm confident that with a wooden leg you could at least get rid of one crutch and have a free hand. I might even be able to fit a wooden leg that would allow you to stop using crutches altogether."

There was never a moment while he was addressing Mr. Lund that he wasn't keenly aware of Mary sitting next to him. While he was explaining about a wooden leg, he was wondering to himself—as he had so many times over these last weeks—why he had made that promise to his father. It had been stupid. He could manage his life just as he chose; he shouldn't have agreed to attend Miss Worthington's come-out ball. All he wanted to do was spend time with Mary. His promise to his father had prevented him from forming a real attachment in these two-and-a-half weeks they had spent together. If he had never made that promise, he would have walked Mary home every day, met her family, tried to get an invitation for dinner. But the promise to his father kept him from it all.

Instead, he had spent every day with Mary resisting his feelings for her. He knew he'd already broken his promise to his father in a way: he would never be able to sincerely try to attach Miss Worthington. His mind and heart were too full of Mary to leave any room for the Duke of Cheltenham's sister.

Mr. Lund had seemed to consider Walter's words quite carefully. Finally, he replied, "All right, Doctor. I'm willing. But I don't want no duchess watching while you take those measurements."

"Duchess?" Walter questioned.

"You know. Mary, here," Mr. Lund said, gesturing to her.

Mary stood up quickly, "Don't say another word, Mr. Lund. I'll wait outside."

She was out the door in a moment.

Walter first gave Mr. Lund a dose of laudanum so the man would sleep. Many with amputated limbs found the prodding and measuring quite painful. After Walter set up the cot he had brought along, he helped Mr. Lund to lie down on it and stepped outside for a few minutes to talk with Mary while he waited for the medicine to take effect.

"Is that your nickname?" he asked her. "Duchess?"

"I'm no duchess, and I don't think he meant it as a compliment," she said with a laugh. Walter thought she looked uncomfortable. "Maybe that's just what Mr. Lund calls all interfering females like me."

It was too good an opportunity to pass up. Walter joined her in leaning against the outside wall and asked, "Would you be a titled lady if you could?"

Walter expected she had probably daydreamed fondly about the idea of a life a leisure, but she seemed taken aback by the question.

"I don't know. Do *you* think a title or that sort of status would be of value?"

"Maybe it can be," he answered. Little did she know, he'd spent quite a bit of time wondering the same thing. Enough time that he had formed a definite opinion.

"How do you mean?" Mary asked.

"I think value is within a person," he explained. "A title or status could give a principled person the means to do a great deal of good. For someone with few principles, a title would be useless or even cause harm."

Mary's smile gradually overtook her face. "I think my grandfather would have liked you." The way she said it made him feel like it was the nicest compliment she could have given.

"When Mr. Lund is asleep, it should be fine if you come back. He'll never know, and I could use your help if you'll write while I measure."

There had only been one time over the last fortnight when he had taken care of someone in an emergency. Seventeen-year-old Frank had been working too close to another farm hand and had taken a scythe down his arm. Walter had put in a dozen stitches and considered the boy lucky. The scythe could have done a lot more damage. Mary had been there to assist him.

He was certainly faster with Mary's help, and luckily, she agreed with his suggestion now, saying, "I suppose Mr. Lund will never have to know."

It was only one more day until he would attend that ball in London and keep his promise to his father, then he'd be back in Aldwickbury the following morning and free to tell Mary how he felt about her. Walter turned so that his shoulder rested against the wall and looked closely at this young woman he had come to care about.

She turned to him with a smile and said, "You're doing it again."

"What am I doing?" he asked.

"You're lost in thought," she replied. "You do this when we practice dancing too. You look at me, but I can tell your thoughts are far away."

That was not true. His thoughts were never far away from her. He reached his hand out and touched hers, then with a little more boldness, he wrapped his hand around hers and lifted it and held it tenderly between his own. He looked back up into her green eyes and was almost lost in thought again. Her quick intake of breath brought him back to himself, and he released her hand.

Just two more days; he could wait.

Walter checked and found Mr. Lund sound asleep a few minutes later, and they began to work. She sat on one side of Mr. Lund, and he on the other. Out of respect for his patient's wishes, he kept the amputated limb partially covered so it was out of Mary's view. He measured and dictated in a quiet voice, and Mary took notes. With Mr. Lund sleeping, Walter felt the intimacy of being alone with Mary. Of course, they'd been alone together quite a bit out of doors, but this felt much more private.

Trying to focus, he asked, "Did you write down the anterior to posterior measurement?"

Mary leaned across their patient to show him the paper and her hair brushed his cheek. He looked up from the paper and studied Mary's face instead. It was mere inches from his own and far too beautiful and tempting. The last few weeks of fortitude melted away, and Walter couldn't help himself then. He barely had to move as he turned and kissed her cheek. He felt her softly sigh and his own heart kicked. He either felt or imagined her raise her chin slightly, and he was happy to oblige. He slid his lips along her skin down to her lips and increased the pressure ever so slightly. He was sure she kissed him back briefly before they both pulled away at the sound of something hitting the floor.

Mary bent down quickly to retrieve the quill and paper. Her hands seemed unsteady.

"Luckily, no ink splattered," she said in a quiet voice, then cleared her throat.

Walter released a shaky breath. "I'm sorry," he quickly apologized. Then realizing that he wasn't sorry at all, he said, "No, that's not quite right. Er, I think we're done here, let's talk outside, can we?"

Mary nodded and stood up. He wanted to hold her hand again, but knowing now that he couldn't trust himself, he gestured for her to precede him out the door.

They stood in their previous positions, leaning against the wall. Walter looked at her for a moment, wondering how he could explain. He began to feel the pull again to touch her and made himself take a step back.

"Mary, I shouldn't have done that," he admitted. "The timing's not right, is all. I'm going to London tomorrow. I have to see my father about something." She nodded as if she understood, even though it wasn't really an explanation at all. "When I get back, we can talk about what just happened … and the possibility of it happening again."

It was more of an admission than he should have allowed himself. Mary quickly looked down at the ground as her hand covered her mouth. Walter was worried for a moment that she might be upset, but when she looked up he thought she must be covering a smile because her eyes sparkled with a mischievous look.

"It's getting late. I'll finish with Mr. Lund," Walter offered. If she stayed, he'd just be more distracted at this point. Mary agreed, still trying to look solemn but not managing it very well.

As soon as he got back from London, he was going to try to win Mary's affections.

For the last fortnight, Mary hadn't gone a day without seeing Dr. Tyndale. It had been the best fortnight of her life. But today, she wouldn't see him. Dr. Tyndale had told her he was going to visit his father and would be gone for two days again. Mary had hoped that Dr. Tyndale would never find out who she was. After their kiss, however, she realized that she wanted him to know everything about her. She touched her fingers to her lips, remembering the sensation of Dr. Tyndale's lips on hers. Even more than the kiss, though, Dr. Tyndale had said that a title didn't matter. She was going to tell him who she was when he returned from London, and she was confident that he wouldn't let the difference of their stations matter to him.

"No, no, no." Mr. Faucheux said, each "no" getting louder than the last. "Your hand goes in the air, like so."

He made a flourish that Mary instantly copied. She had gotten good enough at the dance steps, that she had forgotten she was still dancing in front of her instructor. She hastily removed her finger from her lips and finished the rest of the dance flawlessly.

After that, Mr. Faucheux was remarkably cheerful. "My accomplishment in teaching you to dance in so short a time is nothing less than astounding to me. The duke promised me a large bonus if I could teach you enough that you won't embarrass him at the ball. I've definitely earned it."

Mary didn't refute it. She didn't bother with talking to Mr. Faucheux much in an effort to keep their lessons as short as possible. But the real credit for her learning to dance so quickly was Dr. Tyndale. They had practiced together most days. Even without those practice sessions, the credit still would have gone to him. Mary was only applying herself to impress Dr. Tyndale. When she returned to Aldwickbury after her come-out ball, she was going to attend the assembly ball and make sure he was there too.

"Well then, let's be off." It was an unexpected thing for Mr. Faucheux to say.

"Where?" asked Mary.

"London, of course."

"We're leaving for London?" Mary asked, amazed. "Today?"

"We're leaving within the hour," he replied, sounding more amazed at her ignorance. "Your ball is this evening. Didn't you know?"

Mary ran up to her room and quickly grabbed a few things to put in a traveling case. Of course, Oliver hadn't bothered to tell her when her ball was. She couldn't fault him completely though; she had been too preoccupied to ask.

Her first journey to London was over in four short hours. The carriage delivered her right to Oliver's London house with only a couple of hours until the ball began. Mary was taken to Oliver's library where she said hello to her brother. He quickly dismissed her to go to her room and prepare for the ball, but Mary wandered for about twenty minutes, poking her head in different doors, getting to know Oliver's London home. She finally made her way to the private family bedrooms and soon found a room with her trunk in it, as well as a lady's maid waiting to help her.

Before leaving Cheltenham Manor, Mary had quickly packed her finest gown so she could wear it to the ball. Now, however, she saw there was a much finer gown waiting for her. Oliver was thoughtful when he didn't want to be embarrassed.

In fairly good time, Mary was ready. Oliver came to Mary's room to speak with her shortly before the ball began.

"Hello, Oliver. What an interesting day it's been!"

"How so?" Oliver asked.

"Well, for one thing, the journey to London was fascinating. I loved seeing the different villages and towns we passed through and then seeing so many more people walking everywhere when we came into London. I had no idea it was so big!"

"Oh Mary," Oliver said with some despair. "Did you gawk out the carriage window the whole way?"

"No. Not the whole way," Mary replied.

She had spent a few minutes in polite conversation with Mr. Faucheux before he had fallen asleep. Oliver was obviously worried, as he should be, that Mary was going to embarrass him this evening. His lecture proved it.

"Mary," he began quite seriously, "I think you should take my recommendations this evening on whom to dance with."

"Oh, do I choose whom I dance with?" she asked, feigning surprise. "I thought the gentlemen asked the ladies to dance."

A month ago, Mary couldn't have imagined being disrespectful to Oliver. He didn't notice. He just assumed she was sincere.

"Of course, the gentlemen ask the ladies," Oliver replied. Usually he was condescendingly amused at her social errors. Now he seemed genuinely annoyed and slightly worried. With impatience, he explained, "Every gentleman will be asking you for a dance, you'll have to choose from among them. Since you won't know anyone, it will be best if you let me choose for you."

Mary smiled innocently as though she understood now. Honestly, she didn't care who she danced with. Dr. Tyndale wouldn't be at her ball, so she didn't mind letting Oliver have his way. Mary was certain that everyone who asked her to dance would have been bossed into asking her by Oliver himself.

As if to confirm her views, he said, "My good friend Mr. Webster will be asking you for a dance. The first dance, in fact. You may say yes to his request."

"Do I need your permission every time someone asks me?"

"Well, not every time—" but Oliver stopped there and thought about it for a moment. "That's not a bad idea, actually. I'll be standing by you in the receiving line. If you get asked for a dance, just look at me. I'll give you a nod if you should say yes." He paused and then added, "And if you should definitely say no, I'll clear my throat."

"Wouldn't it be easier if you just answered for me?"

Oliver narrowed his eyes, and Mary tried her best to look innocent. She'd better not push Oliver further today. It seemed like he couldn't decide if her question was genuine or impertinent.

Oliver heaved a big sigh. "This is an important night for both of us. If she says yes, I will be announcing my engagement to Miss Attwell by the end of the night."

"Oh, that's wonderful news, Oliver." Mary smiled at her brother. It was a little surprising to think of Oliver making himself pleasant for a young lady. At least now she was looking forward to meeting one person at the ball, her future sister-in-law. "Congratulations," she said sincerely. "She must be quite an exceptional young lady to win your love."

She thought it was a very kind, sisterly thing for her to say, but Oliver didn't.

"That's not how it works, Mary," he said in his condescending tone. "This isn't about love at all. Miss Atwell is the finest young lady in London this season. Her good taste and mine will be equally complimented by the match." With a shake of his head that indicated she was hopeless, he added, "Your goal tonight is to try to find an equally complimentary match for yourself. Don't embarrass me."

With a last pointed look, he left the room.

Mary allowed herself a small chuckle and a roll of her eyes at Oliver's strange way of approaching marriage. As for her finding a complimentary match this evening … impossible. She'd already found him in Dr. Tyndale.

Walter walked into the ball with his father nearly pushing him along. Before entering the ballroom, Walter turned and reiterated what he'd said earlier to his father.

"When we get to the front of the line, I will ask Miss Worthington for a dance. When she turns me down, you have to accept that this is never going to work."

"I find it hard to believe that my son is so opposite to me. How do you think I rose so high in this world? By not seizing opportunities?"

"She's a young lady, not an opportu—" Walter cut himself off and grasped fistfuls of his hair in frustration. His father was never going to see it his way. "I'll ask for one dance," he repeated firmly, confident that Miss Worthington wouldn't have any available dances to give by the time he reached her.

Walter's father licked his own hand, then used it to smooth down Walter's disheveled hair. "Be optimistic son. Your future wife could be through that door."

He gestured with his chin to the door behind him, where a receiving line to be introduced to Miss Worthington already trailed out of the ballroom.

Walter pushed his father's hand away. His hair could go to the devil for all he cared. "Let's get this over with, then."

The line moved forward slowly. Walter reached the doorway eventually and found himself inside the Duke of Cheltenham's grand ballroom. It was ornate, but he hadn't expected less. He didn't give the details of the room much thought, wondering instead if he would get to see Mary tomorrow if he left for Aldwickbury first thing in the morning.

Out of nowhere, Walter heard a familiar laugh and glanced up to the front of the line. Walter suddenly quit breathing. The receiving line he was standing in was leading him to Mary. His Mary. His mind needed a few moments to make the connection, but finally, there it was.

Mary and Miss Worthington. The same person.

Walter felt a push from behind and glanced back to see his father nudging him forward as the line had moved. He took an automatic step. How could Mary be the sister of the Duke of Cheltenham? The family relation was almost as shocking to him as the fact that Mary was the most sought after young lady in London. He had seen her weeding the Morris's garden and sweeping Miss Westerlee's cobblestone floors! The elite society of England was lining up to meet her. This shallow, civilized crowd wouldn't give Mary any attention if they knew.

It was a few minutes before Walter could reconcile his thoughts. His idyllic afternoons in Aldwickbury with Mary did not in any way relate to the present ballroom with Miss Worthington. There was no sense in this. He felt as though the rug had been yanked from underneath his feet. He must not be very imaginative because he couldn't have fathomed such a shock.

The absolute worst part was that the future he *had* imagined wasn't possible now. The granddaughter of the fourth Duke of Cheltenham and the sister of the fifth Duke of Cheltenham with her 50,000 pounds would never be allowed to choose a brand new baronet who was really a doctor by trade.

Though he didn't think it was possible, suddenly everything became even worse. Walter noticed that the man in front of him, just steps away from Mary now, was Lord Keswick. Everyone knew that he was nearly broke and was a desperate fortune hunter. But Mary didn't know. Walter remembered his conversation with Joseph at White's a few short weeks ago. Joseph had mentioned that there were several men scheming to get Miss Worthington and her fortune for themselves. Lord Keswick had the charm of ten fortune hunters put together. How would Mary deal with it? As Lord Keswick stepped up for his turn to be introduced to the illustrious Miss Worthington, Walter watched to see what would happen.

Lord Keswick bowed low over her gloved hand as he held and kissed it.

When he straightened, he said, "Miss Worthington, I have anticipated meeting you since the moment I heard of your existence. You were described to me as the most beautiful young lady to ever live, and that description simply didn't do you justice."

Walter watched Mary closely. Her eyes widened, and she looked very focused on Lord Keswick. The slight smile that she had plastered on her face for all the other introductions grew. Walter recognized her expression. She was trying to repress a full grin.

"Thank you, Lord Keswick," she replied. "I don't think I've ever received such a lovely compliment."

Walter suppressed a growl. He couldn't believe she was falling for Lord Keswick's charm!

Lord Keswick took the encouragement she gave and said, "To be in your presence is a privilege I had only hoped to enjoy. If you would do me the honor of allowing me to dance with you, I would be the luckiest man on earth."

Mary bit the side of her bottom lip and glanced over at her brother, who dropped his chin in a perfunctory nod. So, Cheltenham was not even letting her choose for herself whom she would dance with. Walter wasn't surprised.

Mary turned back to Lord Keswick. "I'd be pleased to dance with you. Perhaps the supper dance."

Lord Keswick put his free hand over his heart and declared, "I am honored beyond anything I've ever known. My greatest aim will be to not disappoint you, Miss Worthington."

Walter's father suddenly nudged him and said quietly into his ear, "Wipe that expression off your face. You look like you're about to meet an executioner, not a lovely young lady. Come now, Walter; you promised to give this your best effort."

Walter tried to not let his emotions show. He was beyond disappointed that Mary couldn't be his, angry at Lord Keswick, frustrated with his father, livid with the Duke of Cheltenham, and—more than anything—worried about Mary.

With her hand still ceremoniously held by Lord Keswick, Mary couldn't believe that anyone could take this conversation seriously. She was trying so hard not to laugh as Lord Keswick gave her another ridiculous compliment. Did the man only know how to speak in superlatives? She glanced at her brother again, wondering if she could catch a look that showed his thoughts were similar to hers. But he didn't seem to notice anything awry. Surely, she couldn't be the only one within earshot who had any sense. She looked at the line of people still waiting to meet her to see if anyone—anyone at all—was trying as hard as she was to keep from laughing.

All in one movement, Mary's jaw dropped and she yanked her hand away from Lord Keswick's grasp. She didn't know how it was possible, but Dr. Tyndale was the next man in line to meet her. She instantly recognized him, but then taking in his fine ballroom attire, she looked again to be sure it was really him.

It most definitely was. He didn't look at all amused by Lord Keswick, but perhaps that was because he was too surprised to see her standing here. She certainly wished she had confessed who she was before this moment.

Lord Keswick found her hand again, and she turned her attention back to him

"This most memorable meeting will stay with me always. It is only in anticipation of our dance that I can bear letting this moment end." He bowed over her hand once more and affectionately kissed it.

With very little patience, Mary said, "Yes, until later."

She pulled her hand away again and gave a brief dismissive smile, then turned to speak with Dr. Tyndale.

There was the silly introduction ritual to get through. The footman standing next to Oliver collected the cards of the guests and said their names as they reached the front of the line. Just like with so many things, this had been unexpected.

The footman said in his clear voice that carried through the crowded hall, "Mr. John Tyndale and his son, Sir Walter Tyndale, Baronet."

Oliver greeted them first. "Mr. Tyndale. Sir Walter. We're delighted you could come."

It didn't hit Mary until she heard Oliver call Dr. Tyndale "Sir Walter." That's why he was here. He was a titled gentleman! What had the footman said? A Baronet? This was the first good thing to happen to her all evening. She couldn't wait to ask Dr. Tyndale all about it.

The polite greeting was returned first by Mr. Tyndale.

"Thank you so much for having us, Your Grace." Then he turned to Mary. "Miss Worthington, it is a very great pleasure to make your acquaintance. My son, Sir Walter, has been particularly looking forward to it."

And finally it was her turn to speak to Dr. Tyndale. Before she could say a word, he greeted her quite formally, saying, "Miss Worthington, how do you do?"

Apparently he wasn't going to acknowledge that they were already acquainted. Mary knew what she was supposed to do. She should return his formal greeting and pretend that this was their first time meeting, too.

In that instant, she realized why grandfather had protected her from society: it was this ridiculous pretending. Lord Keswick had been the worst example by far, but to see Dr. Tyndale pretending not to know her just because they were in a ballroom made her realize that she had no desire to pretend. Here was someone who knew her; she could finally drop the pretense.

Mary smiled, and just as if she had run into him while tending John Morris, she said, "Dr. Tyndale! What a pleasant surprise to see you here. You are the first person to come through this line that I actually know." He looked at her brother and then at his father, but Mary didn't spare them a glance. "You never told me you were a baronet. I guess I may call you Sir Walter now. It's a bit funny isn't it?"

If only he would laugh!

After such a speech from her, he couldn't pretend he didn't know her, and stumblingly he replied, "It is funny, or rather it's quite strange to see you here. I, well, I don't exactly know what to say." Just then his father nudged him, and Dr. Tyndale closed his eyes and let out a soft sigh before opening them again and addressing her once more. "May I have the honor of a dance with you this evening, Miss Worthington?"

Again, he was so formal, as if he wasn't the very one who had taught her to dance in the meadow, when it was just the two of them.

Before she answered, she looked to Oliver for permission, as had been her habit each time she had been asked for a dance this evening. Oliver cleared his throat, his sign for her to decline the invitation to dance. Mary gave a slight negative shake of her head.

Turning back to Dr. Tyndale she said, "Of course. How about the first dance?" She knew that one wasn't engaged yet.

Oliver took her by the elbow and interrupted before Dr. Tyndale could reply. "A moment please, Sir Walter." He pulled Mary back a few feet and said in a low voice, "Mary, you were supposed to decline."

"But he's the only person I know here besides you."

"How do you know him?"

"He's been filling in for Dr. Milner in Aldwickbury."

"You don't even make sense sometimes. Do you know that?" He looked at the receiving line and said with finality, "I can see Mr. Webster in line, and I already told him he could have your first dance. You'll just have to tell Sir Walter you can't dance with him. I'm sure he'll understand. He's probably quite used to being turned down. Pretend you didn't understand his question before and politely decline."

He wanted her to be a perfect, docile young lady and do his bidding. But in the face of him asking her to be rude to the one man she wanted to impress, Mary lost the last vestige of respect for Oliver's opinion.

"No. I'm dancing my first dance with Dr. Tyndale. You can stand up for the first set with Mr. Webster if it's that important to you."

It was the most defiant thing she had ever said to her brother, and he looked furious. They both knew there was nothing he could do in this crowded ballroom. She turned away from him and stepped back to Dr. Tyndale, who, she realized now, was close enough to have possibly heard some of their conversation if the noise of the ballroom hadn't drowned them out.

She smiled at him with as much warmth as she could. "The first set is yours, Dr. Tyndale. I think we'll be commencing soon, so don't go far."

He glanced back and forth between her and Oliver. He looked unsure of her answer.

"I won't, Miss Worthington," he solemnly replied. "And thank you for the honor."

His stiff manner must be a result of finding out that she was Oliver's sister, but she would explain away her deception during their dance and cheer him up. She was sure of it.

Mary had been prepared to dislike every gentleman who she met this evening simply because they weren't him. She had practiced speeches telling her brother that she planned to marry a country doctor. She had imagined being his permanent apprentice for as long as they both lived. Finding out he was a baronet would make some of that easier, and she felt optimistic.

When she was introduced to Mr. Webster several minutes later, Mary gave him her last dance of the evening as a compromise to Oliver's wishes. Now that her dance card was finally full, Oliver broke up the receiving line and instructed the musicians to begin. Mary stood on tiptoe and looked for Dr. Tyndale to come find her.

The musicians were tuning their instruments, and Walter's father, who hadn't stopped talking since the receiving line, said, "Finally, it's time. Now remember, you have the advantage over everyone here since you know her."

His father couldn't have been happier to discover his convenient acquaintance with Mary. He really needed to start thinking of her as Miss Worthington before he slipped and said her given name out loud.

His father was still talking. "...the first dance, even. You must smile and charm her so that she'll be so in love with you after one dance that she won't have any thoughts left for all the other fellows."

Walter just shook his head. He had tried to explain to his father that even if Miss Worthington liked him, the duke most definitely did not. After he had asked her to dance, Walter had heard the conversation between brother and sister. It was just as he had already known: he would not be considered worthy of Miss Worthington.

He slipped through the crowd. When he found Mary, he bowed before offering his arm.

"Shall we, Miss Worthington?"

She beamed at him, and Walter tried not to let it get to him.

They walked to the center of the dance floor, and Walter felt the stares of the entire room on them. The harshest glare of all was from the Duke of Cheltenham, whom Walter could see over Mary's shoulder.

The music began, and with the noise of it, they were able to have a somewhat private conversation.

"I'm so glad my first dance is with you," Mary said confidingly. "I can just feel how everyone is watching us. It would be so much more intimidating if this first dance was with someone I'd never practiced with."

"Miss Worthington, I think it would be best if—"

Mary interrupted him with an impish grin and said, "You don't need to call me Miss Worthington now. No one can hear you."

Walter let out a small sigh and quickly but quietly said, "I think it would be best if we forgot about our previous acquaintance." Mary's smile froze in place, and he knew he was hurting her feelings. Better now than later. "I would never have been so ... familiar with you if I had known who you were. I meant no disrespect." Feeling almost frantic to explain himself, he continued, "I could never have guessed that you were the duke's sister." Lowering his voice even more he said, "You held a bucket while Miss Westerlee vomited! You swept her floor!"

Mary gave him an uncomprehending look. "Surely every young lady here does those things too. Well, maybe not holding a bucket, but isn't it common enough for ladies to do charity work?"

"If they do, I've never seen it, at least not how you do it." Walter shook the thought away as he hit on another reason her identity had remained a mystery to him. "You wander all over the village without a chaperone."

"Why would I need a chaperone in Aldwickbury?" she asked, as if he were the one who'd lost his reason.

"I'm just trying to explain that I would never have guessed that the Duke of Cheltenham would allow his sister to be ... like you are."

"My brother has nothing to do with it. My grandfather didn't want me to be part of a society that he considered absurd. I told you about my grandfather, you'll remember. After meeting all these gentlemen this evening, I'm convinced my grandfather was right."

"When you spoke of your grandfather, I certainly wasn't picturing the fourth Duke of Cheltenham." In a calmer tone he said, "Regardless, Miss Worthington, I apologize for being far too informal with you."

He could see she was unhappy with his apology.

When she had the chance, she said, "Then I must apologize as well *Sir* Walter."

"A lady such as yourself has no need to ever apologize to a mere baronet."

"Not even if she steps on his foot?" Mary asked as she overstepped and landed her slippered foot on his boot. She stomped hard, but he still hardly felt it.

Walter felt like smiling for the first time since he had seen her tonight. "Even then."

"Well, I disagree. I didn't tell you who I was, and I should have, so

I'm apologizing." She gave him a challenging look. "I think the gentlemanly thing to do would be to accept my apology."

"Very well, I accept your apology, Miss Worthington." Despite the fact that everything between them must come to an end, Walter couldn't help but be proud of Mary. Since he wanted to change the subject anyway, he said, "You are dancing flawlessly and are even able to converse without missing a step. Your attention to detail is superb as ever, Miss Worthington."

"You really need to stop this 'Miss Worthington' nonsense. And you know very well I never would have learned to dance without you. It's probably only because I'm dancing with you that I'm finding it so easy."

"Your brother didn't seem at all pleased that you accepted my invitation to dance."

"I don't know why he was so annoyed. I let him choose all my other dance partners."

Walter looked at her closely. Did she really not know? "He knows I'm not good enough for you."

Mary pulled her head back in surprise. She really hadn't known. "Why would he think that?"

"Because I'm only a baronet and your brother is a duke. Besides, I was only made a baronet eight months ago. That's nothing compared to the generations of your family that have been part of the aristocracy." She really had been sheltered to not understand these facts. "Your brother will never consider me a good choice for you. For a dance or anything else."

There. Now she knew he was too far below her for the possibility of marriage. He almost wished he hadn't said it. She would have probably realized it on her own by the end of the evening.

"You know, I don't really care what my brother thinks."

Walter just smiled a sad smile. He couldn't have her, but he didn't think anyone here was good enough for her, either. Eventually, her brother would talk her into marrying one of these gentlemen, but he would at least try to protect her from the men who were plotting to trap her. There could be more schemes than the ones he knew about. But he'd focus on the ones he had learned about from Joseph.

Although it was by accident, Walter had hopefully already frustrated Leonard Webster's blackmail plot by preventing him from taking Mary's first dance. He'd have to keep a close eye on Charlie Hampton, whose plan was to get Mary in a compromising situation. He'd have to watch carefully for Mark Hayes too, who was Charlie's co-conspirator. Walter had gone to school with both of those men and knew that they were certainly capable of the scheme. Then there was Lord Keswick, the charming fortune hunter. Maybe he could warn Mary about him, at least.

Their dance was at an end, and Walter offered Mary his arm so he could lead her back to her brother.

"Your brother seemed to think Lord Keswick was a good choice for you. And it seemed like you were inclined to agree with him."

"Lord Keswick? The one whose flattery was so exaggerated?"

"Er, yes. You seemed to be enjoying his flattery."

"I was trying not to laugh. I couldn't believe anyone could talk that way and be taken seriously."

"Well, good. I was just going to warn you that Lord Keswick has a reputation of being a fortune hunter."

They were approaching her brother now, and even though the ballroom was noisy, Mary dropped her voice to say, "Do you really think I should listen to my brother, who would let me choose Lord Keswick, but not you?"

"What I think doesn't really matter. It's just the way it is."

She dropped his arm, and Walter turned and walked away.

Mary had only caught a few glimpses of Dr. Tyndale since their dance. He hadn't looked at all happy while she danced with Mr. Hayes or with Lord Everton. She hadn't been able to catch his eye while dancing with Mr. Langford, but Dr. Tyndale hadn't seemed to be able to take his eyes off her while she danced with Lord Keswick.

Mary had let herself enjoy her dance and supper with Lord Keswick. She tried to pay close attention to every silly compliment he gave her. At least she would have funny stories to tell her friends back in Aldwickbury. It seemed as if nothing else good would come out of this night.

When supper was finished, she was claimed by her next partner, Lord Tolley. Then, Mr. Laughlin, then the Earl of Stapleton. She was getting quite tired by the time Mr. Hampton claimed his dance with her. Mary hadn't appreciated her own talent for remembering details, but it had never helped her so much as it had this evening. She couldn't remember everyone's names—she had met too many new people for that—but she had made herself remember the name of each gentleman she had agreed to dance with. Her dance with Mr. Hampton was the cotillion, and Mary was pleased to feel confident about the steps.

Just before the dance began, as she had all evening, she looked for Dr. Tyndale. He looked miserable, and now almost angry, she thought, as she took her place on the dance floor across from Mr. Hampton.

Mary performed the steps beautifully, but she wished Dr. Tyndale could have been her partner. Mr. Hampton made a few comments which she answered as politely as she could, but she knew her conversation was insipid.

She was sure he would be glad to turn her back over to her brother, but he surprised her when the dance ended by saying, "The musicians seem to be taking a break. Would you like to step out on the balcony?"

Mary glanced around. She had explored a little when she had arrived. She didn't quite know how to get to the balcony from the ballroom, but it was upstairs. She felt a little guilty for practically ignoring Mr. Hampton through the whole dance and going with him might make up for it.

"I suppose that would be all right," she hesitantly replied.

They were already quite close to the door, and Mr. Hampton held her arm just above her elbow as they stepped out of the ballroom and up the stairs. His steps didn't hesitate, and she realized that he knew his way around Oliver's house better than she did.

His grip on her in the crowded ballroom was fine, but now away from the room full of people, Mary didn't like it.

Trying to pull away, she said, "Actually, let me just run back to the ballroom and let my brother know where I've gone. He'll be put out with me if he can't find me."

"We'll be back before the next dance begins," Mr. Hampton said, still pulling her forward.

Mary instantly felt frightened. He wouldn't let her go. Her first instinct was to struggle, but she repressed it, knowing she wouldn't overpower Mr. Hampton.

They reached the top of the stairs, and she tried to quickly think of how she could escape. It was so odd how fast she had gone from the safety of the ballroom to alone with a man and frightened. But she tried to reassure herself that Mr. Hampton couldn't really have ill intentions. Someone would surely come looking for her when the musicians were ready, and he must know that.

The stairs and the hallway were all well lit, but when Mr. Hampton pulled her into Oliver's long gallery, it was dark.

They only took a few steps into the room when Mr. Hampton stopped and said, "This will do."

He finally released her arm only to pull her into a tight embrace and begin kissing her neck. Mary was shocked by the touch. This man —her brother's guest—thought he could get away with this!

She tried to push away from him but was only able to pull her head back.

"Stop! Stop it this instant!"

But his arms didn't loosen and now he had full access to her face. He tried to kiss her mouth, but Mary jerked her head back even further and to the side.

"Mr. Hampton, I insist you release me. I don't even know you. Someone could catch us at any moment!"

He paused his arduous conduct briefly to answer, "That's the plan,

Miss Worthington." His arms stayed tight around her even though she was trying with all her might to break his tight grasp. "You and I will be caught in an embrace, and the next step will be to marry to cover up the scandal. You can fight if you want to, but it will be much more enjoyable if you just relax."

Mary almost laughed at that and realized she might be nearly hysterical. Relax while a man she didn't know kissed her? Relax while he spoke of their marriage as inevitable? As soon as someone caught them, she'd be forced to marry this vile man and would never be able to carry out her plan of convincing Dr. Tyndale that they weren't so different.

Thinking of him made her that much more determined. She really couldn't escape Mr. Hampton's grasp; her arms were pinned to her sides, and his hold on her was too tight.

It had probably only been a minute or two since they left the ballroom. Everything was happening so fast, and Mary wanted it to end just as fast. She looked around, trying for any idea, and noticed a statue of an ancestor just behind them. One of the previous Dukes of Cheltenham stood on a pedestal in the vaulted gallery. Mary had to push against Mr. Hampton, and perhaps to him, it felt like she was leaning into the embrace, because he buried his face in her neck once more. Mary shoved so he took a few steps backward. As hard as she could, she swung them both so that his head bashed hard against the stone boot of the statue, which pointed out at the base of the tall pedestal.

She was instantly free of Mr. Hampton as he crumpled to the ground. Perhaps that had been too hard. It was too dark in the room to see much, but he was now unconscious at her feet. She felt like he deserved what he got and was considering whether she should just leave him there or go for help when Dr. Tyndale came into the room.

"Mary. There you are," he said somewhat breathlessly.

He was holding a candelabra that lit up the room. Drops of perspiration on his forehead and temple shone in the light. He leaned his head out the door and called down the corridor,

"I've found her. She's here in the long gallery." Turning back, he came toward Mary. "I've been looking all over—" He finally noticed Mr. Hampton on the ground. "What happened? Is that Mr. Hampton?"

Mary nodded. She was giddy with relief. She looked up at the statue that had saved her. It was the first Duke of Cheltenham. Mary recognized him from the portrait that hung in Oliver's library at Cheltenham Manor.

"The old Duke of Cheltenham kicked him in the head." She reached over and patted the stone foot affectionately.

Dr. Tyndale's eyes were wide with disbelief as he stared between her and Mr. Hampton's crumpled form on the floor.

They were joined a moment later by Dr. Tyndale's father, who was also slightly breathless. "Is everything alright?"

Dr. Tyndale seemed to recover from his surprise at his father's question. "I think so. Mary, are you hurt?"

"No, but Mr. Hampton is." Mary looked down and noticed a small dark spot on the carpet by his head. Suddenly more worried she said, "I think he's bleeding, actually."

She knelt down by Mr. Hampton, and Dr. Tyndale did the same across from her.

"Careful," he warned her. "Don't get blood on your gown."

Mary made sure to keep her white lace away from the dark pool of blood while they rolled the unconscious man onto his front so they could get a good look at the back of his head. Dr. Tyndale set the bank of candles down a few feet away and reached into his coat for a handkerchief. He held the handkerchief tight against Mr. Hampton's head to stop the bleeding.

"Once the bleeding stops, I'm probably going to need to stitch this wound." Dr. Tyndale looked back at his father, accepted the handkerchief he was already holding out, and placed it on the wound over his own. "Can you fetch my small kit from the carriage? It's in the squab behind the seat."

"Are you certain you want to stitch him up?" Mr. Tyndale asked his son.

"No, I'm not certain. But I'd better do it anyway."

Mr. Tyndale left with a shake of his head.

It was quiet between them for a few moments. Mary pulled out her handkerchief to add to the other two just in case the blood seeped through. She folded it two more times and placed it over the top of his. He had moved his hand away so she could apply her handkerchief,

58

now he placed his hand over hers and they both held them in place with gentle pressure. Finally, he broke the silence.

"Why did you leave the ballroom with him?"

"I didn't know I shouldn't."

"What did he do, exactly?"

"He held me tight so I couldn't get away, and he tried to kiss me."

Dr. Tyndale narrowed his eyes and looked down at Mr. Hampton with an angry glare. Mary was partly gratified at the jealous anger she saw, but partly annoyed. Dr. Tyndale had kept a careful distance from her since their dance at the beginning of the evening.

"Why did you leave the ballroom to come find me?" she asked.

"I was worried when I saw you dancing with Mr. Hampton. I had heard that he might ... try something like this."

Mary was angry that she knew so little. Was abducting young women from ballrooms common? Her brother certainly hadn't tried to protect her. She looked over her shoulder at the statue behind her. At least the old duke had. She heard a sharp intake of breath from Dr. Tyndale and turned back around.

"What is it?" she asked.

Dr. Tyndale spoke haltingly. "It looks, well, it looks as though Mr. Hampton tried to open, or rather, he um, undid a tie and maybe some buttons on the back of your gown."

Mary could feel her hands underneath his become sweaty and her arms started to shake a bit. Her eyes stung, and she didn't think she could hold back the tears.

Dr. Tyndale rescued her when he said, "I'd like to kick him in the head myself."

Mary was able to take a deep breath and smile just a little instead. He pulled his hands from over hers and took off his suit coat. Mary closed her eyes when he placed it over her shoulders.

Very kindly, he added, "When my father gets back, he can escort you to go find your maid."

Mary looked down at Mr. Hampton again, so harmless now, but still so vile.

She met Dr. Tyndale's eyes again. "You realize that this is the type of man my brother approves of?"

"I wish I could control your brother's opinions, but I can't."

"Oliver's opinion shouldn't matter to you," she said, her annoyance driving away any lingering desire to cry. "I assure you, it doesn't matter to me. The last time I saw you in Aldwickbury, you—" Mary couldn't quite bring herself to say, 'You kissed me,' so instead she said, "I thought you wanted to court me. Up to that point, it seemed as if you hadn't decided, but it felt like you had finally made up your mind."

"I thought I had, too, but I could never have made that decision if I had known you are practically a duchess."

"I didn't tell you who I was because I was worried you wouldn't let me visit patients with you. But if you had admitted that you are a baronet, then I would have told you that my brother is the Duke of Cheltenham."

"Those are not anywhere near the same thing."

Thinking of what he had told her during their dance, she said, "You're right. A new baronetcy is more impressive than an inherited title. It means you actually earned yours."

Mary thought her argument was valid, but Dr. Tyndale just rolled his eyes. Before he could argue further, Mr. Hampton began murmuring.

With no sympathy that Mary could detect, Dr. Tyndale said sharply, "Lie still. You've got a cut on your head. If you try to sit up, you'll just make it worse."

Ignoring the prone man face down between them, she asked, "So are you saying that if my brother would approve of you, then you would court me?"

"That would never happen."

"But if I can convince Oliver, then would you consider it?"

Mary knew it would be the most difficult argument. Oliver really was quite stubborn, but so was she. If Dr. Tyndale would just admit there was a chance, she would argue with Oliver without ceasing until he agreed.

"Of course I'd consider it, Mary," he said quietly. "But it will never happen. I think your grandfather did you a favor by sheltering you from society, but you just don't understand that your brother would never pick me to be your suitor."

Mary looked up as the doorway suddenly filled with people. First her brother, then Mr. Hayes, whom she had danced with earlier, then an older woman, then Mr. Tyndale returning with Dr. Tyndale's kit. They all pushed into the room at the same time.

Dr. Tyndale looked over his shoulder at their entrance, and Mr. Hampton pulled his arms up and tried to push off the floor, perhaps still hoping to make his plan work.

Mary made up her mind in that instant. If Dr. Tyndale needed her brother's approval, then she would get it. These society rules were ridiculous to her, but apparently, if she were caught kissing a man then they could marry. Even a devious man like Mr. Hampton could use the method to get married.

Mary was sitting back on her knees. She shifted forward and placed one knee on Mr. Hampton's back, preventing him from rising as he was trying to do. He grunted as she leaned over him. She reached for Dr. Tyndale's chin, pulled his face around, and planted her mouth on his.

Dr. Tyndale froze in what she assumed was surprise. She wasn't entirely inexperienced with kissing, but she thought she must not be doing it quite right. She had kept one hand on the handkerchiefs covering Mr. Hampton's wound, but now she used both hands to hold Dr. Tyndale's face against her own.

Strange that it was just yesterday that they had kissed like this, only it had been Mr. Lund lying between them instead of Mr. Hampton. That kiss had been so gentle and like a shock at the same time. Remembering it now, Mary softened her lips against Dr. Tyndale's and let her hands relax and her finger-tips trail gently down his face and neck. Paying attention to details had never served her so well. Dr. Tyndale rose up to meet her and wrapped his arms around her to pull her closer.

Mary tried to ignore the angry, bewildered and excited voices around them.

"That's not Hamilton. Who is she kissing?"

"That's my son, Sir Walter Tyndale!"

"Mary, what do you think you are doing?" That one was Oliver's voice, and she smiled against Walter's lips.

Dr. Tyndale seemed to recognize her brother's voice as well, and he pulled away. "I shouldn't have done that."

"That's what you said last time," Mary replied. She still held his face in her hands and she leaned closer again to add, "But you had better not say it next time."

Mary turned to look up at Oliver, who was standing, arms crossed, glaring at Mary. "You know the implications of what you just did? What you've just given up?"

"Yes, Oliver," she replied. Interestingly, she adopted the same tone he usually used with her when he tried to explain something as though she were dim-witted. "I've given up Mr. Hamilton, and Lord Keswick, and all the rest. I suppose you'll condone a marriage with Dr. Tyndale?"

"Nothing else to do about it now, is there? Although please, at least call him Sir Walter." He heaved a great sigh at the inevitable. "I've secured Miss Attwell's hand. Wait until I announce my engagement to let this news spread. I don't want to give her a chance to reconsider."

He left to see to his future in the ballroom.

Mary couldn't believe what Oliver was giving up. Didn't he know he could find love rather than merely secure the hand of the most sought after young lady?

Mary stayed with Dr. Tyndale while he stitched Mr. Hamilton's head. He cut away more hair than was necessary to access the wound, which pleased Mary quite a bit. Gossip had spread down below, and several guests made their way to the long gallery.

Mary and Dr. Tyndale overheard them as they asked each other, "Is that Miss Worthington helping a doctor?"

"Why would she?"

"Someone just said they are betrothed."

"It's preposterous!"

Dr. Tyndale met her eye, but Mary couldn't tell if he agreed with the bystanders or not. Finally, when the stitches were in place, Dr. Tyndale stood up and reached a hand down to help Mary up.

He kept her hand in his as he turned to Mr. Hayes and said, "He's your responsibility now."

When they were out of the long gallery, Dr. Tyndale led her down the stairs but turned away from the ballroom toward the back of the house.

"Where are we going?" she asked, not really caring where he took her but curious.

"I'm looking for the kitchen. I'm sure there will be a basin where we can both wash up."

Mary hadn't remembered the way to the balcony, but she had paid attention to the quickest route to the kitchen. She showed him the right door, and soon they were both standing in the corner of the kitchen with clean hands while servants washed dishes across the room.

"Are you angry with me?" Mary finally asked.

Dr. Tyndale shook his head then set down the cloth after drying his hands. "No, just worried that your brother is right. You've just given up a great deal to be with me."

A smile slowly lifted her face. "I just gave up a future with a pack of men that I never want to see again and instead got everything I wanted."

Mary was relieved when he smiled back. "Mary, you are everything I want and more." He reached for her hand and held it. "My father insisted I come to this ball tonight and try to win over Miss Worthington. He made me promise, in fact. It was so frustrating these last few weeks to be wishing I could pursue you but having to wait until my promise to my father was fulfilled."

"That's why you withdrew after our kiss at Mr. Lund's? Because you were going to try to win over another young lady?" Mary pulled her hand away from his. She had been worried about Dr. Tyndale forgiving her, but now she folded her arms and gave him a challenging glare.

His smile just grew, and he lifted his hands to the lapels of his coat still on her shoulders.

He pulled gently, and she stepped closer as he said, "It wasn't another young lady; it was you."

"But you didn't know that at the time," Mary pointed out, squinting at him, not giving in quite yet.

"My father insisted, but I already knew that the Duke of Cheltenham's sister could never tear my heart away from you. I had very low expectations when I arrived to meet the elusive Miss Worthington tonight."

"It did seem as if you were disappointed when you saw me."

"Only disappointed because I thought my future happiness with you had been taken away." Dr. Tyndale pulled her closer still, and when he leaned toward her, Mary thought he was going to kiss her again. Instead, he whispered in her ear, "If my father hadn't wrung that promise out of me, I would have told you I loved you before now."

Mary uncrossed her arms and wrapped them around Dr. Tyndale as she stood on her tiptoes. She turned her face just an inch and kissed his cheek, then gently slid her lips down to his, and he kissed her back. With her lips so preoccupied, she'd have to tell him later that she loved him too.

About the Author

About Paula Kremser

Paula Kremser began writing while living in England, so choosing to write about the Regency era was no coincidence. She is an avid reader but decided to write because sometimes stories just didn't go the way she wanted. She obviously has control issues; just ask her four kids. She hopes to someday win an award for her writing. In the meantime, she brags about once winning a bubble gum blowing competition. She continually practices that skill (along with writing) in her new hometown of Sandy, Utah.

Other Books by Paula Kremser

Sophia

To Suit a Suitor

Unexpected Love: A Marriage of Convenience Anthology

Oregon, United States, 1880s

Hiding Gems

MANDI ELLSWORTH

MATTHEW

The last couple of months felt long as a Texas summer, but I was finally home, and the sigh that welled up from my toes expelled itself as relief. The forested hills and distant snow-covered mountains, the corrals and barns and livestock made up the place I had lived my whole life. I'd helped Pa fight off the encroaching forests, and the bears and bobcats that came with it. I'd planted Ma's garden, both flowers and vegetables, year after year. I knew this land better than my Pa knew me and understood it far better. This was my work, my playground, and my passion. Happy didn't quite convey how I felt to be home again, but that was certainly part of it.

Ma stood on the wraparound porch of the main house, listening to me ride up, smiling her grim smile, waiting for me to come to her. Her blonde hair had faded to a tired noncolor, and her sightless eyes were a weary blue, but her body and mind were as lean and strong as ever. It looked like she'd won the recurring debate over what color to paint their wood-slat house again because it was still yellow with brown shutters.

Pa strode across the hen-pecked, patchy grass yard to meet me.

He'd taken to shaving his head and growing a cayenne-colored beard when his red hair started thinning out. It made him look mean as a dog fight when he removed his hat, but no one who saw him with my ma would ever think of him that way. With her, and my sisters, he was soft as cotton fluff. With everyone else, he was about as fluffy as steel.

My littlest sisters, Regina and Florrie, raced to see who could reach me first. Of course, Reggie was winning, since one of Florrie's legs was shorter than the other. Florrie had been born that way. Hard to believe she'd been around for eight years already. They'd both grown in the two and a half months I'd been gone, and I felt a pang that I hadn't been here to see it.

Dismounting my faithful roan, I scooped Reggie up and twirled her just to hear her giggle. At eleven years old, she was almost too tall for such treatment. Then it was Florrie's turn, but I was gentler with her since being rough caused her pain. I nuzzled into her ticklish neck and blew loudly against her skin while her laughter rang across the yard and got sucked into the Douglas firs beyond. I settled Florrie on the ground in front of me, and she grabbed my hand to hold while Pa shook the other and slapped my shoulder.

"Good to have you home, son."

"It's good to be home. Where's everyone else?" Work was continuous, but I'd hoped to see the rest of my siblings welcoming me.

We walked toward my mother.

"Reggie," Pa said, "you'll see to Matthew's horse, won't you?"

"Yes, Pa."

She gathered Sput's reins and led him to the barn. The horse's full name was Sputum Sneeze for reasons only Pa knew and thought were funny. Regina talked to Sput the whole way to the barn, promising him all sorts of fine treatment in her little girl voice.

I was only half-listening to her, since Pa started answering my questions.

"The boys are fixing the fence line in your south pasture. Gettup went straight through it. Again. You ought to make mincemeat of that bull. Belinda is off with that Ferguson fella for the afternoon. A picnic. If he ever gets up the courage to ask me for her hand, they might get married."

I already knew about the Ferguson fella, and knew that Belinda didn't fancy him as more than a friend. Pa was slipping if he thought that would get a rise out of me.

Reaching Ma, Pa left off talking while I greeted her. She didn't like it much when people hugged her right off. Made her feel captured since she couldn't always tell who was doing the hugging. She'd never said as much, but I could tell by the way she stiffened. So, I took her hands in mine and let her hug me.

"Oh, my boy," she whispered in my ear. She patted my back once, sniffed, and released me. "You been by your place yet?"

Ma didn't like getting sentimental.

"I thought I'd see you all first." I rubbed Florrie's head. "Get you off my back."

Florrie grinned up at me with a missing tooth, and I thought life was just about perfect.

Then Pa opened his mouth and ruined it. "We had us some trouble while you were away."

Well, of course we did. Pa came from a family that led trouble around like a lion on a leash. They called it the McKinney curse of Good Intentions and Bad Timing. Mostly Pa's brothers and sister didn't look for trouble, but it came at them anyway, unlike Pa, who seemed to think life wasn't any fun without a bit of danger thrown in. It was like he'd light his own pants on fire, then try to outrun the flames, laughing all the way.

Pa always said I had too much of my ma in me because I didn't want to join in his hell-raising. I wanted a quiet life with plenty of work and as little disturbance as possible, and he thought I was a dead bore. I imagine that's partly why he sent me off with my least favorite cousins to visit my least favorite uncle. It had been something of a joke to Pa to get me to leave my new cabin since he knew it would annoy me, and he'd been grinning when he explained that my uncle Henry needed a man to take his two daughters, Millie and Hannah, to visit Uncle Jack. I knew Uncle Henry would have liked to take his daughters himself, but couldn't get away from his job. Also, knowing Uncle Henry, he likely wouldn't trust anyone but a McKinney to protect his girls properly.

Pa sniggered when he said that while I was gone he'd get my brothers to check in on the cabin into which I had poured every spare moment and every cent I had saved over the last two years. I didn't find it very funny. But since I'm a dead bore, and dedicated to duty, I accepted the challenge in late autumn and rode the rails from my home in Oregon to Texas to collect two of my sniping cousins, then on to New York so they could experience Christmas in the big city courtesy of our Uncle Jack.

"What trouble?" I asked, dismissing my thoughts, and though I was eyeballing Pa, Ma answered.

"It was nothing you need fret over now, Matthew. Just had some of those Orientals find their way to our place. Got a might tearful when we wouldn't give them work. We sent them on their way, right enough."

I nodded, satisfied that Pa hadn't gone looking for a prank and causing worry for Ma.

Rubbing his red beard, Pa said, "Probably won't have much more trouble from Orientals. Most have settled by now in the cities, and I can't imagine there are many more headed this way after they were forced out of Seattle. It's been almost two years now since those Knights of Labor sent them scattering like dandelion seeds."

"I guess."

I wasn't terribly interested in Pa's views of the Chinamen and their "rightful place." I'd heard it too many times before. On a selling trip to Seattle a couple years back, Pa had gotten himself involved in a rally of some kind. The leader of that rally, Daniel Cronin, had spouted off why all the Chinese had to be sent back to where they came from: they were taking jobs that belonged to whites; they were lowering the value of our currency by sending it to their families outside the United States; they were making it hard for whites to keep steady jobs because a Chinese man would come along and do the same job for less money.

It all sounded like the kind of talk that roused men to action, and that had worried me. Pa didn't need much to rouse him. Evidently, where the Chinese were concerned, others didn't need much either. Over several months, the Knights of Labor party riled up plenty of other men and two winters back got most of the Chinese rousted out of their city. Some left by boat, some by train, some on foot. Ma had convinced Pa not to do anything foolish, which seemed her primary job in life, but Pa had never looked at the Chinese the same way after that. Ma trusted almost nobody, so her life view didn't change much—she just rearranged her mental list of "unworthies." I kept my head down and my opinions to myself. No sense in ruffling feathers.

Keeping my mouth closed seemed to be my primary job in life. Having a Pa like mine made it harder than it should be, but since I preferred peace to being right, I'd gotten good at keeping my thoughts to myself.

"Also had two bobcats on our land," Pa went on. "One tore into the sheep and had herself a feast before I shot her. Wasn't big enough to make a nice pelt, but Michael wants it for his collection anyway."

I nodded, letting Pa know I was listening and waiting for him to get to the news I could see he was bursting to share. It didn't take long.

"You know those Nilssons? The ones who foul up our stream by dumping all their garbage in it? Well, the boys and I detoured the stream so it don't cross their land anymore. They came two days ago asking if we knew anything about it. I had to cross my eyes to keep from laughing until they'd gone."

I guessed it didn't matter that Pa had four water sources and the Nilssons only had the one. I also guessed it didn't matter that they were our closest neighbors and would probably hold a grudge against us. That was just Pa's sense of humor. He didn't set out to be mean—he didn't think of it that way—he just thought it would be funny. I also knew enough about Ma to know she'd already made Pa go and fix his stream detour.

I resisted the urge to roll my eyes or to tell Pa how much harm he'd done because that was exactly what Pa wanted from me. If I didn't react, he was more likely to leave me be. I wasn't much for the arguments Pa seemed to thrive on. I didn't like feeling that itchy, hotheaded anger that came from using harsh words—words that were meant but shouldn't have been said.

Throwing a punch was all in good sport. Getting angry was something else entirely.

"You want to join us for supper?" Ma asked, ushering Florrie in the house to wash up. "Your pa made bread and corn chowder, fresh today."

"No, but thanks for the offer, Ma. I'm anxious to see how my cabin held up. I'll see you in the morning for breakfast though." It was a sacrifice to pass up a meal of Pa's since he was a better cook than anyone I knew, but I had a longing for my own home that couldn't be shoved off anymore. I looked at Pa, "You made sure no skunks took up residence in my cabin, right?"

Pa offered a gesture of disappointment. "Skunks! I shoulda thought of that!"

Ma shook her head, wearing her grim smile, and went into the house, followed closely by Pa. I didn't miss the fact that he hadn't answered my question. I'd have to be on my guard until I found the extent of what he and my brothers may have rigged up.

Regina stepped onto the porch on her way in the house from the barn. I snagged her arm and lowered my voice. "I'm counting on you to tell me the truth, Vegetable. Anything out of the ordinary happen while I've been gone?"

For a few years the nickname had bothered her, since we weren't the only ones who thought she resembled a string bean, but now it seemed she didn't even notice as she teetered her head from side to side. "Pa and John had another run-in with the Mowbry crew, but they was all drunk and let Pa and John thrash them without much of a fight. Michael sure was disappointed he wasn't there."

I nodded. Pa had raised his sons to be good in a fistfight. Each one of us itched to prove our salt, even me, and I was the least like Pa of any of his sons. The only reason I'd found my time in New York City tolerable wasn't because of the fancy dances and teas my cousins had forced me to escort them to, it was the illegal boxing club I'd stumbled into the end of the first week there. Boxers had good camaraderie and very few fights involved anger, which I appreciated. Uncle Jack knew why I'd come home with new bruises every other night, but Aunt Penny and the other girls weren't enlightened. I only had three weeks to hone my skills as a boxer with ring rules, but it was time I considered well spent, and even though I didn't rise straight to the top in the ring, I was close. If I could have stayed a few more months I might have been a contender for the top.

The bruises had only just faded.

"Were the Mowbrys on our land?" I asked. It had happened before.

"Not this time. Just on the road from Molalla, but John says they started it."

"Sure they did." That's what we all said. I was the only one who ever meant it. "Anything else happen?"

She shrugged. "You were gone a long time, Matthew. I can't remember everything."

I gave her a smile and tugged on her braid. "Ma's headaches gotten worse?"

"Nope. And Florrie's doing just fine at school, too. I make sure no one picks on her."

"Good girl."

"You eating with us?" She moved toward the door and the mouth-watering smell wafting from it.

"Not tonight, but I'll see you tomorrow. Then you can come keep house for me."

She giggled. The idea of keeping house for me tickled us both, as she got to play house, even though she was getting too old for that, and I got a clean house and a meal cooked by someone that wasn't me in my own kitchen.

When she went inside I went to the barn to get another animal to take me home since Sput was tuckered out.

My place wasn't more than two miles from Pa's High Noon Ranch. In fact, I'd bought the land from him, since he had more than he could handle. I'd walked the distance between homes often enough, but I was eager, and walking would take too long. I mounted an animal with all my gear—a mule I'd sold to Pa last year that wasn't above taking commands from a rider—and headed out. The sun was sitting atop the trees to the West like a candle on a Christmas tree before setting completely, and it warmed my left shoulder as I headed north.

About a half-mile from my cabin, I ran into an ambush of my three younger brothers. John and Michael, twins, swung out of the trees on ropes like sailors from the rigging, their cries of attack piercing the solemn woods. Patrick, my youngest brother, braved the mule's kicking and silently pulled me off its back from behind. Patrick wasn't as filled out as John and Michael yet, but he was trickier because he'd learned the art of being quiet.

I hit the ground with a grunt and was immediately swarmed with three sets of fists and elbows and knees. I'd have new bruises to replace the ones that'd just healed, so I set out to give a few. The grimace on my face turned to a feral smile as I attacked.

To some, our good-natured tussle would have seemed brutal, but to us McKinney boys, it was pure enjoyment. We didn't play by many rules, but we kept the rules we had, which was really just one rule: no hits between the legs. Scratching and biting were allowed but considered beneath us. Being the oldest, I'd always pulled my punches, so to speak, but John and Michael sure didn't, and they were nearly as big as me now.

By the time we'd all had enough, our chests heaved with the exertion, our clothes were covered in mud and fir needles, and smiles abounded.

I clapped a hand on John's back and he tried to elbow me in the stomach.

"Hey, now." I said, gripping his shoulder harder than necessary. "We all know the reason none of you took me on by yourselves. Don't go starting something you can't finish." I was taunting, but they all knew it was true. "Pa said you were out fixing the fence around Gettup."

Michael, trying to brush the mud from his trousers, said, "We did. That old snort ain't worth the trouble he causes." Which was why they'd left him in my corral, alone, while I was gone, instead of taking him to the main house with the rest of my animals. "Then we figured we'd wait here to welcome you back home. Belinda is going to have a hissy fit when she sees this mud."

John and Patrick started cleaning themselves up.

Since Ma couldn't see, Belinda was in charge of most of the cleaning and organizing around the main house. To me, it was another reminder of why I was happy to live on my own. If I didn't want to upset Belinda with more washing, I either did it myself or got rid of my clothes, and she was never the wiser.

As they cleaned themselves off, I took a minute to eye the boys. John and Michael looked like brothers, but not twins. Michael's hair was blonde with red strands sprinkled throughout. John's was red as Pa's beard, like mine. Michael was missing a front tooth that got knocked out while trying to tame a mustang a few years ago, and John's nose was crooked from being broken in a fistfight. With a tall Pa and a tall Ma, we had no choice but to grow tall, too, and the twins were six feet, at least. Working on the ranch provided us all with the opportunity to bulk up, and our shoulders were wide enough to carry loads most men would find impossible. But seeing as I was four years older than the twins, and they weren't done growing, I was still taller, and still outweighed and outfought them. Especially with the things I'd learned in New York.

Patrick was just starting that transition from boy to man, but his dimples, blue eyes, and blonde hair were already turning female heads. All that attention drove Regina loco, as she had to listen to the other girls fawn, while Patrick lapped it up like a hungry kitten laps cream.

"Which of you boys was the last to check on things at my place?" I asked.

Their confusion wasn't reassuring, and I started up another tussle when it came to light that no one had been to my house in the last week to check on anything. The corrals were built away from the house, so they could have seen to Gettup without actually seeing my house through the trees.

Finally, when Patrick had a split lip, John's eye looked to be swelling shut, my finger had been bent backward, and Michael was wheezing, we called it quits. This time for good.

The boys, in one last bid for dominance, stripped the mule of all my gear, dropped it in the mud, then sent the animal running for home before I could stop them. I'd have to walk the last half-mile carrying everything I'd taken to New York. They ran to their horses, laughing all the way back to the ranch. I watched them disappear into the trees, sighed, then gathered my things: a leather satchel with my clothing and shaving gear, a fancy suit in a special bag of its own, and a box of things I'd bought in the big city for my family.

I wasn't sure the boys would be getting theirs.

The walk wasn't difficult, just awkward, especially trying to keep my things out of the mud while opening the gate that marked the beginning of my land. I'd always loved this dell and knew it was exactly the place I wanted my home. It had turned out better than I'd imagined and even walking down the hill through the trees felt ineffably right. By the time the walls of my own wood-slat house came into view I was more than happy to see it. The trees I'd cleared myself, using them as building materials. I'd had the lumber milled, taken out the stumps, built the house, outbuildings, and corrals. My own animals filled my pastures and barns, and next spring I would have enough space cleared to plant a little grain along with a vegetable garden. It made things easier to clear when the animals ate through most of the undergrowth. The year after that, I had plans to plant fruit trees. I couldn't live off my pa's food stores forever.

It wasn't that I was trying to get away from my family—if I had been, I would have moved a sight farther than two miles—I'd just decided it was time to have a place of my own.

Though, it may have had something to do with needing a little distance from Pa.

Halfway across the dusky clearing, I realized there was smoke coming from my chimney. Even though I knew I wouldn't see my brothers or the main house through the woods, I looked behind me in their direction. They might be mischief-makers, but I could tell they hadn't been lying when they'd said no one had checked on my place recently. Who would have lit a fire?

It was possible one of the girls had come without telling anyone and made things comfortable. Possible, but I wasn't convinced. If someone else was in the house, it was too late for me to go unnoticed, since I was right in the middle of the clearing. Even though the sun was down, it was probably light enough to see me if they looked out any of the windows, so I decided to be cautious and angled myself toward the back door instead of the front. I kept a hammer in the lean-to shed by the back door and could use that as a weapon if need be.

Guns were among the things I didn't agree with Pa about. He thought a man wasn't a true man without one. I could use one and had gone hunting all my life for food; I just thought they were unsporting against a man. A gun didn't give a man a real chance to fight back.

I placed my gear inside the lean-to and snatched up the hammer. If someone was in my house, they'd soon wish they weren't.

I tightened my hold on the hammer and cleared my thoughts as I slowly pushed open the wooden door to the back of my house. Aside from the light of the fire in the open stove, and the dimming light from the windows, the place was dark. Looking into each of the darkened corners, I finally spotted a face and straightened up. The face was lower to the floor than it should have been. Either the person hiding in my cabin was kneeling down, or they were awfully short. A child, perhaps? The eyes shone brighter than anything else in the place.

I stepped forward, the hammer at my side, hoping to get a better look at what I was up against. My footfall sounded like thunder echoing against the walls in the silence. A whimper escaped from somewhere, and I noticed a second pair of eyes hiding behind the first. The second pair of eyes were even lower to the floor than the first. Two children?

Belatedly, I looked behind me and shifted the door to check behind it. If there were two, who'd say there weren't more? Finding nothing more than clean floors, I turned back to the corner that held my intruders.

The one in front held up their hands, took a step into the light, and a girl's voice said, "Please, mister. Don't hurt us."

It took me a single heartbeat to realize this was a full-grown woman, just a very small one. But then, most people were small compared to my family. She and the child were Chinese. Her long curtain of straight black hair shone like obsidian in the low light, with delicate facial features and fingers—birdlike. But the strength and sorrow in her eyes were what captured me. One look into those eyes and I could see she'd been through more difficulties than could be counted. Knowing recent events just north of the Columbia River, I could imagine her life hadn't been easy.

The child behind her was frightened. Of me. I couldn't abide that.

The region in my chest around my heart pained me, and the look in the woman's eyes, the fear in the child's, bound me tighter than cords. She and the child might be trespassing in my house, but I had a feeling it was me that was lost.

PEARL

Mud and fir needles clung to the giant man who had crept into the house. His short, dark red hair was mussed like he'd purposely stuck it on end, and the blue of his eyes was visible even in the near darkness. Li's four-year-old hands tightened into fists on the back of my dress, making me wonder if his heartbeat was as loud as mine. I wanted to push my hair behind my shoulders or put it up in a bun like it should be, but I kept my hands held in front of me to show the man I meant no harm.

I almost snorted, bitter. Like I could harm someone as big as he.

The big man straightened, pulling the hammer behind him like he didn't want us to see it. His voice was deep as still water.

"Sorry for scaring you, but what are you doing in my house?"

Li's little hands shook, and I pulled him around to my side and patted his back to better comfort him. I took care to speak confidently, hoping it would fool the man into thinking I was.

"It was empty and the door was left open. Mengzhi is sick and we needed food and rest. We couldn't find anywhere else."

The giant nodded at Li. "Is that, uh, Meg shi?"

"Mengzhi. No. This is Li, her brother."

I probably shouldn't have given him that much information. It seemed the more information a person with power had, the more they'd use it to hurt me. I patted Li's hands, comforting him when I so desperately wanted the comfort.

The giant rubbed his head, messing his hair even more. Then he attempted to smooth it down, all while trying to keep the hammer hidden.

"Uh. Oh. I guess she's in the bedroom," he said. I gave a quick nod.

His feet shuffled, and I found it in me to be amused by his discomfort. He, with all the power, discomfited by a few trespassers.

"I'm calling the sick one Meg, unless she has an easier name. I don't think my tongue could make those other sounds."

I nodded because I knew Meg was a perfectly respectable female name in English. I also knew that some Americans liked to give the Chinese names that were not so respectable, expecting us not to know the difference. But I was born American. My Irish father worked on the transcontinental railroad, where he met my Chinese mother, who worked in the laundry. They'd only been married fifteen months, long enough to create my older brother and me, when an accidental explosion killed my father. I was born eight months after that, and my mother stayed with the railroad until finding work in Seattle. Because of that, I knew English as well as I knew Cantonese and spoke both without an accent, which surprised many people. I could also speak a little Italian and Greek from listening to the other women in the laundry and the men who spoke to them, but there wasn't much use for that skill anymore.

The giant, still shuffling his feet, cleared his throat. "My name is Matthew McKinney. I guess that little guy behind you is Li. And you are?"

I was tempted to tell him the name my mother had called me, Xiaohua, because I knew that would confuse him, but I took pity on him at the last second. "I'm called Pearl."

Matthew reached up to tip his hat to me, realized he wasn't wearing one, and sort of nodded awkwardly in my direction. "They yours?"

He meant the children. I would have been twelve when Mengzhi was born. I shook my head no, even though they felt like mine with the three of us being together for so long. "I care for them."

"How long you been in my house?"

If I told him we'd been there nearly a week it would likely enrage him, so I held my tongue and just looked at him.

"All right, then. How's Meg now? She doing better?"

I could see he wanted to know when we'd be leaving. If my answer wasn't what he wanted to hear, I imagined he'd toss us all out the door on our ears, so I continued to say nothing.

He rubbed his hand through his dirty hair while he thought. "Look, I'm glad you found someplace to stay when you needed shelter. I don't even mind that it's my house. But I have someone coming over tomorrow to clean and you can't be here."

He looked at me, waiting. When I continued to keep my mouth closed, he sighed. "She'll be here after breakfast tomorrow. The three of you could move out to the barn—just while she's here—and then you can come back inside."

That wasn't what I expected.

My mouth fell open and I closed it tightly before any words poured out. He'd already gotten more than his share from me.

"If Regina sees you here, she'd tell Pa—his name is Buck—and then he'd come and make my life miserable. Probably your lives too, since he agrees with the Knights from Seattle. You see what I mean?"

I definitely knew miserable. I nodded and decided it would be safe now to twist my hair back and stick it with a few pins. I did so. Maybe that would teach me not to get ready for bed before dinner, no matter how tired I was.

"I'll let you know when she leaves and you can come back in here where it's more comfortable."

He said the words, but I had the feeling he wasn't paying as much attention to them as he was to what my hands were doing.

"If we're staying in here, where will you stay?" Matthew seemed nice enough, but I knew from experience that many men expected something in return for their generosity, and his staring made me nervous.

Rubbing the back of his neck, he mumbled something I didn't understand. When he looked at me and saw I didn't hear him, he said, "The hayloft ain't uncomfortable. I can stay there tonight, but I'll have to wash up and eat in here with you all."

I knew he wouldn't allow a situation like that to last for longer than a day. Maybe two. I'd be locking the doors though because I didn't trust that he'd keep his word. He'd toss us out to the wolves soon enough.

"Have you all eaten dinner yet? I'm starved." He stepped to the hanging cupboards in the kitchen area and stood immobile in front of the one with bottles and boxes in it. There were considerably fewer bottles and boxes than when we'd first gotten here, even though we'd tried to be careful and not eat much. He mumbled something in a growly voice. Growling meant anger and I stepped back from him.

"I'll work for the food we ate," I said. "I already cleaned the cabin, if you didn't notice, and I plan to do more of the like for as long as you let us stay."

He stared at me, his face set in an unreadable expression, then shook his head and went back to mumbling as he looked through the cupboard. His house had been a squirrel-infested dust heap before I'd gotten my hands on it because a door was left open, so the work I'd done wasn't insignificant. The craftsmanship under the dirt was outstanding.

Finally, his growls became audible communication instead of beastly noises of displeasure. "I ain't gonna charge you for food. You eat what you want and I'll see you get more." Taking out a glass bottle of preserved string beans, Matthew opened it and began eating them out of the jar with a fork. "How's Meg? She getting enough to eat?"

Eating cold green beans wasn't all that strange, but his solicitude toward Mengzhi was probably concerning. What did he want with the little girl?

"She have a fever?" he asked between bites.

I nodded carefully, letting him know I wasn't about to give him more information than I thought he needed.

"She sick or infected?"

"Infected. Stepped on a sliver and it isn't doing well now. It's making her fevered." This was the sort of information I would give; it might help little Mengzhi.

Matthew looked around a bit as he ate, finally finding the box he was looking for under a three-legged stool. It was something I hadn't opened while cleaning, but I should have after seeing what was in it. It held bandages, saleratus, brandy, and dried herbs, some of which I was familiar with. Pushing all those things aside, Matthew found a set of small pincers and thrust them in my direction. Li didn't loosen his grip on me as I moved forward, so he came along.

The fact that my fingers touched Matthew's as I took the pincers from his hand shouldn't have bothered me, but I felt the warmth of where my fingers had brushed his extend through my palm, up my arm, and settle somewhere behind my ribs. My face even warmed. It felt like something I hadn't felt since my mother died: peace, warm and safe. I barely knew this man and didn't even pretend to trust him.

Peace made no sense. To hide the oddity of that feeling, I brought my hands to my chest, gripping those pincers like they held my sanity.

I couldn't help but think that Matthew was big enough to shield me and the children from anything that would come at us—should he think to stand up for us—since a shield was exactly what I wanted so often. But it would be a miracle if his work-roughened hands labored on our behalf, and I certainly didn't expect them to. His mahogany-colored hair looked soft, unlike the rest of him, and his blue eyes held promises of protection and safety no one, in my experience, had ever been able to keep. I lowered my eyes, embarrassed to have looked at him for those few moments, and reminded myself that no matter what his eyes promised, it wasn't meant for me.

I cleared my head of everything but Mengzhi and didn't allow myself to think of Mr. McKinney's thoughtfulness or generosity as I scurried with Li clinging to my behind to the bedroom where Mengzhi lay. In fact, I didn't think of him at all, and if the clomping of his boots or the grumbling of his deep voice tempted my thoughts to stray in his direction, I yanked them away with force enough to keep them where they were supposed to be. He was just like all the others who'd pretended generosity and later expected a payment too harsh for me to pay. No sense in allowing myself to think differently.

The bed where Mengzhi lay had to be Matthew McKinney's since it was big enough for ten of her, and she looked comfortable except for her eyebrows drawn together in pain. I explained what I would need to do before I touched her foot so I could coax her into doing what needed to be done. She'd become skittish about letting anyone near her injury because the swelling and infection made it hurt terribly. I used the pincers to take the larger-than-average sliver out of little Mengzhi's foot. She cried. I felt like a monster for hurting her. Li lay his coarse-haired head on her shoulder and tried to soothe her as best as he knew how. She hugged him and hiccuped until her tears stopped.

"It will start to feel better now, Little Bird."

"Thank you, Xiaohua," Mengzhi whispered, using a funny combination of English and Cantonese that was particular to her and Li. They could understand both languages just fine. It was only when asked to speak that they had problems keeping them separate.

I wanted them to know the language of their parents, but also the language of their birth, so I alternated speaking English one day and Cantonese the next. It was an English day.

"Mr. Matthew McKinney is home now. He says we can stay here for a bit, but in the morning we'll need to move to the barn while his house is being cleaned."

At this, Li sat up and said with an earnest expression known only to little boys, "Mr. Matthew is big as a tree! He's bigger than, than ... " Li's arms waved in a futile demonstration of the man's size. "Bigger than a steamboat!"

The biggest thing he'd seen close up had been the steamboat we'd ridden across the Columbia River. I smiled, not only at Li's excitement, but also at his mixing languages.

"Is he gonna hit?" Mengzhi pulled the bed linen up to her nose so only her eyes peeked out.

I smoothed her shiny hair with my own work-roughened hand. "I don't think so, Little Bird. If he gets mean, we'll leave and find somewhere else as quick as can be. You know that, don't you? I'll keep you safe."

She nodded but kept her face covered from the fear of what might happen. These children had known too much fear in their short lives, and even though they had only been our neighbors in Seattle and I had no blood ties to them, I had sworn to keep them as carefree as I could for as long as I could.

"What do you think of having the name Meg as your English name? It's close to Mengzhi, and Meg sounds like a nice sort of person."

"What does it mean?" Mengzhi asked.

I shrugged. "English names don't have to have a meaning. Sometimes they're just nice sounding."

"You think I should?"

I smiled at her. She trusted me more than anyone else. Li too. I was the only mother they remembered. It filled my heart with both trepidation and love. "I think it's a good idea to have an English name. Mr. Matthew McKinney said he couldn't say your real name."

Mengzhi smiled and a small giggle snuck out. "Meg." She nodded her acceptance.

"All right, Meg. I'm going to get something to take that yucky stuff out of your foot, then we'll wrap it up. You'll feel better in a couple of days."

I left the children playing a game of their own creation with small rocks on the bed and went to confront the giant. He was frying eggs with a bottle of tomatoes dumped in. The bedroom door was right off the kitchen area, so he looked up as I came out.

"You hungry? I can make more."

More? He didn't think that entire fry pan full of food was enough? I knew how much the children and I could eat. That left the rest for him. The notion that any one person could eat that much in one sitting left me speechless.

He watched me search for something to say for a moment before turning back to the stove and the food, stirring with enough ease that it was clear he'd cooked for himself often. Finally, I cleared my throat.

"Thank you. The children and I haven't had supper yet."

He nodded, his back still to me.

His hands had been scratched and were bleeding which must have happened when he'd gone out to collect eggs. I would have noticed otherwise.

It would seem Mr. Matthew McKinney had met the occupants of his henhouse, which weren't all hens. There were at least six roosters mixed in. I wondered if he liked the constant violence of the birds. Why else would someone keep six roosters in a hen house?

I watched his enormous shoulders move under his shirt as he stirred, then as he shifted the pan from a hot spot to a cooler one. I supposed a man who had that much muscle and bone and mass would need a lot of food.

On a different train of thought, that much man would be difficult to escape from if he ever turned on me.

Taking a large step away from him, I opened my mouth. "Meg could use some saleratus if you wouldn't mind lending us some. Like I said, I can clean the house and barn, garden, cut firewood, sew, wash clothes, or a lot of other things in exchange."

He flicked a look in my direction as he emptied the contents of the pan onto a plate. It smelled good, and I knew the children were as hungry as I was. We had eaten from his stores, but not as much as we'd wanted.

"Use whatever you need." He took his plate to the table and set it in the middle. "And don't think I'll be making you chop wood. A bitty thing like you would take a full day to do what I could in an hour."

"Then don't you be thinking I'll be doing anything other than chores for you. I may be small, but I won't put up with mistreatment. I'm a good Christian woman, and I expect to be treated like one."

I'd heard other women use this line and liked the strength it showed. Not to mention it seemed to get results. It worked with good men, anyway.

From the look of shock and consternation on his face, I would guess this Matthew McKinney fancied himself a good man. All he said was, "Good."

Then he went back to the cupboards to find something more to cook. From over his shoulder, he said, "The saleratus is in the box."

I gathered it, some bandages, ointment, and some camomile to make a soothing tea with after supper, then went back into the bedroom. The three of us watched in fascinated disgust as the saleratus fizzed on Meg's wound. Happily, it didn't hurt her enough to bring tears. After I cleaned that up, I got out the bandages and ointment. Meg and I were both used to the bandaging process, so it didn't require all my attention, or hers. She continued to play with Li while I let my mind wander. When Matthew left the house this time, I knew it, also when he walked back in with more eggs held carefully in his shirt, more wounds on his hands and forearms.

Before he'd fried up another pan of eggs and tomatoes, I had the children's hands washed and them sitting at the table, their noses twitching with the smells of abundance. I gathered plates and forks for us all and set them around the table. Matthew sat at the opposite end than the rest of us, like a head of the household should. Although, in other households, the head probably didn't have the others in his home cringing away from him in apprehension. I didn't mind the children's mistrust of him because it reflected my own and helped keep us all safer. I just wished my mistrust led me not to think about him.

Matthew nodded politely in greeting to Meg, said a brief blessing over the food, and dug in. After dishing up food for myself and the children from the heaping plate in the middle, I watched in near horror as Matthew shoveled food into his perpetually open mouth. The man barely paused to chew. He also ate everything from the second pan he'd cooked, and when he'd finished with that, looked inquiringly at what the children and I hadn't eaten. Almost with a sense of awe, like one would have when viewing a freak show, I pushed the leftovers closer to him. He took them with no expression on his face and finished every speck of food.

That had to have been close to two dozen eggs he'd fried with two jars of tomatoes. The children and I maybe ate two eggs each. That left enough to have fed two whole families and he ate it all! And that didn't include the bottle of green beans! Had it been a truly long time since Matthew had eaten? Or was this a common occurrence? I guessed if he kept to himself as he said he would, we might stay long enough to find out. Perhaps a couple of days. Longer if he'd let us. It wasn't like we had many options.

I was recalled to myself when Matthew pushed his plate to the center of the table and clasped hands across his flat stomach. "You all come from Seattle?"

It was tempting not to answer, but he wasn't shoving us out the door as he could have done, so I decided to give him a little. "Yes."

"The riots happened two years ago. You been on the go all that time?"

"Yes."

"Did little Meg get that sliver in her foot walking barefoot?"

"Yes. Her shoes are getting small and pinch her feet sometimes."

"Do you have any family you could stay with? I'd likely be able to help you get to them."

"No." His questions were easy to answer; I liked that.

"You seem willing to work. Would you like help finding a job or something like that?"

This question wasn't so easy. "If you know someone who would hire me, knowing that I have the care and feeding of two children, I'd be grateful for the work. I'd be grateful for your help. But as I'm sure you've guessed, finding work hasn't been easy." Few people wanted anything to do with a Chinese person, especially one they assumed was either a widow or an unwed mother.

For a few moments, he sat unmoving. Then he sighed and nodded to himself. "Fine. For now, you work for me in exchange for a place to live and food to eat. Sound fair?"

I couldn't see that he'd be getting much out of the arrangement, but I wasn't about to remind him he was getting the short end of the stick. "Fair."

He nodded again, this time to me, then stood and took his dishes to a large sink on the same wall as the stove. I scrambled to help. After all, he'd fed us when he didn't need to, and we'd just made a deal to trade for that. It should be my job to clean the dishes, especially since the slashes on his hands had to be irritating him.

Loading all the dishes into a bucket I'd been using for this purpose, I bent to lift the bucket and tote it to the sink, but a massive arm stuck itself in front of my face and the bucket was taken out of my hands. A noise like a combined gulp and grunt came out of my mouth as I watched Matthew put the bucket into the sink and pump water into it. Looking at Li and Meg for confirmation of what I was seeing, they looked as confused as I felt.

Finally, I pulled myself together and walked to the sink where Matthew had begun rolling up his sleeves.

"I'll wash them," I said to his back.

He grunted, so I knew he heard me, but he plunged his hands into the water with a rag and started soaping it up.

"Mr. McKinney, I said I would wash the dishes. We have a working arrangement. I need to earn our keep."

He glanced at me, picked up a tin plate, and began washing it. "From what I've seen, you've already earned a surplus of your keep. The chickens were taken care of, even though I'm sure you didn't introduce six new roosters to the brood. That honor had to be my pa. If you stick around, it looks like we'll be eating a lot of chicken in the near future. The barn looks better than it has since it was built, except for the leaky bucket of sap Pa put above my horse's stall. The house is sparkling it's so clean. You even did something to the privy to make it smell better." He handed me the clean and dripping plate, nodding toward a towel.

I grabbed the towel and the plate, careful not to touch him, and wiped the plate dry. I replaced it on the shelf where it lived when not in use. If his pa had brought the roosters and put a bucket of sap in the barn, he sounded like a handful, to say the least. I wondered if that was why the door to the house had been left open.

Matthew continued talking as he washed. "The way I see it, I'm in debt to you and need to catch up somehow so we start from an even field."

I glanced again at the children. They sat close together at the table, worriedly looking between the adults. The fear in the little faces made me wonder if I was doing something wrong by being wary of everyone. Was it ultimately helping or hurting them?

"We stayed in your house without your approval. We ate your food, basically stealing it. You could have me jailed for those things." I snapped my mouth closed, angry with myself for giving him ideas.

He handed me another plate, but didn't let go when I grabbed it. I looked at him, my anger burning with the heat of my gaze. He spoke slowly with no expression on his face. "I owe you. What kind of man would I be were I to take your services and repay you by fetching the authorities? As it is, Reggie won't have much to do when she comes in the morning." He twisted his face to add to the humor in his eyes. "I doubt she'll feel bad about that."

His face softened when he talked about this Reggie, and the gentle way he teased about her had me dropping my eyes. He went back to washing and I to drying, but my thoughts were elsewhere.

No one had teased me since Zhao was shipped away two years ago.

Zhao had been the best older brother, letting me tag along with him, listening to all my concerns, and gently prodding me into a better mood. Walking with me when I needed to go somewhere. Making the whole house lighter with his laughter. Zhao used to tell me after Mama died that he'd take care of everything; he'd take care of me. He'd promised Mama he would. But when it came down to it, he didn't care enough about me or his promise to Mama to do more than wave as he boarded the ship to China. In the face of opposition, his promises meant nothing.

I'd learned the hard way that most men were like that. Most people were like that.

Now I had no way of knowing where my only living family member was, how his life was going, or if I'd ever see him again, because he wouldn't fight for me. I had to learn to fight for myself. No one else would.

❧

MATTHEW

I washed the pan last of all, scraping all the cooked egg off it and gave it to Pearl to dry, trying not to think about how small her hands were. Or how vulnerable she and the children were. Or how much they needed someone to give them a break. Or how lovely the smoothness of her skin was.

"I'll grab a blanket and be on my way." I stepped into the bedroom and snatched the only spare blanket I had from the wooden trunk I'd made when I was twelve.

I stepped toward the back door and nodded at the children still sitting at the table like deer listening for trouble. I nodded also at Pearl, who watched me with the dishrag still in her hands. She looked at me like I was the hunter scouting those deer.

"Latch this door behind me."

I crossed the threshold and closed the door firmly. I waited for a moment, and when I didn't hear the latch, I hollered through the door, "Latch it."

Footsteps sounded, far too quick to be anyone but Pearl, and I heard the latch slide home.

"Good night," I said, though I doubted she heard me.

I didn't expect a reply in any case. A fly in the vicinity of a frog wouldn't bother with polite farewells, and I'm sure that's how she felt.

I knew I should be suspicious of the people in my house, worried they might steal something, or murder me in my sleep, but I wasn't. I had seen so many desperate people, both around home and in my travels, and the three little people in my house had that look. They were desperate for food and shelter. I had so much, and I could share, as I had with others before this. Besides, if they stole something from me, it would be because they needed it more than I did.

Shoot! They needed everything I had more than I did.

I was trying to be a good person and I couldn't, in good conscience, make them leave or treat them unkindly. The working arrangement would hold them over until something more permanent came along.

I hadn't lied when I'd said the barn would be comfortable enough. I'd slept in rougher places and didn't mind bedding down with the hay we had to import from the valley. We could grow our own grain to feed the animals, but alfalfa took more cleared space than we had. Tomorrow I'd bring home my animals from Pa's where he and the boys had been taking care of them while I was gone, and then my comfort in the barn would start to slide downhill. Cows and mules and horses and chickens and sheep and goats all together made a sort of diabolical stink.

Maybe I'd drag some hay to the toolshed and sleep there tomorrow.

As I lay down in the hayloft and pulled the blanket over top myself, I couldn't help but wonder about Pearl, Meg, and Li. They were some of those that had gotten expelled from Seattle. Where had they wandered since getting kicked out? How had they lived? Didn't they have anyone to help them?

No family, at least.

And most pertinent to me, how long did they plan to stay in my house?

I wasn't about to toss them out. I'd build someplace for them to live before I did that because they needed it so much, but I didn't expect them to stay long, despite our arrangement; they seemed like wanderers. I also didn't want Pa finding out I was housing three Chinese people. Ma wouldn't be far behind him in her silent recriminations. She always let other people have their own opinions even if they didn't line up with hers, but if you asked her, she'd tell you that her opinion was the right one.

Pa, though. Ugh. Pa had to convince whoever didn't agree with him that they were wrong and he was right. He'd landed himself in some mountainous arguments because he wouldn't back down. I did not want to find myself his next target.

I reminded myself that Pa had many fine points to his character, despite his joke with the roosters. He was gentle with those under his protection, and he knew when he'd done something wrong. He might not admit he was wrong, but he still knew it. He loved to laugh and to make others laugh. He told the best stories. He was the hardest worker I'd ever seen. And he was a good pa, teaching all of us how to be hard-working, God-fearing adults. I had to remind myself sometimes that he was a good man, because I tended to see mostly his annoying traits.

Getting that settled, I said my good-night prayers, being sure to pray for my new houseguests, tucked more hay under my right shoulder, and drifted off to that land of nod.

I woke, as usual, with birds starting their songs and woodpeckers fighting the trees for food. The sun was struggling to rise like the sleepyhead it was. I washed my face and torso in the stream close to the house and nearly shouted as the cold water touched my skin. Nothing like a good shock to the system to get a body going in the morning, but even knowing that, I still preferred bathing at night.

This morning, I figured I'd get some help to herd my animals back to the barn and corrals and fetch Reggie after I had the livestock settled. Besides, I didn't want to make Pearl hide out more than she had to, and if I had some of the boys with me, it'd be easier to hide the three visitors if they stayed in the house while we delivered animals. No reason for the boys to go inside.

I put that plan into action and found the two men I paid to help care for my animals, along with John and Patrick. We had the barn full of its usual occupants, the corrals full of oxen, mules, and horses, and the sheep and goats under the trees before Pa finished making break-fast. I told John and Patrick to hustle home and to tell Pa I'd be there directly. My hired men had already headed that way.

When I knocked on the door to my house, I had to bite back a grin. Knocking for permission to enter my own house. Sometimes life throws us humor when we aren't expecting it.

Thinking back to the list of Pa's good qualities, I added another: He could always find life's funny little moments.

I saw the curtain at the window twitch and then heard the latch slide. Pearl opened the door, wide-eyed as an owl, and I nodded my hatted head in greeting.

"Morning," she said as I walked in the house carrying a load of fire-wood. I set the wood by the stove and washed my hands in the sink. I hadn't noticed it yesterday because of the darkness, but in the morning light, Pearl's want was obvious. Her dress was fraying around the bottom, stained and patched several times, nor was it in the least bit fashionable. Those kids weren't any better. Meg's dress looked much like Pearl's. Li's pants didn't quite cover his knees and his shirt didn't cover his wrists; both elbows had patches. And the three of them were so skinny it looked like their bones were knocking at their skin.

"You have enough for breakfast?" I asked, noting the small amount of porridge cooking on the stove.

"Yes," Pearl answered, quiet as a fox on the prowl.

"Good. I'll be eating at my pa's house. When I get back, I'll have Regina with me and you'll need to be hid. It'll take less than an hour."

She nodded.

"Don't worry none about cleaning up the dishes after you eat. It'll make Reggie suspicious if there's nothing for her to do."

She nodded again and I turned to leave. "Oh, there's animals in the barn again. So, hide in the loft. It'll be safer."

I didn't wait for her to finish nodding at me before I left the house. I waited outside the door for a moment, then opened it again. "Keep the doors latched until you leave the house. Bears have been known to get into a poorly closed door." But I was more worried about people.

When I closed the door a second time, I waited until I heard the latch being slid home before I walked toward the main house. It might seem loco to tell a stranger to lock the door of my house when I'm on the outside of it, but I wasn't taking any chances. I couldn't guarantee their safety if they were found. It'd keep things nice and quiet if my guests would stay hidden for as long as they'd be my guests.

The walk was pleasant, probably much like it was decades ago when Pa married Ma. Ma had been a widow, and Pa inherited the running of the place with the marriage, and since he wasn't interested in logging, he began supplying a few of the biggest logging operations of that time with meat: mutton, pork, chicken, and beef. The loggers sure could eat a lot, and it made Pa a wealthy man. When I grew to adulthood a few years ago, I decided to cover transportation needs and provided trained oxen, mules, and a few horses to the two biggest companies that Pa worked with, along with selling to individuals. I liked the animals. I liked the freedom to sell to whomever I wanted. I liked the income. But mostly, I liked the peace of being my own man.

I walked into the main house just as Reggie and Florrie finished setting the table. The long wooden plank table was set with enough plates, cups, and forks to feed all five hands and the whole family besides. Ma sat at the head of the table in her customary spot, tatting while waiting for the meal to begin. Ma did as much as she could, but it had always been Belinda, as the oldest daughter, who'd picked up the slack of what Mama couldn't do.

Belinda fussed with the placement of platters heaped with eggs, sausages, hash browns, pancakes, baked beans, and bottled apricot jam. Pa sauntered out of the kitchen, wiping his hands on a cloth he then slung over his shoulder before placing a plate in front of Ma and filling it with the things she liked. The hands all trooped in the house and sat to the table at the same time since Florrie had alerted them that the meal was ready.

Little Florrie had quiet ways and mannerisms that I loved. Mistreatment of her was one of the few things that could and would get me angry. She rarely got mistreated anymore, since all her older siblings got angry about someone mistreating her. The shoes meant to help her mismatched gait were something she'd gotten better at working with and now made hardly any sound at all when she walked.

Pa sat, and we all bowed our heads as he said a quick prayer. "Lord, bless this food and our lives. Amen." Then the race was on to grab the nearest platter of food before someone else cleaned it of vittles. I made sure I got my share and tossed Reggie a pancake when she missed out on them.

"Hey there, big brother," Belinda said, winking at me from across the table. She had grown into quite a beauty: tall, slender, hair the color of her blushing cheeks. All the men round about saw it too. Even the hands had difficulty keeping their eyes to themselves, and two of them were twice her age. I slashed them all with a look and noticed Pa doing the same.

"Lindy," I nodded her way.

Pa took a bite of sausage and spoke around it. "I'm having the trees felled on the east twenty acres."

It took a moment for his words to penetrate my food fog. "You mean the twenty acres you're selling to me?"

He nodded, a gleam of anticipation in his eyes.

Ma took up on my behalf. "Buck, you know that land is as good as Matthew's. What are you hoping for by logging it?"

"That land isn't sold yet, and I intend to get a fistful of cash from it, if I can. And I can. That land has mostly white oak. Good hardwood. So, the fallers will start day after tomorrow. You got a problem with that, son?"

Pa as good as told me that land was already mine—we just hadn't signed the paperwork to make it legal. I had the money saved up to buy it, minus a few dollars, but I'd have the whole of it next month. I took a deep breath and fought to keep my teeth from clenching. It wasn't worth fighting over. If I fought him, it would only egg him on, and I'd be dealing with this sort of thing more often than I did now. Besides, what did it matter to me if he stripped the trees and left me with the stumped leavings? It was the land I wanted. The animals would get more grazing without trees.

"No, Pa. Go ahead and get what you can."

The swift look of his disappointment that I hadn't argued didn't bother me because Ma's proud look set me at ease. That, and my own conscience telling me I'd done the right thing, even if Pa thought I was lily-livered.

Seemed my conscience was having a good run of it lately.

After the meal, Pa and the boys left the house, but I made sure to hug Belinda and Ma and swap a few tales of my time in New York. They were especially interested in the fashions back East where bustles were all the rage. It was a good thing I'd thought to bring home a few of those magazines my cousins had poured over. Bustles? I shook my head, bewildered. Seemed impractical to me.

I left Ma and Lindy and gave instruction to my two workers about what needed doing, then headed back to my property with little Reggie on her own mule next to Sput. Reggie and I chatted some, but mostly we were content to look around.

I'd seen a good many places and people, and there wasn't any I liked better than what I had here. Soft sunlight filtered through clouds and trees, chill enough this time of year to bring frost. The smells of fir and woodsmoke filled the air, and the sounds of fallers two hills away shouting to each other reached my ears. The trees muted sound but also kept things quiet enough to hear everything, close or far. As near to paradise as God could get on Earth.

I encouraged Reggie to allow me to tie up her mule so she could head straight into the house. Then I took Sput into the barn. Keeping my voice down, I called into the loft to let Pearl and the children know I was back. When I got no response, I climbed up. Even with the doors open, I couldn't see into the dark corners and figured that'd be where they'd hole up.

"Pearl? You three up here, safe?"

A rustling sounded in the corner behind where I stood and I eased my way around so the ladder under my feet would stay under my feet. I saw three sets of dark eyes peering at me, but no one said anything. I nodded my satisfaction and climbed down.

Reggie was washing dishes when I stepped into the house.

"I don't think I've ever seen your house so clean, Matty. You should go away more often if you come home and tidy up like this." She grinned at me, and I tried not to look guilty.

"I'm glad you approve Vegetable, but I think I'll stick around anyway."

"I thought you would. You have the nicest house in the neighborhood, aside from the main house. Why would you want to leave?"

"My thoughts exactly. I'll be with the livestock in the birthing barn if you need anything. A couple of the cows are about to calf and I want to have a look at them."

She nodded and I left her to the cleaning. Having two barns was a luxury I was happy to have. Especially today. Steering clear of the hay barn, I felt more than a little like I was escaping—a mouse running for its hidey-hole. Working with the animals had always been my haven, and I needed it twice as much today.

At lunchtime, I headed back to the house, knowing Reggie would be finished cleaning and had probably tried out her budding cooking skills for my benefit. Between Pa and Belinda, little Reggie didn't have much chance to cook meals herself at home, and she liked the quiet when it was just her and me. We ate, and I tried not to think about the hungry fugitives in the hayloft.

"You all right to make it home on your own?" I asked Reggie when we'd finished washing the dishes together and chatting about how schooling was going for her.

The look she gave me about withered me in my boots. "Of course. I'm eleven, not three."

"I beg your pardon, Grandmama." I bowed to her all fancy-like as gentlemen did in New York.

She grinned and whipped at me with the end of her wet towel. I picked her up and carried her as she shrieked with my tickling to where her mule stood waiting in the shade of the Douglas firs. Reggie always preferred riding bareback and had a knack for staying on when others needed saddles, so I plopped her on the animal's back and waved goodbye as she rode away.

As soon as I was sure she wouldn't double back, I hustled to the loft and said, "Hey, you three. It's safe to come out."

Only one of three sets of dark eyes met mine, and I scrambled the rest of the way up the ladder and into the loft. "Where are the kids?"

"There." Pearl's voice was much softer than mine had been. She pointed into a little nest she'd made where Meg and Li curled up together sleeping. I knew Michael would have teased me for the soft look on my face just then, but I couldn't see such a tender sight and not let it show. It seemed I had gotten a double measure of Pa's soft heart where children were concerned.

"You want me to carry them down?" Part of me hoped she said yes. Another part warned me not to become attached.

I wished the look on her face could have been as easy to read as mine had been. "You could carry them down the ladder?"

I nodded. "Or we could let them finish sleeping up here."

Why was I talking about "we"? There was no "we."

She considered a moment more. "I'll wake Meg, but if you wouldn't mind carrying Li into the house, I'd appreciate it. That is if we're still welcome there."

"You bet."

Pearl shook Meg, who woke wide-eyed and immediate. They slipped down the ladder, Meg favoring her hurt foot, and waited at the bottom for me to climb down. I liked to think they were there in case I slipped, but I figured it was because they didn't want me carrying Li anywhere but into the house.

Li was such a tiny little thing. I'd forgotten just how nicely a child could fit with their head on my shoulder. It was a reminder of how long it'd been since Florrie was born.

Turned out I was even broodier than the cows.

We made it to the house, and I deposited little Li on the bed. On my way back through the living area, Pearl called to me.

"Mr. McKinney?"

I turned, privately thinking it odd to be addressed by Pa's name.

"Thank you."

There was so much behind those two words, like a beaver dam that held everything back but a trickle. I didn't want to think about how much she'd suffered and how little kindness had come her way. Plenty of people held the Chinese in dislike and that had to have made things harder for Pearl and the children. I didn't like thinking about their hardships. Instead, I tipped my hat and went back to work with the firm determination that I wouldn't let anything bad happen to my guests for as long as I had them. A good employer should do no less. They needed and deserved a protector. Also a little happiness. As Pearl had said, they didn't have any family, so who better than I to give it to them? At least I was willing.

That night when all the chores had been finished and I'd sent my workers back to Pa's table for supper, I knocked on the house door and waited for it to be unlatched. Li was bouncing on his toes as he waited for me to come through so he could close the door behind me. I placed my hat on his head, then pretended to be surprised.

"Oh! I beg your pardon, I didn't see you there!"

The light that filled the boy's eyes was bright enough to be mistaken for the sun. I winked at him and put my hat on the peg on the wall. I wondered what had caused the change in his attitude toward me but was mostly just happy for it. Meg stopped when I came in but resumed setting forks beside each plate. Four of them. I wondered if I'd be welcome to eat with them and didn't want to assume, but it was my house, after all. Pearl was stirring something that smelled not only edible but delicious on the stove. I went to the sink and pumped some water to wash with. I noticed Pearl didn't say anything, but she did sidle further away.

"You make enough for me too?" I asked.

"I tried." The wry note in her words had me taking another look at her.

Was she teasing me? Her lips twitched, and I shook my head. Amazing. It wouldn't have surprised me to find the cares she bore had stripped all humor from her, but the woman actually had a sense of humor after all she'd been through.

"I eat more than anyone you've ever seen, right?"

She leveled a look at me that confirmed what I'd said.

"But that's only because you haven't been to a mess hall at the logging camps. Any one of those fallers or buckers eats even more than I do at every meal. One winter I worked as bullwhacker, and I couldn't keep up with those other men when we sat to the table."

"No one could eat more than you!" Meg said, then blushed so red she could have been a raspberry.

I washed my dirty face, scrubbing like Ma taught me, until I was the one with red cheeks. "I'd like to believe you all mean that as a compliment, but I'm starting to think you don't." I threw the towel I'd dried my hands and face with onto the worktable, wishing I dared take off my shirt to wash the parts of me that really needed a good airing after working all day. Instead, I said, "How about I make you a treat after dinner? If Pearl doesn't mind, that is."

Pearl shrugged, keeping her back to the room, but mostly to me. "I don't mind."

"What kind of treat?" Meg asked. Li didn't say anything, but he looked eager as a puppy with a tail wagging and tongue lolling.

"You'll see. First let's eat a hardy dinner and make sure to thank Pearl for making it."

"Xièxiè, Xiohua," came the chorus of twin voices. I had no idea what they said, but it sounded sweeter than apple pie in their pint-sized tones. I helped get the children settled in at the table and toted the big pot from the stove. I knew Pearl wasn't happy that I'd taken the pot from her hands, but it was heavy for her, and Pa taught me to help out a woman in need.

No one said much during the meal. Of course, I never said much during meals because my mouth was already too busy to bother with forming words. Eating was the first priority. But when the food was gone, I wanted more time with those two little bits, so I got them to help me wash the dishes. I set Meg on a stool to dry since her foot hadn't fully healed. At one point, I could have sworn Pearl even smiled from her seat at the table. I pretended to myself that my stomach didn't swoop like a hawk in flight when I saw it. I also pretended not to notice that she was particularly lovely. For an employee.

After that, I made sure the fire in the stove was hot, melted a dollop of lard in the bottom of the pot, and popped some corn. The way Li jumped around in excitement, I might have mistaken him for popcorn. We agreed to let Pearl have the first taste, which she did and was sufficiently encouraging that the little ones begged to be next.

While their tiny hands dug into the white kernels, I couldn't help but think this felt like a family. This was what I wanted my own family to feel like. I didn't know Pearl and the kids well enough to harbor anything for them but pity and admiration, but I could get used to having a family of my own if it would feel like this.

PEARL

Later that night as I lay in bed with Meg and Li, I listened to them talk about their thoughts of Mr. McKinney. Li kept bringing up how strong Mr. McKinney must be to be able to carry such a big boy as himself down from the loft, and how much Matthew had eaten at dinner. Li was also enamored with the popcorn.

He finally ended his thoughts with, "Mr. McKinney likes us. He didn't hurt any of us. Do you think he'd teach me to do stuff?"

Meg was quieter, but she seemed to think well of him too. All Meg said was that she liked Mr. McKinney's smile. I had to agree; even though I resisted, I also couldn't deny that it seemed like a nice man went along with that nice smile.

Watching the children interact happily with Matthew was a joy and a worry. I was happy for their happiness and that they had the opportunity to feel safe and full and warm enough to feel anything other than worry. But I knew better. I knew this joy was a fleeting emotion, just like safety and satisfaction. Despite being nice, Matthew would tire of us. Or he would be unable to afford feeding all of us. Or perhaps he would face opposition and, even with sadness, decide we needed to move on. He would wave as we walked away and feel the weight of a burden lift off his shoulders.

It wasn't that I couldn't notice the pleasant feelings that encompassed my little flock, but I could not trust him. I would enjoy the comfort while it lasted, and try not to be hurt when he shoved us out the door. But that shove would come, if we didn't find a reason to leave first.

I knew of families that stayed together. Some men didn't leave, and some women didn't die young. How did their lucky families manage to keep them around? Could I ever become someone that got the good things of life to stay? It almost hurt too much to think about.

The morning after having popcorn I was sitting in the rocking chair, mending a torn seam on Li's shirt, when Li burst through the bedroom door, wearing pants and his undershirt, and interrupted my melancholy thoughts.

"Xiohua, can I go with Mr. McKinney to feed the chickens? Please?"

It was a day for Cantonese, but Li had mixed in the English word for chickens.

Matthew stepped into the room and nailed me to the rocking chair with his blue eyes. The reaction to his clear gaze had nothing to do with the softening around his mouth when he let his eyes linger. I had no desire to encourage any sort of softening. Except that I couldn't seem to break away, and found that I enjoyed looking back at him very much.

"Xiohua?" Li tugged on my sleeve.

Finally tearing my eyes from the giant leaning against the threshold, I looked at Li. The little squirrel couldn't have been more eager, his excitement bringing him to his toes. "As long as Mr. McKinney doesn't object, you may go."

"I heard my name in there somewhere," Matthew said. "I don't know what else you said, but it sounded like music."

Li hopped his way to Matthew and took the large hand with his small one. "Let's go!"

"All right, Mr. Big Britches! You sure you don't mind?" he asked me.

"I'm sure. Li," I said, switching back to Cantonese, "you stay beside Mr. McKinney and do just what he tells you."

Li didn't stop tugging Matthew's hand as he replied, "I will!"

Matthew laughed and allowed himself to be towed from the house as Li chattered in perfect English. It interested me that Matthew was the one who wanted to keep us hidden, but he'd asked me if I minded Li going outside with him, as though it had been my rules keeping the children out of sight.

I watched Matthew and Li from the window, Li walking slightly behind Matthew, trying his best to match his smaller steps to Matthew's much bigger ones.

When Meg came in the bedroom looking for an occupation, I set her to hemming a handkerchief from a scrap of material I'd found a couple of months ago. We'd already been using it as a handkerchief, but it would be nice to have it look tidy. Even better that she'd use it to even out her stitches.

I'd really have liked to have fabric enough for a new dress. The one I was wearing had been turned twice already and had started looking its age a year ago. I dreamed sometimes of having a beautiful new dress —green, with a bustle, and swags in the front held in place by large black velvet bows. I knew I could make myself such a creation if I had the materials, but it was just dreaming, because I'd make the children new clothing many times over before I'd spend any hard-earned money on something frivolous for myself.

Matthew brought Li back in the house after about an hour, then set out by himself. He didn't come back for lunch, and the children and I couldn't eat even half of what I'd made, thinking he'd be there to eat it, so I saved it for dinner.

When he showed up for dinner, I noticed his hair was wet and tried not to notice his bare chest at all, but couldn't help notice it glistened with water too. And dark hair. The man was big enough to seem invincible, like a god. All muscle and bulk. No one would tell him he was unwelcome on their land without worrying about retaliation. No one would cheat him of his rightful pay. No one would call him rude names, or trip him as he walked down the road, or take things that belonged to him. In short, I supposed no one would treat him as they'd treated me and the children.

He walked straight from the door to the bedroom and donned a shirt first thing. All three of us had stopped what we were doing to watch him. It embarrassed me that we'd been staring, and the pink in his cheeks when he reemerged fully clothed told me he was embarrassed by it too. I lowered my eyes.

He stood just inside the kitchen and cleared his throat. "Something smells good."

"Chicken and potato soup." I flicked my eyes to his face, noticing the pink was still there, and lowered my head before he saw my smile. It amused me that such a man would be modest. "I found the cellar. I hope you don't mind I used some of what was in there."

"Of course not. Use whatever's here."

"Thank you." I kept expecting him to tell me I'd gone too far and kick us out to the elements. My gratitude was deep when he didn't. Every safe day was a blessing.

I expected it this time when Matthew took the pot from me to set it on the table. I turned back to the worktable and got the bread that was still warm from the oven. When we were all seated and the prayer was said, I turned to Matthew. "Are you going to be gone for lunch every day?"

When he looked at me, the softening around his mouth was there. "I usually eat at Pa's table once or twice a day. Usually. So, I'll head there for lunches."

I nodded, keeping my eyes on the soup in my bowl. He must keep up the appearance that everything was normal. That we weren't here. The man wasn't invincible. No one was. "That's good to know. Thank you."

"You don't have to keep thanking me, Pearl. I'm doing what any good person should do."

"Should, perhaps, but rarely do."

Meg, having watched our whole conversation with interest, said in English, "Today is a Cantonese day."

Matthew and I shared a look, but I didn't linger.

"True, Little Bird, but Mr. McKinney doesn't know Cantonese, so he speaks English every day." To keep with our rules, I spoke Cantonese.

"Oh." She focused on getting another spoonful of soup to her mouth without spilling. While I appreciated her dedication to keeping herself clean, it worried me too. She shouldn't be so concerned by it. But then, she'd been helping me wash laundry for other people for more than two years, so perhaps her concern was a natural byproduct of that.

Matthew asked, "What is a Cantonese day?"

I explained our method, and he seemed suitably impressed. I made a conscious effort not to be flattered by his reaction.

When we'd finished eating, Matthew inhaling the rest of the soup and loaf of bread, Li jumped from his seat.

"Popcorn!"

Meg even perked up at that.

"Well, now. How could I resist that?" Matthew teased, then

enlisted their help with dishes again before popping their treat. I swept the floor and basked in the warmth Matthew provided, both figuratively and literally.

"Come on in here and we'll play jacks." Matthew led Meg and Li into the parlor just off the kitchen where a padded bench flanked by matching chairs and coffee table all sat on a braided rug.

Unable to hide my curiosity, I stowed the broom in the shed by the back door and joined them to see how it was played. I'd seen other children playing jacks, or sometimes they called it knucklebones, but was never invited to join. It would be nice to finally learn the rules. Meg and Li had settled on the floor beside Matthew and he was emptying the contents of a small pouch on the wood floor. I sat on the bench and watched as Matthew showed them how to play.

When they'd learned enough to take their own turns, Matthew looked at me. "As a kid, I used to play this every day after school. What about you?"

I shook my head. "I've never played." It was no use telling him I'd had no one who would speak to me in school, let alone allow me to play a game.

"What!" He pulled me off the bench to join them on the floor.

I inherited his rubber ball as he pointed out the finer details of the game. When Meg won the first game she threw back her head and smiled for all she was worth, which made me smile along with her. When I stopped grinning, I noticed Matthew's face pointed in my direction. It was unbelievable how soft his expression was considering how the rest of him looked. Whatever was behind that look made me uncomfortable in the same way electrical currents made me uncomfortable. Amazing enough to draw me in and too dangerous to get close to. I won the second game, then helped Li win the last one before putting them back into the pouch and telling the children it was time for bed.

Matthew helped me settle the children for bed, even telling them a bedtime story while I changed the bandages on Meg's foot. We all watched him gather the clothing he had in a wardrobe and shove it in a satchel. I followed him out of the room, thinking that I would latch the outside door behind him when he left, but he turned to talk to me first.

"I didn't realize how improper it would be for me to come in the house after my wash at the stream. I forgot I would need to come in here for a shirt. I won't do that again."

"This is your house, Mr. McKinney. You may do whatever you like in it."

His head was wagging back and forth before I'd even gotten my words out. "No. I will treat you as a good Christian woman should be treated." Not invincible, but honorable. I could live with that. "Besides, now that I know you cheat at jacks, I don't think I should mess with you."

A surprised laugh burst out of me, the first I could remember in years. Matthew looked pleased with himself. I wished I could have said I didn't cheat, but we both knew I did so that Li could win. "It seems I am a dangerous woman when it comes to jacks." It was difficult keeping a straight face while making that declaration.

"You're dangerous any time." I could see the joke not quite making an appearance in Matthew's face. I didn't know what to do with that sentiment if it wasn't a joke, so I ignored it.

"Where are you going to sleep?" I could have asked where was he going to live while we were pushing him out of his home, but thought it more politic to ask the way I did.

He stepped outside and pointed to a wood-slat shed just visible through the nighttime gloom. Not far from the house, but not concerningly close either.

"It's a toolshed," he said, "but I cleared out space for my blanket. Smells better than the barn."

"Would you like me to clean it while you're working tomorrow? I could make it more comfortable."

"That would be nice. The men who work for me don't come that close to the house usually, so you should be fine if you stick to the buildings close by."

Meaning that he didn't want anyone seeing us. It was another good reminder for me where his priorities lay.

"Thanks for dinner and the game," he continued. "Now you have played jacks."

I smiled. "True. Another item crossed off my list."

"What else is on your list?"

Truly, the only things that had been on my list for so long were food and shelter. I said the first thing that came to mind. "I want to read the new Mark Twain book, *The Adventures of Huckleberry Finn*."

He nodded, like making a note of it. "I've heard that's good. Not much for reading myself, but I like listening to others read. Maybe we could work something out?"

"That would require me to have the book. Perhaps you have another book available?"

He shook his head. I wasn't sure if that meant he didn't have access to another book, or that he'd changed his mind and didn't want me reading to him after all.

We stood awkwardly for a moment or two, then Matthew tilted his head in my direction and said a brief good night before walking toward his new living quarters. I did feel a little guilty watching him go to make his bed in a shed while the children and I slept in his real bed, but not enough to call out to him. He was a grown man, and I made it clear he could do whatever he felt he needed to. But I couldn't help the rush of gratitude I felt knowing that I had a warm, soft bed to look forward to. I was also grateful knowing he was within shouting distance.

Before he'd gone too far, he turned around and walked backward as he said, "Be sure to latch the door."

I nodded and he continued on, not looking back again.

Many days passed in a similar fashion. We'd see Matthew for breakfast, he'd work all day— occasionally coming close enough to the house for us to see him briefly—then he'd come to the house freshly bathed and clothed for dinner. After dinner was the time I enjoyed most because the children were so happy to have Matthew there. Especially Li. Little Squirrel needed a man to emulate and he'd cottoned on to Matthew. Even Meg seemed happier when Matthew was around, eager to play any game he thought up and willing to do any chore he suggested. She still felt insecure unless I was close, though.

One of the activities Matthew had initiated after dinner was asking me to read to them all. He presented me with a book—not Huckleberry Finn, but a compilation of some of Mark Twain's short stories he said he'd gotten from the main house. I read one, or part of one, each night, and nearly every story got Matthew chuckling, his shoulders bouncing like boulders jumping rope as he held Li on his lap or helped Meg with some project. His quiet laughter felt like a dew of peace distilling on my heart after a scorching heat. I tried not to read too much into the poetry of the moments. My head insisted to my heart that there couldn't be poetry. But sometimes, Matthew would catch my eye, and the thought that he attracted me like electricity renewed itself. I both wanted to be close to him and feared it.

During daylight, the children and I found many things to do, including cleaning and sprucing the toolshed so Matthew would feel more comfortable there. I asked him if he had any fabric that I might use to sew a tick for him.

The next day, he presented me with a large amount of ugly patterned fabric, and I spent much of my time sewing it. The man was so tall, it could've taken months to sew one long enough. I found some wooden planks that I tacked to the shed wall as shelves for his clothes. One day I washed all his dirty clothing, and he'd seemed irritated about it, but I couldn't see why he didn't want me doing it and he didn't explain. So, I began washing all his dirty clothes along with mending them. He never brought them to me, so I invited myself into his shed every couple of days to gather them.

It got so I felt clandestine sneaking into his room, even though he was never there. It just felt too personal now that it had begun to smell like him.

One day, after he'd been home a few weeks and I was starting to feel comfortable, he came to the house in the middle of the afternoon. The children and I were trying to tidy the woodpile, but Li kept teasing us with a mouse he'd found. All that stopped when we saw Matthew and the blood seeping through the torn sleeve of his shirt.

Li raced to him, his little legs almost going faster than the rest of him, the skin between the bottom of his pants and the top of his stockings flashing in the muted sunlight. Meg and I weren't far behind.

"What happened?" I asked, more demanding than I should have been in my worry.

He picked Li up with his good arm and held him while he answered. Li sank his head into Matthew's neck and held on tight. "I'm training a new team of oxen. The larger bull wanted to show me who was in charge and sliced my arm with his horn. Nothing to get upset about." He patted Li, his large hand covering Li's back completely. The gentleness in those large hands never ceased to draw my notice. "I just came for a bandage."

"Meg, run and get the box with the bandages in it and put it on the table in the kitchen." As she scampered off, I turned to Matthew. "Put Li down and let me see how bad it is."

He whispered something to Li and lowered him. As soon as Li was on the ground, I pulled Matthew's sleeve up as far as I could, but his arm was too big to allow me to see the wound. My first thought was to have him take off his shirt, but I didn't think either of us would be comfortable with that. Instead, I ripped the shoulder seam until the sleeve came off. "I will fix it."

He nodded and held his arm up so he could see the gash in it. "Ornery cuss."

The gash stretched across his upper arm under the shoulder and was the width of one of my handspans. If something had cut me so deep, bone would have been visible, but with Matthew's size, it seemed almost insignificant. Still, better safe than sorry.

"Come into the house. We'll wash it before I stitch it up."

"You think it needs stitching?" He kept looking at it as we walked in the house, Li trotting beside him.

"Yes."

"Have you ever stitched someone up before? Because I could run to Pa's house and get Belinda to do it."

"You do whatever you want after we wash the gore off." I didn't want to tell him I'd never sewn a person before, but I wanted to be the one to take care of him anyway. He'd think I was mother-henning him.

"Pearl." His gentle hand came to rest on my shoulder and I looked into his face. It wasn't a terribly handsome face, but I had grown fond of it, and that made it better-looking than most other prettier faces. "I don't want to add to your list of bad experiences. I can have Belinda look after me."

I shook my head, wondering how much he had guessed about me and uncomfortable with the thought. "I'm sure Belinda does a fine job, but it'd be easier on you to have me care for it. I'll do a decent job."

He continued looking at me for a moment, seeming to search for something. With a deep sigh, he sat at the kitchen table, propping his arm up on the back of the chair next to him. "All right, then. It don't have to be pretty, just be quick."

I nodded and got to wiping the blood off with a wet rag. Both my hands together couldn't wrap around his arm. After that, I spread alcohol over the wound; he sucked in a breath and let it out slowly. Pinching the two sides of the gash together, I began sewing with a needle I'd also washed with alcohol. He didn't make any noise or show any signs of pain except for tensing his jaw and bunching his eyebrows. If we hadn't known him so well, the mean look on his face would have scared us all into running as fast and as far as we could get. Instead, Li sat on the chair next to him and talked about what we'd done that day, dwelling with great enthusiasm on finding the mouse. Meg stood beside me, watching with such intensity she seemed to be memorizing my movements. I finished and spread salve over it. Matthew seemed to relax completely as I wrapped the whole thing with a clean cloth and secured the end with a safety pin. I took a deep breath when I finished, glad to have it over, but also glad to have been the one to care for him.

"Much obliged, Pearl." Matthew rose from his seat.

"No heavy lifting with that arm until the stitches come out. If you make it bleed again I'll ... I'll ..." What on earth could I do? "I don't know what I'll do, but I won't be happy about it." I felt a blush of embarrassment stain my cheeks.

Matthew winked either at me or Li or both of us. "Yes, ma'am, but just so I know, do you mean heavy lifting like this?" Using mostly his uninjured arm, he lifted Li up over his head. Li squealed, a huge smile on his face until Matthew put him down. "Or heavy lifting like this?" Matthew scooped Meg off the floor and swung her in a circle, her eyes wide, but smiling hugely. When he put her down, he walked toward me. "Or heavy lifting like this?"

Not realizing what he had planned until after he grabbed my arm, I was too late to protest. Matthew hefted me up so I lay across his shoulders, my stomach pressed to the back of his head. Then he pretended he'd lost me, looking back and forth.

"Where did she go, Li? Do you see her, Meg?"

The children were shouting my location and laughing hard enough to upset their stomachs. I tried very hard not to think of my own stomach touching him, and the whole rest of me laid out across his shoulders, with his hands holding me in place. I'd never had so much of me pressed against a man, even in fun. It embarrassed me that I liked it so much, but I knew I wouldn't enjoy it if it were anyone else.

After a while, he pretended to find me. I noticed he used only his good arm to help me to the floor. Holding my elbow to steady me, his eyes locked onto mine. For a breathless moment, I couldn't move, couldn't blink. The softening around his mouth extended to his eyes and I could almost taste his thoughts. Almost.

Li spared us further introspection by clinging to Matthew's leg and throwing us both off balance. Matthew tousled Li's hair, still looking at me. Deliberately, Matthew winked. At me.

With that, he walked out of the house and went in the toolshed. When he came back out he had on a different shirt. We all watched him through the open door as he strode off through the trees to the livestock further out.

"Will I get big as Mr. McKinney?" Li asked for the dozenth time as Matthew disappeared.

"No, Little Squirrel, but you'll be bigger than me." Most likely.

"No one's as big as Mr. McKinney," Li said, puffing out his chest proudly like a son speaking of his father.

Oh, how I wished Matthew could be a father to Li! The thought of the three of us being under Matthew's care permanently hit me with such longing I had to sit down on the threshold, which surprised me. Surprised me that I wanted it so much. Surprised me that he had somehow slipped through my defenses to the point that I wanted to trust him. How wonderful it would be to have the safety, the comfort, the care he could provide!

Not to mention his kindness and honor. The heart-throbbing gazes didn't hurt his case either. Shaking my head to clear it of nonsense, I didn't allow myself time to linger over the wistfulness, especially when he had hinted from early on we wouldn't be staying longer than he could keep us hidden. I needed to spend more time figuring out where we would go and what I could do to support the children so I wouldn't be entirely useless. Jumping back up, I herded the children back to the woodpile to finish our chore.

That night after the children had been tucked into bed and I was taking off my dress for a quick wash, a knock came at the door. I didn't rush to open it because I was only in my underthings. Matthew always announced himself as he knocked, so I didn't think it was him. Whoever knocked then tried the latch. I thanked heaven I had secured it, then began scrambling back into my dress. The knock came a second time, and I heard a man's voice holler through the door.

"Matty! Open up!"

"Pa?" Matthew's voice came through the wood. "What are you doing out here so late?"

I hurried to the nearest window and peeked between the curtains, my dress clutched to my front, and had my fears confirmed. Matthew's Pa was the same man who'd thrown us off his land when we came looking for work—Buck McKinney. He'd said something about the Chinese taking work away from Americans. I'd never stolen a job from anyone, mostly because few others would lower themselves to do the jobs I got. But he didn't give me the opportunity to explain anything to him, he'd just told me to get. And with his menacing expression and massive size, he hadn't had to tell me twice.

How could such an unreasonable man have such a caring son?

"I came to check on you. I heard from Al you got gored."

Matthew, wearing nothing but his trousers, laughed and gestured to the bandage I'd put on earlier. "A little cut on my arm is hardly a goring. It's all bandaged up and will be good as new in a couple days. Tell Al to quit using me for his tall tales."

"You had your Ma in fits."

"You mean she pursed her lips?"

Both men laughed, and Mr. McKinney clapped his hand on Matthew's shoulder. "She'll be glad to know you're not bleeding out. Why didn't you come have Belinda patch you up?"

Matthew shrugged. "Didn't need to."

"If you say so. You gonna invite me in for a drink or a chair? I ain't as young as I used to be, you know. Worry for you just about sapped my strength." Mr. McKinney wiped his forehead with a handkerchief, teasing Matthew.

"You still outwork us all, Pa. You don't fool me."

"Did you know your door is locked, and you on the outside of it?"

Matthew grunted. "I have a door on the other side of the house."

"Why's a candle still lit in there?"

"Just came out here a minute ago. Why are you so curious?"

"Bad habit." His pa grinned, his teeth showing like a wolf's in the moonlight. "You sure you're feeling good? You could sleep at the main house for a night or two."

"In the bunkhouse? No, thanks. You know how loud those boys are, and how smelly. I'd rather sleep in a barn."

"Well, that's available, too."

The men laughed again. It would seem Matthew got along well with his father, regardless of the fact that Mr. McKinney had thrown us off his property and that he could be terribly mean. Regardless of the fact that he had played unkind jokes on Matthew. Either Mr. McKinney was a better man than he'd shown me, or Matthew was more forgiving than anyone should be. Maybe a little of both. And I was impressed that Matthew had managed to answer all of his pa's questions without telling a falsehood.

"All right, if you're not going to invite me inside, I'll head back home and tell your ma you're fine." Mr. McKinney strode to the horse he'd tied to a post by the barn and mounted up. Matthew followed behind.

"See you tomorrow," Matthew said.

His pa nodded and rode away. Matthew stood watching for several minutes before turning toward the house. When he came close to the door, I opened it, only realizing I hadn't finished dressing after the evening air fingered my bare shoulders. I clutched my dress to my front harder than before. Being the gentleman he was, Matthew kept his eyes on my face, and I tried to do the same to him.

"Good thing you didn't open the door when he knocked."

I just nodded. It was better than good. If his pa had found us living in Matthew's house, I didn't want to find out what he would have done. Mr. McKinney struck me as a hard man, no matter how jovial he'd been, and I no longer wondered at Matthew not wanting to anger him.

"The kids still sleeping?"

I nodded again.

"I don't want you thinking ill of Pa, but I may as well remind you that even though he doesn't belong to the Knights of Labor, he heard one of their leaders talking in Seattle a couple of years back and decided he agreed with them about the Chinese."

"It isn't like there are many people around here that look kindly on us, Matthew." I only realized I'd addressed him by his first name when his lips twitched before blooming into a smile.

"Well, I like you all just fine."

Of their own accord, my eyes jumped to his chest, bare in the moonlight, and when I raised my gaze, it stopped at his mouth, which wasn't smiling anymore. An ache sprang to life, fully formed, behind my ribs. Despite having terrible influences to the contrary, Matthew had shown kindness to strangers and a gentleness I'd seen from no one else. My heart, impractical as it was, and against the dictates of my head, had decided it belonged to him. I couldn't trust that he'd always be willing to keep us, especially since I'd just seen his father and knew Matthew wouldn't fight him, but Matthew had my love, regardless.

"It's chilly out. I'll see you tomorrow." Matthew nodded at me and went to the toolshed. I closed the door behind me and sagged against it, reminding myself that Matthew had already made it clear that he didn't want to fight for us against his parents. He shouldn't have to, even if I wished differently. But I did wish it! I wished he would choose me over everyone else, and fight the world to have me by his side. He was such a good man.

Shaking my head, I resumed my preparations for bed. That close call tonight had warned me that the children and I would need to be ready to leave at a moment's notice. I couldn't afford to get comfortable again.

MATTHEW

The memory of Pearl's bare shoulders kept buzzing round my head like a late summer fly. I'd truly tried not to look, but they were right next to her face. She was even smaller under those slightly puffed sleeves than she seemed, and it amazed me even more that she carried the burdens as she did. How did someone so slight have such strength of will? How could someone with such soft-looking skin be so tough?

Then she had to go and look at my bare chest and cause the winter air to feel too warm.

I shook my head for the dozenth time since lying down in the shed. I should have been thinking about Pa and how we'd almost been found out. In fact, we might still be, considering how wily Pa was. I was beyond grateful that Pearl hadn't opened the door to him when he'd knocked, but on the other hand, a part of me was anxious to have this out in the open.

Belinda had asked me several times where my dirty clothes were since she usually washed them. I couldn't tell her that Pearl was doing my laundry and mending, but I couldn't lie either, so I just told her I was taking care of it. Same with Michael and John and Patrick. I'd had to give them all excuses why I didn't invite them into the house when they'd been helping with the livestock. Having Reggie come to the house once a week had been a drain on my capacity to worry. I didn't like deceiving my family, but I also wanted to keep Pearl and the children safe. And close.

The stitches in my arm pulled at my skin, and I tried not to scratch at them as I settled myself for sleep. After saying my prayers, I decided there was no use in fretting; everything would work out the way the Lord wanted it to.

The next morning, I went to my house and gathered Li and Meg to help clean the chicken coop. First, we shooed all the birds out, then gathered any eggs we found. We'd eaten all but two roosters, and even those two were trouble enough. I had counted the eggs I'd gotten every day and we found more than that today. Pearl had better watch out for rotten ones since those extras had to be ones I'd missed previously. Then we shoveled out all the roosts and floor, replacing the used straw with fresh. Those children worked as diligently as I did, needing only occasional reminders, and I couldn't have been prouder of them.

When I went to the main house for lunch, I asked Belinda when she planned her next trip into town.

"This afternoon," she replied, "which you'd know if you paid attention. Why? What do you need?"

She went directly to where she'd left a list of things she'd need. When I thought of Belinda, I thought of organization. She was so organized she made bees look sloppy. And lazy. That trait came in handy since she handled most of the chores Ma couldn't do. She had started doing that as a tyke.

I took another look at Lindy and thought of how grown up she'd become. It was no surprise that she had men fighting over the right to court her even though she was taller than a good portion of them. Belinda was a perfect mixture of Pa's features and Ma's, and both of them were handsome enough people.

"I want a bolt of material," I said.

She raised her eyebrows at me, the pencil in her hand poised above her shopping list, waiting for me to spill my guts.

"I have a few projects at home that I need material for, but I don't know how much I'll need."

She nodded as she wrote. "I'll leave it at that. For now. But I expect to know the full of what's going on with you in the near future, Matty."

Everyone would insist on knowing the full story of what was going on with me if they knew anything at all about what I'd been up to.

"If I don't hear it from you, I'll start sneaking around and find things out for myself. You know I will. Any preference on color?"

"Green." I answered a little too quickly, trying to change her mind, which I knew wouldn't work, but couldn't help.

"You know you look like a leprechaun when you wear green."

"I know. I'm not wearing it."

"You want cotton, surge, bombazine?"

I laughed. "I don't even know what those last two are. Just get something nice and durable. Something you might make a dress out of.

How much will it be?" Once again, I asked the last question a little too quickly, hoping she'd forget that I said anything about a dress. I was no good at dissembling, which was why I hadn't asked for the cloth before now.

"I'll let you know after I buy it."

I thanked her and left. Sput had carried me to the main house, but I had some thinking to do and felt like a walking, so I pulled the reins in front of him and led him behind me. It was obvious, even to me, that Pearl and the children hadn't had any new clothes in too long, and by something Meg had said, green was Pearl's favorite color. It was good then that she lived in Oregon, considering the abundance of green. Even the ground was green and springy. The air smelled green, especially compared to Texas where my cousins lived. Here, everything brown or gray had something green growing on it. I found it restful. Green was a quiet color. Peaceful. It was home.

I liked that Pearl liked it.

I wasn't sure that Belinda would pick out the right material needed for their clothing, but I figured it would be better than what they were wearing through now. Besides, I was happy to be able to give them something.

When I got back to my place, I put Sput in the barn and waved to Meg as she swept the dirt in the yard. Sweeping the dirt seemed a futile thing to do since it was always damp, but Pearl had heard somewhere that it would make a hard-packed surface, eventually becoming like tile. Outside. I shrugged, secretly thinking nothing could make soil like this hard, and let them sweep.

On my way to the corrals, I spotted Patrick walking in the trees and hailed him. "What are you doing out here?"

"Pa said you'd need some help, what with your arm being split."

I snorted. Sure that's what Pa said, but what he really wanted was a spy. Pa could never be accused of being slow on the uptake. I took Patrick by the shoulder and walked with him the rest of the way to the animals. "You and Pa both know my arm ain't that bad and that I also have Al and Wilbur working for me. Anything that needs doing, we can do, but I will put you to work now that you're here."

He grinned at me, the same grin that got the girls in town all swoony over him. I shook my head and let it be. He'd help me mend fences out here. That should keep him out of mischief. Keeping those bulls fenced in kept me busy at least once a week. They were almost more trouble than they were worth, and they were worth a fair bit.

Later, I sent Patrick, Al and Wilbur to the main house and kept an eye on my tail for anyone following behind. When I was sure no one was watching, I washed in the creek and headed to the toolshed for a shirt and a shave. The bank of the creek was as muddy as usual and I had to scrape the stuff off before stepping anywhere near indoors. If sweeping the mud down by the creek would make it hard like tile, I wouldn't mind those women working on it.

Knocking on the door to my own house had become so ordinary I rarely thought about it anymore, unless I was worried someone else would see me at it and report it to Pa.

Meg came to the door and asked, "Who is it?" through the wood.

"Matthew, Little Bird."

She opened the door, a shy smile on her lips in welcome. "How are those blocks coming?" I asked, knowing she'd been working on painting the blocks I'd made for her and Li to play with.

Her smile blossomed. "Real good! Come see!" I left my hat on the hook as she grabbed my hand and skipped through the kitchen to the sitting room to show me her work. On the way through, we passed Pearl, and I winked at her, happy to see it brought some pink to her cheeks that wasn't there before. Wooden blocks, all different sizes, littered the braided rug Ma had made for me. The children had painted some white, some blue as the winter sky, and some blue as the deep ocean. Meg knelt down so she could hand me one of each color.

"Those colors are almost as pretty as you, Meg. You sanded them down real nice too, so you wouldn't get splinters. Those will be perfect to play with. Good work."

"We'll paint some red tomorrow." She took the blocks from my hand with a quiet pride in her face that wrung my heart like a wet rag. This little woman was a gem and the more time I spent with her the more she sparkled like one. All of them were. It didn't matter that none of these visitors was blood-related to me. It didn't matter that the kids were orphans and not related to Pearl, either. I would be happy to keep them with me even if Pearl didn't come with the package. But since Pearl was part of the parcel . . . A ball of emotion lodged itself in my throat, making it impossible to finish my thought. I didn't know if I could finish the thought, or should. I felt like every feeling I'd ever had in the whole of my life was backed up against those thoughts I couldn't finish, and if I let them out a flood would ensue.

With her eyes on the blocks, Meg said, "These darker ones look like your eyes."

"You reckon so?"

She nodded. "Xiohua says they're a gentle color, but I think they're kind."

"My eyes or the blocks?" I couldn't help but ask. I also couldn't help shooting a look behind us at Pearl. Did she think my eyes were gentle? Was that a good thing?

Meg giggled. "Both, I guess."

I grabbed her up and tickled her until she let out a screech like an eagle on the hunt, then Li jumped on my back and tried to rescue his sister from my attention. I worked them over good until Pearl told us dinner was ready.

The children raced each other to the pump to wash up. Li put up a fuss about Meg winning, but I told him it was only fair that she be allowed to win sometimes. Then we all washed our hands with some pansy-scented soap Pearl had made. That woman was sure productive. I liked my hands smelling the way her hair did. Made things seem more personal than they were. I wanted them more personal.

I'd looked forward my whole life to having a family of my own, and nights like this made these people feel like family. My family.

After we started eating, Pearl directed her eyes to me. "When I went to your shed to get the shirt that was ruined yesterday I couldn't find it. Where have you put it?"

The thought of her in my shed shouldn't have caused my stomach to tense up, but it did.

"I gave it to Li." I turned to him. "And where did you put the shirt?"

He mumbled something to Pearl I couldn't understand. She replied, but I still didn't understand. Either I needed to learn Cantonese or they needed to only speak English because it was making things difficult not knowing what was going on. I had gotten to recognize a handful of their words, but I hadn't caught any just then.

I leaned closer to Pearl, close enough to her soft skin to send my mind reeling back like a retreating boxer, and whispered, "What did he say?"

She wiped her mouth with the tablecloth, which didn't do much to help my punch-drunk thoughts. Her lips invited words to my mind, like kissable.

"He said you gave it to him and he's going to keep it with his prize possessions so he'll be sure to have it when we need to leave."

I felt like I'd just been kicked in the gut, and I wasn't sure if I actually grunted or if it was only in my head. I knew from the beginning that Pearl, Meg, and Li were wanderers and probably wouldn't stay in my house long, but now that I knew them, now that they could be family, I couldn't just let them leave. Surely I could think of a way to get them to stay.

The first and easiest solution I came up with would be to marry Pearl. I wasn't opposed to it. In fact, I had a feeling I'd like it as much as I liked everything else about her. The real question was would she like it? It wasn't as though I was refined, and I was too big and broken up to be considered handsome. Next to her, I was like one of my oxen in a tea shop. And she was so small and lovely and loving. I may have sighed at that point, but no one would get me to fess up to the cause.

If Pearl didn't want to marry me, maybe I could legally adopt the kids and hire her on as housekeeper or maid or whatever other title she'd want.

Did they let bachelors adopt children?

Did I want her to marry me just so she could keep the children fed? Because she likely would be doing just that. When I looked at her, quietly cleaning Li's face with the tablecloth with love shining on her face like water in the sunlight, I had to admit I would.

And then the flood hit despite my feeble defenses. Overwhelming, invading, covering every other thought and feeling. It had been sneaking up on me so stealthily that I hadn't known it was coming. I loved Pearl. I wanted her to marry me. I would take her under any circumstances.

The problem would be my pa and ma. They wouldn't take to being related to Chinese people. They'd likely cause problems.

I finished eating the meal Pearl had made without tasting it. I did taste the preserved blackberry pie she'd pulled out of the oven for dessert. It would have been a sin to overlook that. Then I helped the children wash dishes and tucked them up for bed. Li begged to wear my old shirt to bed, and I promised him he could after it had been washed, even though the bottom would drag on the ground behind him like a fancy lady's train and it was still missing a sleeve. Pearl kissed their foreheads and I followed her from the room.

"I know you've been caring for Meg and Li for a long while, but how long exactly?" I asked, distracting myself from the flood roaring through me.

"More than two years. Li still had to be carried when we walked anywhere out of doors."

"And their Pa died of lockjaw, right?"

She nodded. "When Li was a baby. Their mother couldn't handle the strain of working and seeing to the children, and she died of exhaustion a couple of months after Li's second birthday. They have no one else. We used to live next to them in Seattle and took them in."

"You and your mother?"

From the look on her face, I was about to hear something she wasn't sure I should know. "And my brother Zhao." Her voice had gotten impossibly small.

"What happened to Zhao?" I already knew her mother had died six months before the riots, cause unknown. She had simply not woken one morning. But since Pearl had a brother, I'd need to talk to him about marrying her. I'd also need to have a talk with him about leaving her to fend for herself and the young'uns. I wondered why she hadn't talked about him before this; she'd had plenty of opportunities.

"He was put on a boat and sailed away without looking back." He was one of those sent from Seattle, then.

Her shoulders slumped, and with the flood directing my actions, I reached out to take her hand. "I don't know your brother, but I would bet he didn't get on that ship easily, or without thinking of you."

"That's certainly what it seemed like. He barely took the time to wave goodbye to me."

I shook my head to clear myself of any need to respond to that. So, he wouldn't be close by. If I ever found her brother, I may have to strangle him after I asked to marry his sister. No wonder she didn't talk about him.

Surprisingly, Pearl kept talking, which she'd never done before. Usually I had to pry answers from her closed lips. "After Zhao left, I was able to keep working in Seattle for a woman whose husband was gone most of the year. He was a bucker and only came to visit her once a month or so. When he found out she'd been paying me to do laundry and housework, he wasn't happy, and I lost my employment. After that, I couldn't find work in the city, and I took the children into the country. Some people were kind enough, but never kind enough to keep us for long."

I was only reminded that I still held her hand when she made a sound of distress and I realized I'd been gripping it too hard.

"Thanks for telling me." I stroked the back of her hand to ease the pain, the feel of her skin causing me to lose my head. "I've been thinking," I said, still stroking. I had to approach this the right way. I wanted her and the children to stay and be safe and be with me. "Would you be willing to marry me?" I nearly palmed my face after uttering the question so baldly. But I was in it now, and couldn't take it back. "I want you and the children to stay with me. Permanently. The best way to do that is for us to be married." At the look on her face, I began trying to dig myself out of the hole I was in. "I'll understand if you don't want to. I mean, you can stay here even if you say no."

I backed away from her, my face flaming. Any moment now I would combust with embarrassment. "I'll let you think about it."

Before I could make more of a fool of myself, I raced out the door, stopping only to make sure Pearl secured it. Once inside my shed, I sat on the milking stool I'd put in there, my head in my hands. The flood had created a disaster! If Pearl decided to stay with me now, it would be in spite of the way I'd asked her. I hoped she would say yes anyway.

I fell asleep trying to keep my mind off a set of bare shoulders and woke to someone knocking softly on the door the next morning. I tumbled off the tick Pearl had made for me and fumbled into a shirt before opening the shed door, only to realize it wasn't someone knocking on the shed door. It was Pa knocking on the house door. Again. This time he carried a bolt of green fabric.

I smoothed my hair as best as I could and rubbed the sleep from my eyes so it wouldn't look like I'd just spent the night in the shed, before saying, "Hey, Pa. Back again?"

Pa turned to watch me walk toward him and narrowed his eyes. From that look alone I knew the jig was up. I tensed with the expectation of confrontation. I'd so much rather him throw a friendly punch.

"You're sleeping in the shed." It wasn't a question, it was an accusation.

I nodded and tucked my shirt into my Levis.

"Why?" By his tone, he was already angry, which meant he already knew why.

"Why don't you tell me?"

"I don't know particulars. Just that you have a woman and children hidden in your house. Why don't you tell me the rest of it?" I knew then it was Patrick that had ratted me out. He must have come back and snuck looks in through the windows last night.

I sighed, any hope I had that I could skirt around this fight flying south with the birds. "You really sure you want to hear this, Pa?" I waited for a tense nod from him before continuing. "When I got home from New York, I found a woman and two children in my house. I couldn't kick them out; they have nowhere to go. They've had a hard time of it too. What was I supposed to do?"

"If I'd have known this was how neglecting your cabin would turn out, your cabin would have been under watch night and day. How about giving them a few dollars and pointing the way to town?" His lips were hard, a sure sign he was angry.

"Is that what you'd do?"

He nodded and I shook my head in answer. I knew what he would do and guessed how he'd already treated this little family I wanted to think of as mine. I'd do better to let Pa see the faces of the people he was determined to hate because I hoped their sweetness would win him over.

"I want your word, right now, that you'll not hurt these people." He grunted and slightly inclined his head. Pa was as good as his word, even if he only grunted, and that was good enough for me. I went to the door and knocked, calling out so she'd know it was me.

It took a moment for her to unlatch the door and open it enough to peek out. "Pearl. Will you come out here, please?"

At my request, she swung it wide and marched out, her carpetbag in one hand and Li's hand in the other. Meg followed close behind. It looked like Pearl was ready to leave, and my heart immediately flung itself up and choked me. She'd decided she'd rather leave than marry me. I had been ready to confront Pa about keeping them with me, but now I was scared, and being scared made me mad.

When I faced Pa, he was sputtering, red-faced. "I told these vermin to get off my land!"

The suspicion I'd had that these were the people Pa had been talking about the day I got home was confirmed.

"They're not on your land," I said, my own face burning as hot as his. My voice every bit as loud. "And they're no more vermin than you are."

"I will not have them anywhere near my family!"

"Well, too bad, because I want them to be my family! I've asked Pearl to marry me, and I'm not going to let you or anyone else drive them away from me! I'm a grown man, and I don't need your approval or help!" By severing ties with Pa, I'd be hurt, both emotionally and financially, but I could do it, and I would if I had to.

"Marry you? I've told you time and again what these people do! They're leeches, sucking the life out of our economy!"

I had never been so angry in all my life, and I knew my voice conveyed it. I could see Pa was itching to take a swing at me, but he wouldn't unless I started it. I was tempted.

"You told me your opinion, Pa. I don't share it. Pearl, Li and Meg are good, kind and strong and I love them! If they want to stay, I'm keeping them here and there's nothing you can say or do that will change my mind!" I was breathing hard at the end of this tirade and glaring at Pa hot enough he'd start smoldering in a minute.

Pearl made the same noise of distress she'd made the night before when I was crushing her hand, and I glanced back in time to see her drop her carpetbag and cover her mouth.

I turned back to Pa. "You better pray she doesn't leave because of you."

Pa looked at me and then at the three huddled behind me, confusion on his face. That made me nervous because I'd just threatened him, in a manner of speaking, and I had no idea what he was thinking.

But I wouldn't take back what I'd said. None of it. I kept the scowl on my face, daring him to call them vermin one more time.

"You seem pretty determined about this." Pa's voice almost sounded surprised. Angry surprised.

I nodded.

"I can't believe you chose this!" He sounded angry, but his face looked amused.

Then he smiled full out. When he stepped toward me, I actually took a step back. I'd seen my aunt Mildred smile like that just before punching a man in the jaw and yelling her head off. Pa kept walking toward me, dropping the bolt of fabric. Then he shocked my socks off when he hugged me, pounding my back hard enough to knock the wind out.

With anger and confusion still filling my head, I didn't hug him back and waited with clenched teeth for him to step back. When he did, he kept his hands on my shoulders. "Son." His eyes were a fierce kind of soft he got when he looked at my sisters, and I worried more than ever. "You're a dadburn fool. Who would have thought this would be the thing to get your dander up?" He chuckled once. "Still can't believe you chose this, but I couldn't be more proud of you."

"What?" My stiff shoulders hunched in disbelief, the anger draining out of me like water from the sink.

"I've tried for years to get you to fight back. I've worried you'd be the kind of man other people would walk over simply because you'd let 'em. You're a hard worker, a decent shot, and a better-than-average boxer. And even though it'll take me a while to learn to accept your choice of bride, I can see you want her enough to stand up to your old man. That makes her worth more than all our acres put together since you've never fought me for any of them." Pa's voice sounded hard as ever, but I heard a slight wobble in there and thought he might not be angry anymore.

Then my world tilted on its end. Did I hear that right? Pa had been testing me all this time? Trying to get me to stand up for myself? If I wasn't overwhelmed with the revelation, I'd probably get mad all over again.

"Of course, you'll have to be the one to tell your ma. I ain't taking that bullet for you."

Of course, he wouldn't fight for my choice of bride when Ma had his same disinclination. That was fine. I was standing up to Pa, I could do it with Ma too.

I nodded to show I'd heard him, but I couldn't quite make myself believe he was taking the situation so calmly.

Pa went back to the bolt of fabric, picked it up, and brushed it off before thrusting it at me. Leaning in and speaking quietly, he said, "You better take care of your woman, son. She looks about to faint."

I spun, and at the look on Pearl's face, I dropped the fabric again and was at her side in two steps. When I touched her elbow, she shook herself out of whatever daze she'd been swaying in. Her fathomless brown eyes rooted me to her side; I could no more leave than I could allow her to leave me. A feeling of rightness settled over me. This woman belonged beside me, for me to tease and coddle and care for. To drown her in the flood of my love.

Then, quite suddenly, I had my arms full of her. Her thin arms stretched around my neck, my own arms lifted her from the ground and secured her to my chest. She wept openly, sobbing only once and sniffing every couple of breaths. I buried my roughly shaven face in her smooth neck and breathed.

I had faced down my pa and come out the other side. I didn't want to think of how many times he'd use the fact that I had gotten angry about this to get me angry again. He'd use this to poke at me often. I didn't think of that longer than it'd take to blink because I had the woman I would choose over every other in my arms.

"Please say you'll marry me, Pearl." The plea came out hoarse and quiet.

Pearl gulped twice like she was trying to say something, her head resting on my shoulder. As long as she was in my arms I could be patient.

Finally, she whispered, "I didn't want to leave you. Packing that bag was the hardest thing I've ever done, but you've said often enough that you didn't fight your pa. I couldn't expect you to on my behalf."

She gulped and wiped the tears from her cheeks on my shirt. Using handkerchiefs was overrated.

I kissed her temple because it was close to my mouth and I had to kiss her immediately.

"You really want to marry me?" she said. " You're not just saying that because you feel bad for us?"

"I really want to marry you, Pearl. More than anything. Will you be my wife?"

Burying her face in my neck so I couldn't see her, I felt her nod. The grin that overtook my face felt like it would never leave.

Something tugged on my pant leg and looked down to find Li's concerned face. "Mr. McKinney, why's Xiaohua sad?"

I put my armful down reluctantly and even more reluctantly handed her the handkerchief from my pocket. Pa was standing a little ways off watching the whole thing. He probably could only hear snatches of what was said.

I hunkered down to Li's level. "I don't think she's sad, little man."

When we looked at her, Pearl shook her head, still wiping tears, but her words sounded like a smile. "Sometimes people cry when they're happy."

I pulled Meg over and sat her on my knee, then took Li by the shoulder. "Your Xiaohua and I are going to be married." They looked at me but didn't seem to understand. Looking back at them, I asked what I wanted the most from them. "Could you . . . do you think you could call me Pa?"

My own pa groaned and ran a hand over his face. "Never thought my first grandbaby would be Chinese."

Then he mumbled to himself in words I was grateful we couldn't hear, but he didn't leave. He continued watching.

"You're going to be our papa and we'll live here with you forever?" Meg asked.

I nodded, solemn as she was. Li began hopping all around us happily chanting, "Pa-pa, pa-pa!" The look I shared with Pearl was reminiscent of so many we'd shared over the past weeks. We loved these children. Then my arms were full of little Meg, weeping as much as Pearl had just done. I sure had a way with the ladies. At least this time I could look pleadingly at Pearl. She clutched the handkerchief in both hands and smiled at me, which was nice, but not helpful.

I looked at Pa and he was smiling too but in a different way. His smile looked a little bitter, but I got the feeling it wasn't directed at us. I smoothed Meg's shiny black hair with the hand not patting her back and kissed the top of her head in a gesture I'd seen my own pa give to his daughters.

Strange that Pa baited me and petted his daughters, but I guessed both were done with love.

I stood, picking Meg up and carrying her in one arm, then wrapping the other arm around Pearl. She fit there so nicely I thought I might keep her there always. She took Li's hand and we walked the short distance to Pa.

"I'd like you to meet my family, Pa. This is my bride-to-be, Pearl. This little angel is Meg, and that spinning top down there is Li. Meg and Li, I'd like you to meet your grandpappy."

To Pa's credit, he didn't turn away, even though a month or so ago he'd turned his back on all three. Instead, he hunkered down and solemnly extended a hand to Li. Pearl nudged Li with her knee, and he hesitantly stepped forward to touch the hand of the enemy.

Pa shook the little boy's hand and said, "Nice to meet you."

Even though Pa didn't like the Chinese, he couldn't resist a little kid like Li.

Li nodded and stepped back to hide behind Pearl's skirt. Pa rose and held out a hand to Meg. Her natural bashfulness showed in the way she barely extended her hand and made Pa come the rest of the way to meet her.

"Nice to meet you, Meg." She nodded her acceptance and tucked her hand between me and her stomach when Pa released it like she didn't want to have to give it out again.

When Pa turned to Pearl, I was ready for anything from violence to fawning and tightened my hold on her. I got neither. Pa, as polite as I've ever seen him, took off his hat and blinded the world with his shining bald head in the morning light.

"I got me some prejudices, Pearl. I hope you'll forgive me of them."

Pearl didn't respond but kept her steady eyes on Pa. I could have kissed her for knowing how best to win concessions from the man. I decided to kiss her anyway. But later.

After a short silence, Pa continued. "I know I didn't treat you as a good Christian ought to treat his fellow man. I'm proud of my son for taking up my slack. Matthew here looks at you like you made the sun shine." He gave me a taunting look. It was almost a relief to know not everything Pa did to annoy me was altruistic. "When you marry him you'll be my daughter, and I hope that you and I can eventually rub along together as family should."

After another intense moment between the two of them, Pearl nodded. "I will accept your apology as long as you make sure that you treat the children with the love they deserve and treat me as you'd treat any other decent woman, regardless of how you feel. I will be honored to carry the McKinney name."

Pa looked confounded when he looked at me. "She don't sound like a Chinese."

I rolled my eyes. "She was born in California." I could see the metaphorical egg on Pa's face and wondered if he felt it.

"The lot of you come on up to the main house. Your gramma will be happy to make your acquaintance." Then as an aside to me that everyone else could hear, Pa said, "Maybe if we don't say nothing she won't know they're Chinese."

"You know better than anyone, Pa: Ma's blind, she ain't stupid. She'd find it out and then refuse to talk to you for a month for trying to keep it from her."

"I guess so." Pa had calculation all over his face, but at least he wasn't dismissing my new wife and children-to-be out of hand.

With Pa being so polite, I decided to tell him what I wanted. "Now, Pa, I'd like you to leave so I can kiss my bride."

Pearl's cheeks turned the dark pink of an almost expired sunset and Meg giggled. Li was peeking at the world between my leg and Pearl's.

"Not a chance, son. I'll leave you alone when you're married. Until then, someone has to act as propriety demands."

"Then send Reggie or Florrie or both girls. They should meet their niece and nephew anyway. And since when have you cared about propriety?"

"I care when my daughters are at risk."

Well, that was true, though he hardly could think of Pearl as a daughter yet.

Pa continued. "What good would your baby sisters do? They couldn't keep you from mauling your woman any more than a lamb could."

"Pa."

"Where's the nearest preacher?" Pearl asked, her sweet voice one of logic. "No reason to wait, is there? We could be married today or tomorrow."

Pa and I both grinned at her. She truly was a marvel, and I didn't care who saw me show her how I felt. Wrapping her up tighter than a goose at Christmas, I kissed her long enough that Pa had to clear his throat and punch my shoulder. When I finally came back to my senses, I wanted to lose them again. I couldn't wait to marry this woman.

Stepping back from her so I could keep myself in check, I said, "Right. Um. You three want to come with me to find the parson? We'll get married and come back to the main house to meet Ma."

"Good idea. Seal the deal before telling her." Pa cracked a laugh. "That's what I did to my ma. I'll head home and act superior so everybody'll know something's up."

I loaded Pearl and Meg onto a saddled mule and myself and Li onto Sput. I'd need to get a wagon soon. The trip to Molalla didn't take more than an hour. The parson wasn't hard to find, but before anything could be made permanent, I pulled Pearl to the side.

"You know you don't have to go through with this, right? I'll take care of you and the little ones even if you don't marry me. I mean, I want you to because I love you, but if you don't want to marry me, I'll understand."

Before I'd finished speaking, she was shaking her head and smiling. "I want to marry you, Matthew. I love you too and I'm happy to belong to a man who'll fight for me."

I sighed. "Good. Because I lied when I told you I'd understand."

I married her happily and felt that God had rained blessings on my head.

Epilogue

PEARL

I had been married nine months and expecting a baby for about six of those when I spotted a stranger walking through the trees to our house.

Pregnancy had been a difficult joy, making me ill for months on end, then rewarding me with feeling my own child move. And to make things even better, Matthew held me every night as we slept. I cherished my marriage to him and the tenderness he showed in every look and touch and the way he cradled my growing stomach in his big hands, talking as though the child could hear him. I loved carrying his child.

Another thing carrying his child had accomplished was to soften his mother toward me. To say she didn't like me would have been like saying fish didn't care for being out of water. She didn't speak to me at all for the first five months I was part of the family. She didn't speak much to Matthew, either, but the thought of having her own flesh and blood grandchild did much to help reconcile her to my existence.

Buck hadn't made a great improvement, as he wasn't always civil in the things he said to me, but I could see he tried. Meg and Li were no longer afraid of him, at least, as he couldn't seem to help himself from playing with them. The rest of the family had taken to our oldest children without any time or prompting at all. Florrie had promised to take care of Meg when she started school next year and seemed pleased to have someone she could protect instead of always being on the receiving end.

Shading my eyes with a hand from the autumn sun, I waited to recognize the stranger headed my way or for him to introduce himself. His stride was uneven, which was odd because it was the only thing about him that didn't seem familiar. He wore ragged pants, his shirt was homespun, and his boots were falling apart. As he came into the clearing around the house, my feet started moving before my head could catch up, and soon I was running.

"Zhao!" I shouted, throwing my rounded self at him.

He laughed, hugged me, then drew back to look at my protruding stomach. "What happened?" His voice was full of dread.

"I got married. His name is Matthew McKinney and he's wonderful."

"Married?" He looked into my face. "You can't be old enough to be a wife. And a mother!"

"I've been a mother for much longer than I've been married. You remember Li and Mengzhi, don't you?"

"You took care of them all this time?"

I felt my spine stiffen. "What else was I to do? I couldn't just wave at them and walk away."

Zhao's spine curved. He took the hat from his head and wrung it in his hands. When he spoke, his voice was sorrowful. "I know that's what it must have seemed like I did to you, Xiaohua. I don't blame you for your resentment. My intent was to get off the ship in San Francisco and come back to take care of you like I'd promised. The ship didn't stop in San Francisco. Our first stop to take on food and water was in Russia. As I was sneaking off the ship, I was discovered and beaten. Badly." He slapped his hat against the leg that had made his walking look painful. "Since I don't look completely Chinese thanks to our father, they thought I was a stowaway and left me. A kind woman took me in and nursed me back to health. Even got me a job at the docks. About a year ago I bought a return ticket to Seattle. They let me off the ship because the boat was from Russia, not China, but when I got to the city, you were gone. It's been a long search trying to find you, knowing in my heart that every hardship you suffered was because of my foolishness."

I listened to his story and felt the punishment weighing him down. He'd been hard on himself. While his heart was heavy, I was overjoyed he hadn't left us willingly, and the hurt his leaving had caused vanished like fog in the sunlight. I hugged him again. "I'm so happy you found us."

"Forgive me, Xiaohua." His words heated my shoulder under his mouth.

It felt strange to hug a man so much shorter than Matthew.

I felt the peace of having found security and comfort. I doubted I would ever have found Matthew if Zhao hadn't left. How could I fault him for things out of his control? And now I could have two men who fought for me, something I would have thought impossible a year ago. "Forgiven."

He wept for a moment, and I did too, speaking words that we each needed to say and hear. My brother had come home to us. He hadn't forgotten his promise. My joy was complete. "Come. Let me introduce you to your brother by marriage."

When Zhao saw Matthew for the first time, his eyes got bigger than I've ever seen, and I couldn't help but laugh. My husband was impressive, especially with a child on each shoulder and a litter of puppies trailing behind.

About Mandi Ellsworth

Mandi is an avid reader, a slow jogger, and disinterested in board game of any kind. She lives in Utah with her husband, three children, and no pets.

Other Books by Mandi Ellsworth

Uneasy Fortunes

Unexpected Love: A Marriage of Convenience Anthology

Utah, United States, 1920s

Bootleggers and Basil

E.B. WHEELER

Helen clutched a picture of her betrothed and wondered what her future husband would be like. Yiannis. His name was Yiannis. She looked again at the dark eyes staring at her through the portrait, trying to decipher what she saw there. His sternness reached through the photograph to stir nervous flutters in her chest. Maybe he'd been tense posing for the photographer. She'd been terrified when having her own picture taken to send to the stranger she was going to marry.

"Approaching the Rio Grande Depot, Salt Lake City!" the train porter called.

Helen fumbled for the handles of her bag, though it would be a few minutes before they arrived. She leaned toward the window, hungrily taking in the glimpses flashing by of snug little homes with gardens and a haze-wreathed city dominated by a great castle-like building.

She'd watched the land of opportunity glide past on her journey: the dizzying skyscrapers of New York, the suffocating green forests of the east, and the lonely and vulnerable flatness of the Great Plains. Here in the West, the arid landscape and springtime flowers reminded her a little of Greece, but everything was too new. Even the mountains here were young—still sharp and tall, not worn and stooped with age like the hills of Greece. In this familiar-but-foreign landscape, she had to hope there was a place for her.

She smiled to herself. No matter how strange it was, at least she would no longer be sitting on a hard bench that bit into her legs and left her backside numb. She hadn't had a chance to really stretch out since they'd left Denver.

An American woman sat across the aisle from her. She was dressed stylishly in a low-waisted dress with her blonde hair bobbed. Still, she didn't look much like the outrageous flappers Helen had been warned about.

Helen smoothed her own long, loose-fitting dress—rumpled after weeks spent in her bag—and adjusted her headscarf. The dress was the finest thing she owned, embroidered herself during the few moments around sunset when she'd had the luxury to dream of the future. A future where she was more than an unneeded younger daughter.

"That scarf will never do," a deep voice said in Greek.

Helen gave a start and looked at the dark-haired man sitting on the bench behind her, watching her with a quirky smile in his amber-colored eyes.

"Excuse me?" she asked. He hadn't said a word to her on the day-and-a-half long trip, though she'd noticed him in the pre-dawn gloom when she boarded in Denver.

"The headscarf. It's too old-fashioned. You need to get a hat like the American ladies." He gestured with his eyes to the other women sitting on the train.

She studied his face—handsome, she had to admit, and not much older than herself. "Do I know you?"

"I doubt it. Demetrios Nikolaides, at your service." He grinned and rested his elbows on the back of her seat.

Perhaps living in America had made him mad.

"I'll thank you to leave me in peace, Mr. Nikolaides. I'm on my way to meet my husband."

"I guessed as much. A picture bride." He leaned back and stretched his arm across the empty seat next to him. "I hope the picture he sent you was really his own. A lot of men send a false one to lure their pretty brides over, and once they get here, there's nothing to do but go forward." His grin widened. "I imagine you sent your real picture. You have nothing to be ashamed of, anyway."

Helen stared at him in horror. "Your Greek is good, but you have adopted some terrible American manners."

His gaze turned more serious. "I suppose you may be right. I do not know what I am—not Greek and not American. Soon you'll understand, too. It's too late to do much about it, but be warned that not everyone here is friendly to us Greek wanderers. We have to face our own cyclops and sirens, just like Odysseus."

She turned away, pushing aside the ominous warning, and secretly glanced again at the picture in her hand. Had Yiannis sent his own picture? Did it matter? As soon as she'd boarded the boat, her course had been set. She would marry Yiannis, even if he did not look like his picture. Besides, her cousin, Alexander, would not have let him send a false one.

Demetrios glanced over her shoulder. "Yes, that's probably the real thing. He would have chosen someone handsomer to fake the photo if that was his intention. Oh, wait!" He laughed. "That's Yiannis! I didn't recognize him all dressed up, with the soot and oil off his face."

"How do you know him?" Helen asked, trying not to think about a husband covered in soot and oil.

"The world is small when you are a Greek in Utah. And I really do think Yiannis would prefer you in a hat."

Helen glared and adjusted her headscarf as she turned away from the obnoxious man. The sooner she found Alexander, the sooner she would meet Yiannis. Then she could start her new life. Here, in the land of opportunity, she would finally find a place where she belonged.

The train lurched to a stop. Helen grabbed her bag and pressed forward with the crowd exiting the train in Salt Lake City.

Cousin Alexander had warned her what to expect. An Italian band and singers would greet them. Helen thought that a very strange custom, but he assured her it was common in America, born of a friendship between Greeks and Italians forged in the mines and railroads. She would see her groom for the first time. They would be officially engaged, and the wedding would be on Sunday. Soon she would be a married woman with a home of her own. No longer a slave to her brother's wife and children. It would be hard work, yes, but it would be her own.

As she stepped onto the platform, she remembered Demetrios's teasing. She hoped Yiannis would be pleased with her appearance, though after weeks of traveling by steamship and train, she wasn't at her best. She also hoped she would be pleased with his appearance—and with his character. His face in the picture was not unpleasant, and Alexander had promised that Yiannis would make her an excellent husband. He was well off from working on the railroads. They would have a house with running water and electricity—luxuries Helen had never even dreamed of while hauling water from the village well.

The crowds pushed her along into the Rio Grande Depot, a soaring building with huge arched windows. She scanned each face, looking for one that resembled the cousin she remembered or the picture of Yiannis. Where were the greeting party and the Italian band? She shifted her bag from hand to hand and stood stupidly as the crowds dispersed.

What had happened? Perhaps they had been expecting her on the wrong day, though she had cabled ahead to tell them when she was supposed to arrive.

"Do you need help?" Demetrios stood watching her with sympathy.

"No," she snapped.

His gaze lingered, but she ignored him, staring straight ahead until he finally went on his way. She was tempted to jump right back on the train, but it would not take her back to Greece. She didn't have the money for the return trip. Certainly, everything would be fine. It was only embarrassing because that obnoxious Demetrios Nikolaides had witnessed it. Somewhere in this large city were her cousin and Yiannis. They would laugh over it later. She had endured Ellis Island, being poked and prodded and examined for lice and disease like a mule for sale; she could also endure this.

A figure emerged from the haze beyond the depot, and Helen stepped forward in relief. Alexander, come at last! But he was alone, his face stricken. He saw Helen, and his shoulders sagged. Had she disappointed him somehow? She clung to her bag. Had Yiannis seen her from afar and changed his mind?

Alexander threw his arms around her and held her so tightly, she dropped her luggage. "Oh, cousin Eleni. I am so sorry."

"Alexander?" she asked, her voice muffled by his coat. He smelled of smoke and oil like the city had seeped into him, and the fumes choked her.

He pulled away. "It's Yiannis." Helen held her breath, waiting for him to deliver the blow. "He's been killed."

"Killed!" Helen covered her mouth.

"In a railroad accident. Two days ago." His voice choked. "He was crushed. I'm so sorry."

Helen just stared, not knowing what to say. She couldn't focus. This railroad station, the smell of smoke, her dead bridegroom. They were all a dream, and she would soon awaken from it. "Killed?" she echoed.

"Come. The funeral is today. You should be there too. We will bury Yiannis. And then...then we must decide what to do with you."

His words penetrated the fog of unbelief. What to do with her? She was trapped in a foreign land with no money and no future. No one wanted her there, any more than they had wanted her in Greece. She lowered her head and followed Alexander without a word.

Alexander led Helen out of the train station to the confusion of the American streets. Men and women bustled by, automobiles and horse-drawn carriages competed for space on the road to pick up passengers, and the bells of streetcars rang out over the din. Helen stood for a moment, stunned by the chaos. Alexander gestured her toward one of the streetcars screeching to a stop on its tracks.

Helen hesitated. She had never ridden a streetcar before, but she imagined they were not free, and she had no money—just the hand-made linens and a few pieces of family jewelry she brought into her marriage.

That had been the problem in Greece, too. No money for a dowry, so no one willing to marry her.

"Come!" Alexander called again, his voice as impatient as the clanging of the bells.

She scurried over to him, nearly tripping on the rails laid over the street. Wires crisscrossed overhead as well, each tied to one of the streetcars like a leash. Her cousin paid for two tickets and handed one to her. She relaxed a little. If Alexander was wealthy enough to pay her way around, perhaps America really was a land of opportunity. She clutched her bag and stepped into the streetcar.

As soon as she was aboard, the car lurched forward. The few bench seats were full, so she clutched a pole to keep her balance, trying not to bounce against the men and women standing near her. Each time the streetcar swung around a turn, she had the opportunity to practice one of the English words she had learned before her journey: "Sorry."

She could hardly catch a glimpse of her new home, though she saw flashes of dirty streets and raggedly-dressed people not so different from Greek cities. The heads around her were blond and light brown, though, and the faces fair, pink, sometimes almost translucent—no familiar dark hair or olive skin touched by the caresses of the Mediter-ranean sun. Even Alexander looked paler than her as if America had bleached some of the Greek out of him.

They zoomed past a department store with a sign reading ZCMI in huge letters and windows full of clothes. The streetcar reached the huge white stone building with six spires pricking the sky and turned past it to go uphill to a cathedral overlooking the city. Alexander helped her out, and the streetcar was off again.

Helen looked up at the cathedral and blinked in surprise. "This is a Catholic church."

"This is the best place we have to hold the funeral."

"Isn't there an Orthodox church here?"

"We sold the old one, and the new one isn't finished yet. We still have some meetings there, but this church has more space, and it's closer to Mount Olivet, where Yiannis will be buried."

He took off his hat and entered the church. Helen looked back over the hazy city below, then turned her gaze to the eastern mountains barring the way back to Greece. Mount Olivet meant the Mount of Olives, but there were no olive trees here—only soot and smoke in place of the familiar scent of meadows and sheep. At least the name sounded comforting. It would be a good place for her prospective groom to be buried. Again, an unreal sensation swept over her, and she expected to awake at any moment. But she did not, so she followed Alexander into the cathedral.

The somber reverence of the place stilled her taut nerves. Smooth pillars swept up to the ceiling far overhead, where they opened out like branches supporting the vaulted roof. Light poured through the colored windows showing familiar scenes from the Bible, and the air was rich with the scent of incense. It was strange stepping into a church belonging to the Catholics—like going to a quarrelsome cousin's house for an awkward dinner—but at least they weren't so different from the Orthodox Greeks.

A keening wail reminded Helen why she was there. Men wore their best suits and spoke in hushed voices where they gathered around the coffin. A priest, obvious by his dark robes and long beard, oversaw the somber gathering. A few women in traditional dresses and headscarves gathered around, singing the songs of mourning over Yiannis. Helen approached slowly. She had seen death before, but she felt suddenly shy, seeing the man she was supposed to have married only to bury him instead.

She peered into the coffin. As was the custom for single men, he was buried in what would have been his wedding clothes, and he wore a little pouch around his neck containing a pinch of Greek earth. His mother would have sent it with him for this very reason, hoping it would never be needed. There was little evidence he had died in an accident. His face looked solemn, as it had in his photograph, and also very sad. He had been pleasant looking. Helen wanted to apologize for not arriving sooner. Then he would have had someone to mourn him properly—family. Her eyes stung, and warm tears rolled down her cheeks.

Whispers rose behind her, and she quickly turned away from the watching crowd.

"You did make him happy," Alexander whispered to her. "He died looking forward to the wedding."

Helen nodded. She sat through the rest of the funeral with a stoic face, though she felt as though pieces of her heart and her hopes were snuffed out with each word. As the funeral came to a close, her chest tightened. When she stepped out of the cathedral, she was facing an uncertain future in a world where she didn't belong.

"Come, Helen, it's time to go home," Alexander said as the crowd began to disperse from the funeral.

Helen gave a start. "Home?"

"Yes, to my home. My wife will appreciate the help."

"Oh." Helen followed him in a daze. So, she was to be a servant again, raising another woman's children, cleaning another family's house. She was grateful to have a roof over her head, but she ached for the loss of the home she had dreamed of on the long journey.

The babble of American English pressed around her on the streetcar. The little English she had learned when her family could spare her long enough to go to school in the neighboring village didn't sound much like the noise around her. She caught people staring at her and looked away, willing herself not to blush.

Finally, she and Alexander escaped the noise and stale stench of the streetcar, and her cousin led her down a block lined with small houses and coffee shops. The slightly-burnt scent of roasted coffee beans mingled with that of bread baking in outdoor ovens, and the aroma of basil growing in sunny windowsills welcomed her. Greek conversations drifted from the nearby houses, soothing Helen's frayed nerves.

Alexander led her into one of the little homes. Helen smiled to see an electric bulb dangling from the ceiling. It cast a bright, happy glow over the interior. Three young children ran about, giggling and calling to each other in a mix of English and Greek.

"Dear, I have brought my cousin home. Helen, this is my wife, Agatha."

Agatha gave her a quick, dismissive look. "Good. I can use some help in the kitchen."

Helen steeled herself with a deep breath. Yes, just like home.

"Fetch some water in that pot," Agatha said.

Helen picked up the pot and peered out the window. She hadn't noticed a well on her walk into the neighborhood.

Agatha rolled her eyes. "From the sink."

Helen followed Agatha's gaze and hurried over to the sink. How to make it work? She lifted the handle and fresh, clear water poured out.

Helen had to remind herself not to gape and quickly filled the pot. What a wonder! Having fresh water right in their home and not having to walk down to a village well every day to fetch it. America was a land of ongoing amazement.

That night, Helen slept on a mat in the children's room. As she listened to the children's quiet breathing, she thought over life in America. Here, she didn't have to haul water from a well. She was living in a house with electricity. The physical toll of her work would be lightened. In Greece, she had no future, because no man would accept a woman without a dowry, but here in America, there were so few Greek women, she might still capture someone's eye. It could be possible for her to find a new future, with a family and a home of her own.

Since Helen didn't have time to wash her travel-weary best dress before Sunday, she put on her second-best for church. The fabric was a plain blue, but she had sewn it herself, each stitch carefully placed. Alexander's family all wore crisply tailored suits and dresses.

Agatha stopped at the mirror to put on a hat with a little feather before stepping outside. A hat! Helen smoothed her headscarf. What did it matter what Agatha wore to church?

The entire Greek neighborhood converged on the unfinished Orthodox church building. Greek columns guarded the steps leading up to the entrance, and two round towers crowned the front corners. Someday, it would be beautiful, and its Byzantine design was as familiar as the melting sweetness of baklava, but the tools and rubble of construction littering the grounds struck Helen as sacrilegious. Her church back home had been as ancient, it seemed, as the Greek words of the New Testament.

Inside the building, Helen clung to Agatha and the handful of other women, vastly outnumbered by the horde of men. The women gossiped, their hats almost touching as they whispered together, sometimes in English too fast for Helen to understand. Only one old woman wore a headscarf. She smiled a toothless grin at Helen, who wished she could pull her scarf over her eyes and vanish. In Greece, she had been considered pretty enough—her fatal fault was that she had no dowry—but here she felt as shabby and out of place as her plain, handmade dress. In Greece, her family's proud name of Botzaris—associated with those who fought for Greek independence—had meant something, but here she sensed it carried much less weight. She was playing a new game and did not understand the rules.

Despite her shabby appearance, some of the men watched her with interest. A little thrill rushed over her at being an object of attention, though she knew it was because she was one of the only single Greek women in the city. She would have to find a way to get to know more about the eligible young men, but there were probably no match-makers here. How did one court in America?

The service, at least, was familiar, until Reverend Karahales reached the end and invited John Condas to speak.

Helen gave Agatha a curious look.

"The president of the board of trustees," she whispered.

Helen wasn't sure what that meant and didn't dare ask. John Condas stood and reminded the congregation to continue contributing to the fund for finishing the church. He swept the congregation with an imploring glance. "And please, remember the great country that we represent." His gaze rested on a few individuals. "As long as you're here, be law-abiding citizens."

A wave of rustling and throat clearing rolled through the room, then John Condas sat, and the tension broke. Helen looked to her cousin for an explanation.

Alexander shrugged. "There has been a little trouble—nothing to worry yourself over."

"What kind of trouble?"

"Greeks and Americans do not always see eye to eye. Prohibition has been especially troublesome. Try telling a people from a land of vineyards that they cannot drink a little wine with dinner... Well, a few Greeks have been arrested lately for making their own alcohol—moon-shine, the Americans call it. The police are watching us closely now." He hesitated. "There are others, too, who don't like immigrants coming to America. We hope, if we keep our heads down, they will leave us alone."

Helen frowned at the strangeness of America.

After the service, the congregation lingered. Helen held back, trying to learn the patterns of her new life. A young woman dressed all in black approached her cautiously.

"You are Alexander Botzaris's cousin, are you not? The one who was supposed to marry Yiannis?"

There was no morbid interest in the woman's voice, only a gentle sympathy. Helen nodded.

"I'm sorry," the woman said. "I was a picture bride too." She met Helen's gaze, as though searching for understanding. "My husband died several months ago in the Castle Gate Mine explosion."

"I'm so sorry," Helen said. Greek widows did not remarry. Helen wondered how this woman survived.

"I'm Katherine," the woman said. She looked like she would have said more, but someone called her name. She smiled at Helen and hurried away. Helen was sorry to see her go.

Helen drifted back to Alexander's family and stood near Agatha, trying to hide under the comforting weight of her headscarf.

"Mrs. Botzaris," said a familiar voice behind her.

She turned with Agatha to see the Greek man from the train smiling at her. Her face flushed. Of course, Demetrios Nikolaides attended church with the rest of the Greek community.

"What a lovely hat you're wearing today." He spoke to Agatha with perfect seriousness, but laughter danced in his eyes, and Helen knew it was directed at her. She refused to meet his gaze.

"Thank you, Mr. Nikolaides." Agatha seemed a little befuddled at the compliment, which almost made Helen smile. Almost.

Demetrios nodded to both ladies and strode away. Agatha shrugged and said nothing about him, leaving Helen to try not to think about the way his amber eyes had lit up when he teased her. The last thing she needed was to have that troublesome man making her feel foolish at every turn. Well, when she had her own place—a settled role in the community—then he would have to leave her in peace.

"Today, I'll send you out to wash the laundry," Agatha told Helen a few Mondays later.

Helen sighed inwardly. She'd spent the last three weeks trying to find tasks she could accomplish to Agatha's exacting standards. Alexander left early each morning and worked until late each night, so every day except Sunday, it was just Helen and Agatha and an unending line of chores, many of which were different from those in Greece. Helen's favorite part of the day was helping the children get ready for school, serving their breakfast and brushing their hair while they taught her more English.

Still, doing laundry for Greek bachelors was an important part of the family's income. If Agatha trusted her to do it, Helen must have finally gained her cousin-in-law's approval.

"The men leave their shirts by the back fence," Agatha said.

Helen thought that strange, but she started some water boiling on the stove and readied the washtubs outside near the beehive-shaped oven for the bread. It was a pleasant morning. Helen could almost imagine herself back in Greece, though the air here was sooty from the nearby smelters and factories. The sun sat lower in the sky than it had in Greece, and the light never seemed as brilliant.

When the water was ready, she fetched the clothes from the pile by the fence. As soon as she touched them, she understood why Agatha kept them outside. The sweat-stained shirts crawled with lice. Helen jerked her hands back and shook them off, though none of the little creatures had made their way to her skin. Was this what Greek men in America were reduced to? She had ridden the streetcar with all those Americans, and she didn't think they were so lousy.

She frowned and looked around the yard. A long stick lay near the fence. Holding it at arm's length, she used it to pick up the clothes and dip them into the boiling water. She rubbed her hands off, itching at the thought of the lice, and poured the lye into the steaming water. Agatha had left her a box of soap flakes. Soap was an expensive rarity in her village. The little brown flakes smelled luxurious. She sprinkled a few in, afraid to waste them. They seemed to make little difference in the stench of the steaming tub as she stirred the mess with her stick. Only when she was certain all the lice would be dead did she scrub the shirts on the washboard, rinse them in the second tub, and hang them to dry.

Agatha wrinkled her nose when she examined Helen's work flapping in the evening breeze. "Didn't you use any soap?"

"A little," Helen said sheepishly.

"Well, I suppose the smell will remind the men of home." Agatha shook her head.

Helen bit back a bitter retort. Laundry was not a source of pride for her, but she'd been doing it for years, and none of her family had ever complained. In America, even the simplest tasks made a fool of her.

The next day, Helen ironed all of the shirts. She heated the iron in the fireplace and took the time to make certain that no shirt had a single wrinkle or a crease out of place. By the time she was done, sweat dampened her face and her arms ached from the weight of the iron. She grimaced as she folded all those white shirts. By the end, she could do without ever seeing another one, but no one could complain that she did not know how to iron and fold shirts.

What an accomplishment, though. Laundress was not a job she aspired to. It wouldn't be so bad if she were just doing the laundry for her own husband and children, but for the whole neighborhood?

The next week, Helen was more liberal with the soap, and Agatha gave her a nod of approval when she surveyed the shirts flapping from the laundry line.

"When the men come to fetch their laundry and pay you, take the money to the store," she said. "We need more currants and a new shirt for Nikoleta."

Helen nodded, excited for the opportunity to get away from the house for a while. "Where is the store?"

"A block southwest of here."

Helen could find that easily enough.

As the men came throughout the day to collect the shirts, Helen gave each of them appraising looks. Most seemed glad to do business with her instead of Agatha, and she suspected they were sizing her up as the only eligible woman in the neighborhood. She tried not to think of the lice crawling through all of their clothes. The bachelors mainly slept in boarding houses, and they could not help being lousy. Having their own home would fix that problem.

They seemed to not know how to speak to a single woman, though. They probably had little practice since leaving Greece, and there they would have had the help of their family or a matchmaker.

One man handed her his coins, blushing bright red, and just pointed to the shirt that was his.

"Thank you," another man said. He fidgeted in the doorway. A fly buzzed past Helen into the house, and she grimaced.

"Um, you do nice washing," the man finally said and hurried away. Helen tried not to laugh at the poor fellow.

She wasn't sure how she was supposed to get to know any of them better. In America, most Greek women came as picture brides. Helen didn't fancy the idea of Alexander or Agatha arranging a husband for her, so she would have to discover how the Americans managed it. What did courting couples talk about?

She went to the store with a heavy purse. Some of the men had paid in canned fruit or coal, but enough of them had cash that she was excited to see what bargains she could find at the dry goods store. Luckily, the signs were in Greek: she would have no trouble communicating here. She stepped inside and was met by the homey aroma of basil and olives. She took a deep breath, letting the scents roll through her and fill her with the feeling of home. Then she opened her eyes and went to work.

The store was a tiny building, badly crowded with merchandise. She had to squeeze past a stack of Greek-language newspapers lying on top of a display of men's long underwear and then around a stand of umbrellas that snagged at her dress. It was like trying to escape from the Minotaur's maze. How did anyone find what they wanted? Eventually, she fought her way through to the center of the store, tripping once on a lumpy rug.

Where to start in this chaos? Buying the currants would be easy, so she headed instead for the shelves of women's clothing. She studied the prices and her coins to get a feel for the way American money worked. It amazed her to see so many ready-made clothes. She ran her fingers over the fabric in the display of women's dresses and wondered if she would ever have enough to buy one of her own. If she wasn't making any money and didn't have a husband to provide for her, she would have to keep wearing the same shabby clothes. She told herself it didn't matter—Greek men would still look at her, just because she was a Greek woman—but how lovely it would feel to wear something pretty and fresh.

Helen paused at the hats. They were attractive, forward, enticing. She glanced back at the bored-looking young clerk behind the counter, who was doodling on the Greek-language newspaper. She carefully untied her headscarf and placed the hat on, tilting it a little, then peeked in the mirror. The hat let her dark curls flow free and framed her face, bringing out her deep brown eyes.

"Charming," a deep voice said. Demetrios's face appeared in the mirror beside hers.

Helen scrambled for her headscarf and clutched it in front of her as she turned to face him. She'd managed to avoid him at church for the last few weeks; why did she have to run into him now? "What are you doing here?"

He smiled and leaned closer. He smelled like the brilliantine styling his dark brown hair, inviting her to step closer, inhale more deeply. She pulled back.

"I'm watching one of my customers try on a very fetching hat," he said.

"Your customer?" She glanced around. "This is *your* store?"

He grinned, and the laughter danced in his eyes. "It is. Didn't anyone tell you? If there's anything you need, Demetrios is the one to ask."

Helen whipped off the hat and tugged her scarf back on. "I just need a shirt for my cousin's daughter. And some currants." She raised her head. "But the price for the shirt is too high."

"What will you do then? Go to an American shop?" He raised an eyebrow, a challenge glittering in his eyes. "You think you can get a better deal there?"

"I think I can make it myself if I must, but I won't pay such outrageous prices."

He chuckled. "Very good. Most Greeks forget how to bargain when they come to America. Or they get trapped by the company stores, and there's no bargaining there." He shook his head. "What will you give me, then, for the shirt and the currants?"

She named a price that was much too low, and he countered with a more reasonable one until they worked their way to the price she expected to pay. He went to the back to get the currants, and the young clerk made himself busy straightening the counter, his doodling forgotten.

Demetrios returned with the little sack of currants. "Here they are as we agreed. But only if you take the hat too."

"That hat?" Helen faltered. "I have no money for a hat. I don't need one."

"I'm not selling it to you. I'm giving it to you, and you only pay the price you named for the currants and the shirt."

"That makes no sense." Was he teasing her for her poverty? She had a respectable name, and she did not need his pity. "You are mad."

He chuckled. "Not at all. I am doing what pleases me. You looked quite fetching in that hat."

Helen narrowed her eyes. "I won't have anyone playing games with me. I don't want the hat." She thrust her coins into his hands—more than they had agreed upon—and took the shirt and the currants, leaving the hat behind. She turned and wriggling her way past the displays and out of the shop. Demetrios's laughter rang in the store behind her. Insufferable lunatic!

The next Sunday, Helen helped the children get ready for church before she dressed herself. She welcomed the familiar rituals of the Sabbath after a long week of hard work: more cooking, more scrubbing, more laundry. For all the conveniences of America, the work never stopped.

Helen rubbed a little olive oil into her skin to soften her hands and gently lifted her headscarf. The edges displayed a string of embroidered birds taking flight. She had tried to capture that glorious moment when their beating wings first lifted them to the freedom of the skies.

As she covered her hair, she thought of Demetrios's hat but quickly dismissed the thought. What silly vanity that was! She had too much pride to let him know that she wanted it. Or to accept any gifts from him—gifts that would just make him laugh at her. A memory of the way his eyes danced when he laughed flashed across her mind, but she shoved it aside. At church, she would have a chance to mingle with other men in the Greek neighborhood and visit with the widow Katherine again.

She stepped out of the children's bedroom to find Agatha standing in the parlor, clutching a box, her lips pressed in anger. Before Helen could ask what was wrong, Agatha whirled on her.

"What's the meaning of this?" Agatha shook the box.

Helen looked inside. "It's a hat," she said faintly. Not just any hat. The one she had admired at Demetrios's shop.

"A hat delivered to you by Demetrios Nikolaides. How did you pay for it?"

Helen blanched. Did Agatha think she'd been stealing from her? She'd brought back the change from her exchange with Demetrios. Despite turning down his offer, she'd made a good bargain and had been proud of herself. Agatha had seemed pleased too. "I didn't buy it. I guess he saw me admiring it and wanted me to have it."

"Wanted you to have it? Ha! Not Demetrios. He's all business. He doesn't do anything unless there's something in it for him." Her voice turned icy as she narrowed her eyes. "What did you do to earn this from him?"

Helen gaped, realizing what Agatha was implying. "Nothing! I did nothing!"

"Don't lie to me. Nothing stays a secret for long in Greek Town. If you did anything to disgrace the Botzaris family name…"

"It was my name before it was yours!" Helen shouted. The neighbors could probably hear. She didn't care. "Do not tell me how to care for it." She lowered her voice. "He gave me the hat to humiliate me. To remind me that I have nothing of my own. Does that please you?"

Agatha shoved the hat at her and stormed away. Helen stifled a sob and rushed into her room. She was tempted to throw the hat in the gutter, but then everyone would see it. She stowed it inside her bag instead and checked the little mirror to make sure her eyes showed no tears.

The family marched to church in stony silence, gaining curious looks from their neighbors. No doubt they would fuel the neighborhood gossip for the rest of the week, if not longer. If only Demetrios did not hear of it. Helen did not want to see him laugh at her again.

They sat through the church service, the words buzzing around Helen's ears without finding any place to land. Her whole concentration was on looking calm and ignoring the stares she felt directed at her and Agatha.

As soon as the service was over, she tried to make her way out of the church. Demetrios cornered her before she made it to the exit.

"Please let me go," she whispered.

"What has happened? Didn't you receive my gift?" He asked. There was a hint of amusement in his voice.

"Your gift!" Helen's voice echoed off the unfinished walls. She squeezed her eyes shut, and when she opened them, there was no laughter in his eyes. "Your joke has cost me enough already," she said quietly. "Please do not speak to me again."

She pushed past him without meeting his gaze and rushed outside. The hazy air made her squint. Beyond Greek Town, people strolled by in their Sunday best and the bells rang on the streetcars. Oh, how she longed for her village in Greece! There, the rules were clear, and she never would have been so humiliated.

A gentle hand touched her arm. She jumped and turned to find Katherine watching her with sympathetic eyes, her pale face offset by her black mourning clothes.

"Do you want to tell me about it?" Katherine asked.

Helen shook her head, but a glance at Katherine's understanding gaze and the whole story came spilling out.

Katherine put an arm around her, and Helen leaned into the comfort of a friendly shoulder, like having one of her sisters back again.

"Demetrios is a stubborn fool," Katherine said. "He thinks he knows what's best, and he's forgotten too much of Greece to understand why he's wrong."

"It doesn't matter why he did it," Helen said. "I have never been so embarrassed. How can I live with Agatha, knowing she thinks I'm the kind of woman who would disgrace myself and my family name? And over a hat!"

Katherine smiled. "There will be some new gossip or scandal soon enough, and this will blow over, especially because everyone knows how Demetrios is. As for Agatha..." Katherine gave Helen a heavy look, as though she were wrestling with some weighty secret. "This may be hard to consider, but why not live somewhere else?"

Helen pulled back to stare at Katherine and laughed a little. "Where would I go? I have no other family here. Not even the means to go home to Greece."

"Do you want to go back?"

"Yes." She hesitated, imagining the shame of returning home a single woman. "I don't know."

"Listen. I know how important tradition is, but in America, things can be different. You could get a job, support yourself."

Helen stared at her. "A job? Doing what?" In her village, the only work for women was taking care of their families or minding the goats —the unclean animals the men did not want to tend.

"Do you speak much English?"

"I understand a lot now, but I...I feel shy speaking it, and the words get twisted up in my mouth," Helen admitted.

"Hmm. That rules out telephone operator, then. You're pretty enough to work in a department store, but not until you're more confident with English and save enough to buy some modern clothes. In the meantime, there are many factory jobs."

Helen flinched a little at the thought of the smoke pouring from the factories, but she was intrigued. "Doing what?"

"Oh, all kinds of things. A lot of Italian girls work in the bakeries and the macaroni factory. I dip chocolates in one of the Greek candy shops."

Helen perked up a bit at that. She'd only tried chocolate once, but it had been heavenly.

Katherine hurried on. "There are no openings at my shop right now—the Americans have accused us of making impure candy, and we are struggling. But the other girls and I, we can look around for you. The canneries aren't bad, but they're not doing as well right now—the farms in Utah have struggled since the war ended." Her eyes brightened. "Do you weave or sew?"

"I do."

"Perfect. There are several textile and knitting factories. They're always looking for more girls to run the machines."

"Machines?" Helen asked. She had only sewn by hand.

"Don't worry—they'll teach you how."

"Yes, I'd like that." If Helen earned money, then she could buy her own dresses and hats—from the American shops, not Demetrios's. "But how do I tell Agatha I won't be working for her while I'm living under her roof?"

"You won't be. You can come to the ladies' boarding house with me."

Helen lowered her voice. "Is that respectable?"

"Very much so. A few other girls live there. An Italian widow runs it, and she's very strict. No improprieties allowed." Katherine looked concerned for a moment, but she shook it off and smiled. "Most of the girls are Italian, but there's one other Greek girl there. You'll like it. It's in Little Italy, just west of here, by the Rio Grande Depot, so not too far to walk to church. You just have to show Mrs. Alberti that you have a job, and she'll rent you a room. She's a great cook too."

"Thank you!" Helen embraced Katherine and looked back over Salt Lake City. It promised a whole new kind of hope now. Her heart beat faster—nervous excitement pumping through her body and lifting her spirits. "I'll start looking tomorrow."

Helen helped the children dress for school in the morning, then hurried to get herself ready. It helped that Agatha wasn't speaking to her except to issue an occasional command. Helen put on her blue dress and hesitated over her headscarf. She wanted to look modern, and a headscarf might not be safe around machines. Glancing over her shoulder, she pulled out Demetrios's hat and secured it over her long, wavy black hair. Guilt gnawed at her stomach.

"I'm just borrowing it until I can buy one for myself," she whispered to her reflection. "He'll never know."

She forced a smile at the mirror and almost didn't recognize her more modern-looking self.

The hallway was clear, so she fled out the front door, shutting it quietly behind her. Clutched in her hand, she held the addresses of the nearby textile mills. Helen marched down the street, aware that some of her neighbors would likely see her and Agatha would hear about it before the end of the day. She had to have a job by then or her life would become a constant stream of arguments with her cousin's wife.

She had no money for a streetcar, so she walked to the first factory. The racket in the building pounded her ears like the noise of propellers on a ship—a ceaseless, pulsing roar. Lines of girls kept their heads bent over sewing machines, pushing fast streams of fabric under flying needles. Helen hoped she could get the hang of the machines without punching the needle through her fingers. She pressed forward, looking for a man who seemed to be in charge.

"Pardon!" she shouted over the noise. "Pardon!"

The man looked over at her with a bored expression. "What do you need, miss?"

She had practiced these words carefully. "I need a job."

The man squinted at her. "You Italian?"

She couldn't hear well over the machines, but she caught "Italian," so she nodded.

His face darkened, and he shouted a string of words in her face she didn't understand and didn't want to. She hurried off before he had a chance to say more.

Apparently, being Italian wasn't a good thing. At the next factory, it was quieter, but the man in charge kept saying, "closed shop," which Helen didn't understand because the shop looked open, but it seemed to mean that there were no jobs for her there either.

She approached the last address, her stomach a tight knot. She said a prayer to Mary, the mother of the Lord, and approached the man overseeing the workers. He was speaking loudly with another man, so Helen hung back, observing the factory. Here, the girls were running looms. The back and forth of the giant machines soothed her, and the loud whooshing and clacking were not as intimidating as the other factories. This would be it. It had to be.

The foreman turned away from his conversation, shaking his head. Helen sensed it wasn't a good time to talk to him, but as she tried to back away, his gaze fell on her, and he narrowed his eyes.

"What are you doing lurking around here? What do you want?"

"Job," Helen croaked out. She tried again, more boldly. "I need a job."

"I bet that's all the English you know," the man said. "How do I know you can do the work?"

Helen hesitated, trying to put together the words she knew but was afraid to say incorrectly. "I weave," she said. "I weave. I need a job."

"Huh. I don't have time to train some idiot girl who can't even learn to speak English."

Helen didn't know all the words, but she understood his intent. She couldn't quit, though. She couldn't go back to Agatha's house without a job. She stepped forward. "I weave. I work hard. I learn more English."

The man rolled his eyes and turned away.

"Wait!" A familiar voice shouted behind Helen.

She gave a start as Demetrios strode past her to start arguing with the foreman. She cringed. He had been the one talking with the foreman when she had arrived. Now, he was a witness to her humiliation once again. And she was wearing his hat! She turned to slink away, but a firm hand on her shoulder stopped her. Demetrios spun her around to face the foreman.

"She's a respectable girl and a hard worker," he said in English. "If you don't want Greeks to make your fabrics, why should I buy cloth from you to sell to Greeks in my store? You can forget the deal we made. I'll take my business elsewhere." He turned away, dragging a baffled Helen with him.

"Wait!" the man called. He bustled over to catch up with Demetrios. "I ain't got a problem with Greeks. I just don't want to waste time training some girl who's too dumb to understand, or who's going to get married and disappear a few months later. American girls stick around longer, especially if they're already married."

Demetrios smiled. "I can't make any promises about her not getting married, but I guarantee she's brighter than most of the workers you already have."

The man shrugged. "If you say so, Demetrios. I just lost one of the girls who worked on the looms anyway."

Demetrios nodded and shook the man's hand. Helen didn't understand everything that had just happened, but the man motioned for her to follow him. Demetrios gave her shoulder one last squeeze, and let his hand linger there for a moment. His touch sent a warm shiver through her, and she flushed and pulled away. She looked up, prepared to thank him as gracefully as she could manage, but stopped at the sight of his grin.

"That hat really is quite charming," he said in Greek.

Then he was gone, and she was left to hurry after the impatient foreman. She had to banish the odd flutters in her chest so she could concentrate on his slow instructions. He spoke to her like she was a child, but at least she understood and quickly picked up the motion of the machine.

"You have to watch yourself," the man said.

Helen wrinkled her forehead, not understanding.

"Be careful," he repeated, drawing out the words. "Dangerous. You get your clothes caught, you lose an arm. Maybe get crushed." He mimed an arm being torn off and made a smashing motion with his fists. Helen's eyes widened, and she nodded.

"Good." He motioned to the blonde girl at the machine next to her and practically shouted, "This is Annie. She'll answer any questions."

Annie gave Helen a weary smile, which Helen returned as she got to work.

After only half a day, Helen's arms ached, and she could only imagine how they would hurt the next day when she had to return and do the same thing again. But she had a job of her own! If only she didn't have to owe the job to Demetrios.

She approached the foreman again before she left.

"Please, I need..."

"You get paid on Friday. Not sooner."

"For Mrs. Alberti. I need a...a paper for my job."

He looked confused for a moment, then nodded. "Oh, for your boarding house lady? I've heard Alberti is a dragon."

He wrote a note in English for her.

Nearly floating, Helen walked home and prepared to face Agatha. As soon as she entered the house, the tension hit her, like a cold wind pushing her back out into the street. Alexander and Agatha sat in the parlor, their faces steely.

"Where have you been?" Alexander asked quietly.

"I went to find work, and I had to start immediately."

"Find work!" Agatha exploded. "What will people say about us? There's enough work around here, and if you're not earning your keep, I'll be charging you for room and board."

Helen took a deep breath. "There will be no need for that. I'll be staying at a boarding house."

Agatha looked ready to explode again, but Alexander cut in. "Is it a respectable one?"

"It's Mrs. Alberti's—where Katherine stays."

"That woman!" Agatha said. "It's unnatural, her living on her own rather than returning to her husband's family."

"Now, Agatha," Alexander said. "When Georgios was killed, the mining company threw her out of his house, and she didn't have anywhere to go. It would be odd for her to live with Demetrios since he's single."

"Demetrios Nikolaides?" Helen asked.

"Her brother-in-law. Or didn't you know?" Agatha asked, her tone accusatory.

Helen opened her mouth to reply but bit it shut again. Of course, she hadn't known. Katherine had talked about Demetrios as if she knew him well, but Helen assumed everyone in Greek Town knew each other.

Alexander gave Agatha a quelling look. "Katherine Nikolaides has to work to earn her keep and to save enough to sail back to Greece. But why do you want to do this, Helen?"

He didn't sound angry, just curious, so Helen took a steadying breath. "I've been thinking about my future. I came here to be a bride. Since then, I've only been working in this house. I'm grateful that you made a place for me, but I can't stay here forever. If I work, I can save up a dowry, help my parents, maybe return to Greece or make a new life here."

Alexander stood, silencing any protest by Agatha, though she looked like she had plenty to say. "We're your family, and we would never want you to see yourself in a disgraceful situation, but I see nothing to object to in your plan. It's a bit unusual, but these are unusual circumstances. When do you go to Mrs. Alberti's?"

"I was going to leave tonight."

He looked pained at that and gave his wife a stern look. "That won't be necessary. You may stay here tonight and move over there at your leisure. We don't want anyone saying our home was not hospitable to our own flesh and blood."

Helen nodded, but she was determined not to stay more than another day. Her new life was calling her.

The next morning, Helen left early for Mrs. Alberti's boarding house. She passed through Greek Town and into Little Italy, hardly noticing the transition, except that the smell of bread baking in outdoor ovens faded. Children still played in the streets and the tiny yards in front of their small homes, and women hung laundry in the backyard and gossiped over fences. It was strangely comforting to see the sights she had become used to in Greek Town repeated in her new neighborhood.

She found the address for Mrs. Alberti's home. It wasn't much different from the other houses, though it was a little larger and had an attic with windows.

Helen knocked on the door, and a girl about her age with short black hair pinned back answered.

"Oh, you must be the new girl!" she said in English. "I'm Maria. Come in. I'll get Mama."

Helen stepped inside. The air was sweet with the scent of basil and tomato, filling her with a warm sense of home.

A matronly woman with streaks of silver in her black braid stepped out of the kitchen. A colorful apron covered her black widow's garb. She wiped the flour from her hands and stepped up to give Helen a keen inspection. Helen stood straight, careful not to flinch under the searching gaze.

"You're Katherine's friend?" Mrs. Alberti asked, her English heavily accented.

"Yes. I am Helen Botzaris."

"And you have a job?"

Helen handed her the note from her supervisor. Mrs. Alberti looked it over and nodded, handing the paper back with a snap of her wrist. "I lock the doors at nine sharp. When you have a late shift, you tell me, and I wait up for you. No men in the house!" She gave Helen a look that made her feel as though she had a young man stashed in her bag. "Except on Sundays, then only in the parlor with at least one other girl. Breakfast is at six. You keep your own room clean."

"Yes, ma'am," Helen said, understanding the drift of the warning.

Mrs. Alberti smiled and patted Helen on the cheek. "You are a good girl."

Helen smiled nervously.

"Maria! Show Helen to her room," she said to the other girl.

Maria smiled at Helen as Mrs. Alberti swept back into the kitchen. "Don't be afraid of Mama. She's a great cook, and her bark is worse than her bite."

"Thank you," Helen said, deciphering Maria's English idiom with a grin.

"Come on, you have one of the upstairs rooms, right across from Katherine."

Helen trotted up the stairs after Maria, her stomach aflutter. The attic landing was a short hallway with doors on either side. Maria opened the one on the right and gestured Helen inside.

Soft light from the small dormer window fell across a hand-stitched quilt on the bed, a little dressing table with a dusty mirror and a doily, and a worn rug cushioning the bare wood floor.

"It's good," Helen said.

"The bathroom is downstairs—the door next to the kitchen. I'll let you get settled in."

"Thank you," Helen said without looking back.

Maria shut the door quietly behind her. Helen walked forward, running her fingers over the colorful quilt with its careful, hand-placed stitches, then peering out her window into the streets of Little Italy below. A handful of dark-haired boys kicked a ball back and forth in the street, shouting in a mix of Italian and English. Helen watched with a smile, basking in the luxury of her own space, her own special view of the world that belonged to no one else.

The thought of luxury jolted her from her daydream. She couldn't afford this view if she didn't get to work on time. She left her bag on the bed, ready to be unpacked, and hurried down to make the long walk to work. Until she got paid on Friday, she wouldn't be able to ride the streetcar.

She arrived at work out of breath and with a stitch in her side, but she was in her spot when the whistle blew and the giant looms hissed and clicked into life. With time for nothing more than a quick nod of greeting to Annie, her day began.

Helen easily fell into the rhythm of the machines, her hands guiding the loom shaft, and her gaze automatically scanning the cloth for trouble, leaving her mind free to dwell on the little room waiting for her—her own sanctuary. As she watched the machines churn out the huge bolts of woven fabric, she thought what a shame it was that they were all the same. It was fast—so much faster than any human, or even the mythical Athena, could weave—but when they were done, no one would be able to tell Helen's fabric from the fabric of the girls on either side of her, all working in silence. The lack of human voices, the constant hissing and thumping of the machines, and the steady sameness of the brown fabric rolling out in front of her filled Helen with a heavy dullness that she could only shake off by dreaming again of her little window.

By the time she arrived back at Mrs. Alberti's, she was too tired to be interested in more than a few bites of the warm spaghetti waiting for her. She climbed the stairs on aching feet and collapsed into her bed without a thought for the perfect stitching on the quilt.

The week wore on in much the same way, except on Friday, at the end of her shift, when she lined up with the other girls to pick up her paycheck. Some of the American girls talked and giggled with each other, but they took no notice of Helen. Still, she didn't mind them so much when she held her first pay envelope. Money of her very own!

At the bank around the corner, Helen took her place in the long line of factory workers snaking out the door. She grinned at the clerk when she reached the counter. He hardly glanced at her as he took her check and handed her ten dollars.

She carefully tucked the bills into her boot and nearly skipped out of the bank. Ten dollars! Seven dollars a week would go to her room and board, but she could ride the streetcar now—a luxury her tired feet would appreciate—and save some money for herself. In celebration, she rode the streetcar home, feeling sympathy for those who had to walk.

The next few weeks passed in a blur of long workdays, broken only by the peace of Sunday and the excitement of getting paid each Friday. Her bundle of bills grew—money set aside for rent and streetcar fares and a little to send back to her parents in Greece. After a month, she'd gathered enough to spend something on herself. A quick glance in the mirror at her worn-out dress, and she knew exactly what she would buy.

On her next day off, she hoped to take Katherine shopping with her. She knocked on her friend's door.

"Yes?" Katherine's voice sounded weak.

Helen swung the door open to find Katherine curled up on her bed, looking pale. "Are you unwell?"

Katherine hesitated a moment, then nodded, not meeting her eyes. Helen frowned, concerned but not wanting to pry.

"Get some rest, then."

She tucked the blanket around her friend and ventured out on her own.

On her walks around town, she had passed the huge ZCMI department store near the Mormon temple. It looked like it sold everything she could imagine wanting.

She took a streetcar for the short ride up to Temple Square and made her way through the Saturday crowds. She stopped to admire some of the buildings there: the Beehive House, the strange but beautiful temple and tabernacle, and the Hotel Utah, whose Greek columns made Helen smile. She had seen the skyscrapers passing through New York City and Chicago, but she hadn't had a chance to examine them up close. She stood at the bottom of the Deseret Savings building and stared up until her neck ached from watching where the top of the column-like building reached to touch the clouds.

Finally, she turned her attention to the window displays of the ZCMI. The store's sign declared, "America's First Department Store." Its displays were art shows in themselves, with their careful arrangement of clothing, shoes, and machines that Helen didn't know the use of. One of the windows was broken, though, the missing glass boarded over. Someone had painted the letters "KKK" on the board in deep red.

Helen shook off her chill at the strange sight and hurried inside, then stopped in wonder. She had felt overwhelmed in Demetrios's shop, but now she understood how small it was. Here, she strolled past long racks of identical suits and dresses, along with shoes and even women's underclothing on display where everyone could see them, though none of the other women seemed to think much of it.

Helen made a note of where the dresses were and continued to explore.

A polished wooden staircase in the center of the store led up to the next floor. Through some mechanical miracle, the stairs moved on their own, one side rolling up, while the other cascaded down like a waterfall. Helen paused to stare, letting people push past her. Then she realized she would have to ride those moving stairs to go up to the next level.

She cautiously stepped forward and hopped onto the stairs. The wooden step whisked her upward. She yelped and grasped the moving rail. The girls behind her giggled, but her embarrassment couldn't overpower her awe at the quick trip upwards. The ground floor seemed to shrink away as she watched. She felt like a bird and for the first time believed the stories she had heard that people could ride in flying machines.

The stairs reached the top, and she scurried forward, afraid of being sucked back down by the revolving machine. Other people hurried past her, and she paused to get her bearings.

Shining silver machines surrounded her. Machines for washing clothes, for separating cream from milk, for keeping the milk cold. Sewing machines drew a crowd of women, and Helen watched the demonstrations with them, wincing each time the demonstrator's fingers got too near the rapidly-moving needle. Never had she imagined that there could be so many machines or that they could do so much. A desire to be rich and fill her house with machines seized her mind, but she laughed it off. She had no idea how to use any of them, anyway. And could a piece of metal and gears really get a shirt cleaner than she could, or sew a better stitch? Impossible.

She stared until her head ached from taking it all in, then she rode back down the moving stairs—leaping free of them before they quite reached the bottom—and went back to the women's department.

She looked through the racks of identical dresses, studying the price tags and dropping them quickly when she understood what the dresses cost. Fifteen dollars! More than she made in an entire week.

Her eight precious dollars would not last long. She would have to build her wardrobe slowly.

Finally, she settled on a style that only cost seven dollars and was a pretty shade of blue-green that reminded her of the Greek Sea. The stitching was adequate, though the skirt could stand to be re-hemmed. She held the dress up to herself. How did one know if it would fit?

She draped the dress over her arm and wandered among the displays, looking for someone who would help her. Busy clerks talked with other customers and chatted with each other, but each time Helen approached, their gazes slid past her and they would suddenly be busy with something else.

After repeating this pattern for a quarter of an hour, Helen stopped and studied herself in one of the long mirrors hanging on the walls. How wrong she looked, with her long hair and worn out old dress, standing among such luxury with a beautiful dress flung over her arm.

She carefully lifted the dress and shook it out to make certain she hadn't dirtied or wrinkled it. One of the clerks watched her out of the corner of her eye, a smug expression on her face.

Helen understood. Having eight dollars in her pocket didn't mean she would be allowed to buy something in this fine store. How had she not realized she was the only woman in the store with dark olive skin and unfashionably long, black hair? A crow among golden-headed eagles.

She hung the dress on its rack with its sisters where it belonged and walked slowly back toward Greek Town. She glanced at the Greek columns on the buildings she passed. The Americans chose which parts of Greece to love and what part to reject.

But she still needed a new dress. Her old ones would soon be fit for nothing but rags. She worked all day making cloth for dresses she couldn't buy. There was only one place she could shop.

Her stomach tied in knots at the thought of facing Demetrios, but at least he would do business with her. Maybe only his clerk would be there and she wouldn't have to speak to him at all. She pushed the door open, and the bell over the door dinged. She blinked to let her eyes adjust to the relative dimness and saw the store with new awareness: too crowded because everything a Greek family might need had to fit in one little shop where their business was welcome.

"Miss Botzaris, how can I help you today?"

Helen's stomach plunged at the sound of Demetrios's voice, then fluttered strangely at the thought of his touch when he helped her get her job.

She turned with a tight smile. "I need to buy a new dress."

"I'm flattered you would choose my store," he said, leaning on a display and smiling at her with his dancing eyes.

Her pride flickered. "I was going to shop at the ZCMI, but they..." She stopped. That only made her sound pathetic.

His expression turned serious. "They wouldn't help you?"

The understanding in his voice broke through her defenses, and she shook her head, hot with shame.

"Sometimes you get lucky, and one of their clerks will be friendly, but many of them—"

"Don't even see that we're there," Helen said.

He nodded.

"I understand now, why your store is so crowded," she said.

"Crowded?" He gestured around dramatically with a grin. "I like to think of it as full of possibilities."

"The possibility of an accident if someone trips," Helen said.

Demetrios laughed. "How would you do it differently?"

Helen considered the store and compared it to ZCMI. "You might try grouping things in a way that makes sense so customers can find what they're looking for. You have men's socks next to women's hats. If you put the men's socks on that shelf near..." her face burned as she gestured to the men's long johns. "Well, near their other things, they wouldn't be in the way of ladies looking at hats."

"Good suggestions. I ought to hire you as my window display artist." Mischievous laughter lit Demetrios's eyes. "Then you can put the 'men's other things' in their proper order."

Helen almost had to laugh along with him, but her pride stopped her. "I already have a job."

"That you do. So, you're looking for a new dress? I'm afraid I can't afford fancy female clerks like ZCMI, but I do have some dresses."

Demetrios led the way, and Helen was relieved, after sneaking a look at the price tags, to find that they were all around six or seven dollars. The colors, though, were not as vibrant as the blue-green dress. She trailed reluctant fingers over the fabric.

"They're not to your liking?" Demetrios sounded sincerely concerned.

"Oh, they're fine. I had only...I had been thinking of something in a different color. Something like the sea."

"Ah," he said as if he understood, and Helen thought maybe he did. "What about this yellow? It will look flattering on you, and it reminds me of the flowers in Greece. What I can remember of them, anyway."

Helen considered it. "Yes, that will do. But if it doesn't fit..."

"You can exchange it. We don't have any dressing rooms here."

She nodded, and her gaze traveled again around the chaotic displays. "Why don't you have anything Greek made?"

"Oh, I do. I try to only buy from local mills that hire Greeks."

"No, I mean, things that aren't made by machines. I wove and embroidered in Greece, and some of the Greek or even the Italian wives might make things for you to sell."

"Interesting idea," he said. "Don't you like the clothes we can get here?"

"Well, they're fine, but the stitching isn't always as good, and they're all the same. I suppose I don't like machines as much as Americans do."

"But they'll make your life so much easier!" Demetrios grabbed her by the hand, and she instinctively wrapped her fingers around his. "Come see," he said, leading her to the back.

The other patrons in the store watched them with interest, and Helen thought of Agatha's triumphant disapproval when word spread that Demetrios had led her off who-knows-where. She wriggled her hand free.

"Wait! Where are we going?"

Demetrios looked at her in surprise, then his expression turned to amusement. "Oh, don't worry. My living quarters are upstairs. This is just the office, and we'll keep the door wide open so the whole neighborhood can spy on us. In fact, I encourage them to. Greek Town could stand to catch up with the times."

He swung open the door to a cluttered room with a desk and a collection of appliances like those Helen had seen at the ZCMI. The other customers wandered up behind Helen to watch Demetrios's demonstration.

"An electric icebox," he said, opening the door to display the cold milk inside. "Saves money by not letting food spoil. This"—he pointed to what looked like a little fireplace with bulbs where the fire would go —" is an electric heater. No more messes from coal." He glanced up at the crowd, his eyes dark, and a bitter edge to his words. "And no more Greek men killed in coal mining accidents. One hundred seventy-one men died in the Castle Gate Mine explosion—fifty of them Greek— and that was just one accident."

The men mumbled at that, their whispers hissing with sorrow and anger still raw from recent losses. Helen remembered Demetrios's brother—Katherine's husband—was killed in that explosion. No wonder he loved his machines.

"These appliances can free us," he went on. "How much money do you men spend paying someone else's wife to do your laundry? This clothes washing machine will do it for you. You can be independent."

"Most of us can't afford such luxuries, Demetrios," one of the men said, and they drifted back to their shopping.

"One day you will!" Demetrios called after them. He glanced at Helen. "And what do you think?"

She stared for a moment at the washing machine. It was true that she'd never seen him at Agatha's house to collect his lice-infested shirts. She'd never considered why. He didn't need a woman to help manage his home. He could replace her with a washing machine. Make her obsolete. Suddenly, she hated the sight of the inventions.

"I think it's a cluttered mess. I'll just take my dress, thank you."

"What's wrong?" Demetrios asked.

"Nothing's wrong. I just don't like machines. I like things the way they're supposed to be—the way they've always been." She looked away from his wounded expression. "Can I buy my dress now, please?"

She hadn't meant to sound so snippish, and she certainly hadn't meant to hurt Demetrios's feelings, but what could she say? Machines were everywhere—she spent each day hovering over one of them like a serving girl bowing to her mistresses' whims—and they sapped the humanity out of her world. Clothes all looked the same, barely touched by human hands. And she was reduced to just a lever to pull, a button to press—someone who could be replaced at a moment's notice with another set of hands and bored eyes in desperate need of work. She would soon lose herself in such a cold, monotonous world.

Demetrios rang up her dress and wished her a good day. She thanked him dully and headed for home.

The next Sunday before church, Helen rose early to put on her new dress, mark the places it didn't hang well, and re-stitch it to fit as a well-made dress should. She studied herself in her little mirror. The dress flattered her, and she looked much fresher and more modern, but she couldn't help wonder how many other women out there wore the same dress.

It was past time for breakfast, so she hurried out of her room to see if there was anything left. Katherine sat on the floor in the hallway, clutching her stomach, her face so pale it was almost green.

Helen rushed forward. "Are you ill? Did you eat something bad?"

Katherine sat back with a weak smile. "No, no, I'm fine. I thought I was past this stage."

"This..." Helen's eyes widened. "Are you...?"

"Yes, I'm expecting my husband's baby." Katherine sat back and closed her eyes. "When he died, I still wasn't sure. He never knew he was going to be a father. He would have been so proud." Tears trickled from under her closed eyelids, and Helen held her and stroked back her hair.

"What are you going to do?" she asked around the lump in her throat.

Katherine opened her eyes and looked up at Helen, her gaze bright with determination. "I'm going to take care of myself and my baby." She wiped her cheeks. "Everyone in Greek Town already thinks I should go back to Greece, to Georgios's family. When they know I'm having his child, they'll probably try to tie me up and ship me back." She gave Helen a pleading look. "But I don't know his parents. I don't want to go back to Greece. I don't want to give my baby to strangers and spend the rest of my life serving them." Her voice became more frantic as she spoke, and her hands fidgeted as though looking for some escape.

"Shh." Helen embraced her again. "You don't have to. We're not in Greece anymore. They can't make you go back." She had never felt any real dislike of her own culture until that moment. "It's going to be all right." Another concern occurred to her. "Does Mrs. Alberti know?"

Katherine sniffled and rubbed her nose. "Yes. I told her as soon as I was sure I was afraid she would throw me out, but she just said, 'I am a widow too.' She'll let me stay as long as I earn my keep. I get five dollars a week from the widows and orphans fund—from the accident —but that will stop after six years. In the meantime, I'll do housework for Mrs. Alberti and help cook, and... I'll find a way." Her determined look wavered. "I'm scared, though." Her voice caught. "I'm so scared of being alone."

"You're not alone." Helen took her hands. "You have friends: me, and the other girls, and Mrs. Alberti."

"I know. I'm glad." Katherine smiled weakly.

"What about your...your husband's brother? Does Demetrios know?"

Katherine shook her head quickly. "He would tell his parents, and then they would think *they* should have the baby. And me. What if he took me back to them? It's their grandchild, but it's my baby." She hugged her belly. "All I have left of Georgios."

Helen wasn't so sure American-minded Demetrios would send Katherine off to live with strangers in Greece, but she didn't know him as well as Katherine did. After all, he thought a woman could be replaced by a washing machine.

"We won't tell him," Helen said. "You'll be safe."

"Thank you. I had hoped to keep going to the Orthodox church as long as possible, but maybe it's time to stop. I'll go to the Catholic services with the Italian girls instead. I don't think I can hide my belly anymore."

Helen studied her friend. Before, she would have said Katherine had a pleasantly full figure, but now her too-loose dress stretched over her belly. Helen felt foolish for not noticing it before only because she wasn't considering it.

"Yes, do what you have to, to take care of your child."

Helen made the walk to the Greek church alone and sat by herself, keeping her eyes down. Demetrios glanced at her a couple of times during the service. Did he wonder where his sister-in-law was? Did he suspect? Helen wasn't ready to talk to him yet anyway, so she hurried home as soon as the service ended.

That night, Katherine made it downstairs for dinner, though she still looked pale. The Italian girls gossiped and laughed. Katherine didn't join in, but she smiled from time to time. Helen ate her lasagna, relaxing into the daily ritual of dining with her boarding house family.

She caught a sound running beneath the conversation: a shrill whistle. The talk and laughter faded as the others heard it too.

"What in the world?" Maria asked.

They all rushed to the window and peeked out.

A solemn parade marched down the street, their torches bathing the front yards in sharp, wicked shadows. The marchers wore white robes with peaked white hoods covering their faces. They marched perfectly in step, silent except the occasional blast of a whistle. Goose bumps crawled over Helen's skin. The masked men's stern discipline reminded her of the soldiers who had marched through Greece on their way to fight in the Great War. Were they ghosts?

Helen hurried outside, ignoring a cry of warning from Katherine. She wanted to look more closely, to understand the fear that stirred in her at the sight of those men: something primal and animal that made her want to run or to fight. The Botzaris were fighters.

The other girls crowded behind her, peering over her shoulders to watch.

The hooded man at the front of the parade held an American flag high. Others raised crosses or signs aloft. Helen's eyes fixed on the slogans, and she flinched as though the silent words were shouted in her face.

FOR RACE AND NATION
CATHOLICS=TRAITORS
AMERICA FOR AMERICANS

Maria cursed under her breath, and Katherine squeezed Helen's arm.

"Back inside," Mrs. Alberti said, breaking their horrified trance. In her widow's garb, she was almost invisible in the darkness except for her pale, pinched face.

They all hurried in, Mrs. Alberti last of all, and Maria bolted the door. They moved back to the window and watched as the parade marched by, the torches waving fiery streaks in the darkness.

"What was that?" Katherine asked.

"Hate. Fear," Mrs. Alberti said, her voice steely. "The Americans who do not like us are getting bolder. Go to bed, girls. I will keep watch over you tonight."

Helen dreamed of faceless ghost soldiers burning a path through her village in Greece. She awoke with a headache and forced herself out of bed to peek through the curtains. The street below looked the same, but something had shifted. The life and color had drained from it. There were no children playing.

Helen dressed mechanically and ate breakfast without tasting it. All the girls picked at their food, their faces pinched with worry.

"What do we do?" Maria asked quietly.

"We do not give them power." Mrs. Alberti said. "We don't let them shake us. You get dressed. You go to your jobs."

"Go to work, knowing our foremen might be some of the men behind those masks?" Maria asked.

"Yes. You don't let them stop you. And you don't strike back in anger. That gives them more power."

Helen was certain the men in the masks already had all the power. Even if the Greeks and Italians wanted to fight back, how could they? She walked to the streetcar station with her head down. The other workers waiting for the streetcar were subdued as well, only speaking in angry mutters until the streetcar arrived.

As they passed beyond Little Italy and Greek Town, the general mood on the streetcar lightened. Americans went on about their day, unaware or unconcerned about the men in the hoods. Helen regarded them with suspicion, but when she studied their faces, she could only see other people like her. How could any of them do something so sinister?

The mood in the shop was likewise subdued, but the machines clacked on. Nothing slowed production as long as the workers were there to push and pull the machines along. Here, at least, she felt safe in her faceless anonymity. When she stepped outside after her shift, she was conspicuous again. Vulnerable.

Helen stepped off the streetcar near Little Italy, and two men got off behind her. She hardly registered them at first, but they walked in time behind her, silently shadowing her path. She rolled her shoulders to shake off her uneasy feeling. Was she just being paranoid? The streets were crowded. The sun had barely dipped below the horizon, and the sky still held its orange glow.

Just to be sure, she took a winding route toward Little Italy. No matter where she turned, the men followed her. Her heartbeat picked up. What did they want? Would they follow her to Mrs. Alberti's? What then?

She whipped around and dove into a restaurant.

"Gotcha!" One of the men grabbed her long hair and pushed her against the wall in the entranceway. "No one in here wants you dirtying up their clean table. Don't you foreigners ever bathe?"

Helen looked around, desperate for someone to come to her defense. A few women with bobbed hair and pearls gave her curious looks, but none spoke up.

"What's going on?" a man in a waiter's apron asked. "I don't want any troublemakers here. You fellows have to go."

The men leered at Helen and stalked away from the restaurant.

"Thank you," Helen mumbled, trying not to let her voice shake.

"You need to leave too," the man said.

"But..." Helen's shoulders sagged at the man's unsympathetic stare. "May I go through the back?"

He nodded and escorted her out. Everyone in the restaurant stared, and she kept her head down, missing the safety of her headscarf. Once outside, she hurried back to Mrs. Alberti's.

Katherine glanced up when she came into the parlor, then stood, her face full of alarm. She put her arms around Helen's trembling shoulders. "What happened?"

Helen poured out the whole story, her voice cracking several times.

"Oh, Helen, I'm sorry."

"I don't understand what I did wrong," Helen said.

"You didn't do anything, except to be different."

Helen sagged against the sofa, thinking of her wish for her headscarf. That only would have made it worse. The markers of Greek respectability did nothing to protect her in America.

"What should I do?" she asked.

Katherine studied her. "We could cut your hair."

"Cut my hair!" Helen smoothed her long, thick locks.

Katherine pulled her hair gently from her hands. "It's beautiful, but it would be lovely in a bob too. And then you'll look more American. Bullies like those men won't pick you out from the crowd so easily."

Helen stroked her hair, remembering how the men had grabbed it, then nodded. "I suppose you're right."

Katherine borrowed a pair of scissors from Mrs. Alberti and carefully trimmed Helen's hair into a neat bob. Helen squeezed her eyes tighter with each snip.

"Now look," Katherine said.

Helen opened her eyes, and her hand went to her head. How strange it felt! Lighter. Chillier. The thick, dark waves of hair framed her face. She automatically brushed her fingers through the bob, but it jolted her to feel her hair stop so soon.

When she put on her hat, she looked extraordinarily American.

"There," Katherine said with a smile. "It's very attractive on you. You look like a modern, independent woman."

Helen smiled, but her heart was heavy. If she was so independent, why was she letting bullies force her to cut her hair?

She tried to soothe herself by watching the night outside her window. On the eastern mountains, a flickering light caught her eye. A fiery cross stood there like an ominous sentinel overlooking the valley. Helen quickly shut the curtains and sought refuge under her blankets, as though, unseen, the dangers would disappear.

The mood at the Greek Orthodox church that week was somber. Several men stood guard by the front doors. Fear, anger, disbelief, and sorrow warred in the voices and expressions inside as men and women discussed the recent attacks on Greeks and Italians.

After the service, people gathered in small groups to whisper, like mourners at a funeral. Demetrios cornered Helen. She made no attempt to escape him, hoping, instead, that he could offer some insight that would comfort her.

"Your haircut. It's very stylish," Demetrios said, raising an eyebrow.

"Thank you. It felt...safer."

"Safer? Oh." He stepped closer, and Helen hovered between wanting to lean in and wanting to flee from his nearness. "It will be fine, Miss Botzaris. Those in power in Utah don't want to see these Klansmen succeed either."

"Those in power? The Americans?"

"Do you see all Americans as the same?"

"Well... No, of course not," Helen lied.

Demetrios smiled. "It may look like all those blond-haired Americans are on the same side, but there's a long-standing division here between those who are Mormons and those who are not. Luckily for us, the Mormons outweigh the others in numbers and political power."

"Why is that lucky for us?"

"Because, like us, the Mormons are outsiders."

"But...there are more of them."

"Here, yes. But elsewhere in the country, they are considered odd. The KKK doesn't like them—doesn't like their religion, doesn't like the power they have here in Utah. The Klan has been speaking against Mormons as well."

Helen thought back to the shattered department store window. "Like at the ZCMI."

Demetrios nodded. "You see, everything will be back to normal soon."

"But in the meantime, what happens to us?" Helen asked. "And is normal so good for us, either? Don't you see it? The way people look at us? The way they ignore us or call us stupid and dirty?"

"I see it. I think it will change. In another generation—"

"Another generation! I hope I won't be here."

He touched her arm, his eyes serious. "You have to give America more of a chance. All you're seeing is Greek Town—a pale imitation of what you left behind. You have to step outside of it to understand what else is here for us."

Helen was aware—too aware—of the firm feel of his fingers pressed against her skin. She didn't understand why it made her thoughts flutter away. "Like what?"

"How about I show you? On a date?" He used an American word.

"A date?" Helen was familiar with the sweet, dark-skinned fruit. "We eat those in Greece too."

He laughed, a rich sound, like the chocolate Katherine sometimes brought home from her job. "It's a different kind of date. An opportunity for a man to take a woman out, so they can get to know each other better."

Helen's face warmed. "Like with a matchmaker?"

"No, just the man and woman, and nothing quite that...binding."

"Of course," Helen said quickly. Stubborn, independent Demetrios wasn't showing interest in her. He was just trying to prove himself right, that his modern American ways, with his hats and machines and dates, were better than her age-old traditions.

"So, you'll let me take you on a date?"

"I don't know."

"You're worried that it's improper? Americans do it all the time, and you're in America now. Ask Katherine."

"Very well. If Katherine approves."

"Good. I'll come for you Friday night at eight-thirty."

"Okay," Helen said, using the very American phrase she heard other girls say.

He laughed again. "Good girl."

Friday night, Helen modeled her new dress in the little dresser mirror. The pale yellow cotton was crisp and clean, but otherwise unremarkable. Helen chided herself for thinking of how she might have looked in the blue-green dress at the ZCMI.

Maria poked her head in the bedroom door.

"You're wearing *that* on your date?" Maria asked, her Italian accent thickened with disappointment.

"It's the best dress I have."

Maria grinned. "Lucky for you, I have this." She produced a dark blue dress that shimmered with sequins.

Helen covered her gasp. "Oh, it *is* beautiful, but I could never wear that!"

"I think we're about the same size, and it's a loose-fitting style."

"I know, but...it has such short sleeves!"

Maria laughed. "I have a shawl that matches it, if that makes you feel better. And it's not as short as a real flapper dress—Mama would kill me if I ever wore a dress like that. Come, I don't have many chances to wear it, so someone should enjoy it."

"Well..." Helen touched the shimmering fabric. It slid through her fingers, silky and tempting as a cup of cool water on a hot afternoon. "I'll try it on."

Maria stepped out long enough for Helen to change. Helen tipped the mirror this way and that, trying to get a better look at herself. It reflected flashes of a modern, almost sophisticated woman, the type who breezed with confidence through the city, flirted with handsome men, and embraced the changes swirling around her.

A stranger.

Maria tapped on the door. "Please, can I see?"

Helen opened the door and stood back for Maria's reaction. Katherine peeked in behind her.

"This Demetrios of yours is going to be floored," Maria said.

Katherine studied Helen with a worried look.

"Is it too much?" Helen asked. "Too...forward?"

Maria laughed. "No, *bella*. It's just more American than you're used to. Here is the shawl. But we need to do something with your hair."

"I have a hat," Helen said.

"No, this dress calls for an uncovered head, or maybe a Greek headdress."

"What?" Helen asked, exchanging a confused look with Katherine. She'd never seen an American wearing a headscarf.

Maria laughed. "I know, these fashion magazines throw foreign labels on things to make them sound exotic—I like to remember how exotic I am while I can beans—but they mean a headband."

Helen patted her hair. How naked it felt! "The headband, then, I suppose."

She refused to wear rouge or paint her lips, but Maria and Katherine fussed with her hair, so by the time Demetrios knocked on the front door, she felt like a paper doll dressed up in clothes cut from a fashion magazine.

Demetrios's eyes widened when he saw her, and then he broke out in a grin that made her blush all the way down to her neckline.

"Be back before midnight," Mrs. Alberti said sternly. She whacked Demetrios with her rolled-up newspaper. "And be a gentleman!"

"Of course, ma'am!"

He offered his arm, and Helen took it, feeling suddenly shy. Her hand fit perfectly against his elbow, and her steps easily matched his relaxed pace, as though they had been strolling together for years.

"I hope you don't mind walking," he said. "It's not far."

"No, I don't mind. It's very pleasant," she murmured. He gave her a self-satisfied smirk, and she hurried on, "I meant to say, it's a pleasant night for a walk."

He chuckled and drew her closer. She almost pulled away, but he was warm in the chilly evening, and the rich, spicy scent of his after-shave intrigued her.

"You look lovely," he said. "Very progressive."

"It feels like a costume."

"I suppose it is, in a way, but aren't we always wearing costumes? Greek or American, orthodox or progressive. We decide every day when we get dressed what we're going to tell the world about ourselves."

"I'd never thought of it that way." But she'd been aware of it on some level. Wasn't that why she had cut her hair? "Where are we going?"

"It's a surprise. You like music, don't you?"

"Yes, I suppose."

"You'll love this."

He led her out of Greek Town and down a street bustling with people dressed up for the night. Street lights illuminated their path with glowing circles of light, and walking on the arm of a handsome man in a fine suit, Helen felt like a queen.

Demetrios guided her down a side street. The light from the street lamps faded, and she shrunk closer to him in the darkness.

"Don't worry, we're here." His deep voice steadied her nerves and at the same time sent flutters through her stomach.

He stopped and knocked at a door as bland and faded as the others on the side street. A man in a black suit peeked out then beckoned them into a foyer. A rumbling rhythm came from the room behind him. Demetrios exchanged a few quiet words with the man in the suit then guided Helen to the room. When he swung the door open, a wave of drums and brass engulfed her and drew her into the dim space.

The music thrummed through her body, vibrating down her limbs. Despite the foreign rhythms, its bright energy reminded her of dancing in Greece, making her itch to join the crowd on the floor. Men in suits swung around women in short skirts and bobbed hair who moved so smoothly they seemed to be a living part of the music. Boot-legged liquor swirled in glasses and cigarettes hung from the lips of men and women when they weren't dancing. The smoke thickened the air and seemed to swirl in time with the beat.

Helen hovered close to Demetrios, who watched her reaction.

"What is this place?" She shouted to be heard over the music.

"A, uh, jazz club of sorts. A speakeasy, to be honest. Frowned on by some of the stuffier elements of the city, but the music is what matters. It's catching on. Watch."

Helen looked again and began to separate the dancers from the music. Some of the women were definitely flappers, but many wore longer hemlines and longer hair. Not all of them were smoking or drinking. And while many were the white Americans who dominated the city, there were darker heads and darker faces among the dancers— dancing together, swirling into a kaleidoscope under the command of the musicians.

Demetrios drew her aside to a corner of the club where they could hear each other better.

"You see?" he asked.

"You mean, that everyone is dancing together?"

"Yes. The music draws them together, and suddenly it doesn't matter as much, the color of their skin or hair or where they were born. I'm not saying it's going to change quickly, but if those walls can be broken down here, the change will slowly travel everywhere else."

"I suppose it's possible—"

"Not just possible. Guaranteed. No one with white hoods in here. And that's what the Klansmen are afraid of. They know the change is coming, and they are powerless against this."

He gestured to room. The pounding waves of music moved through the crowd, and Helen imagined it moving through the city, flooding the streets, crashing through the factories and the stuffy displays at the ZCMI.

The music turned slow and sultry. Demetrios leaned closer and took Helen's hand.

"Will you dance with me?" His voice blended with the dark, smooth tones of the saxophones. His gaze took hers and held it, and the admiration there thrilled her with a heady rush, like a sip of strong wine. She wanted to spin with him around the floor, free, unafraid.

"I don't know how," she whispered.

"I'll teach you."

He led her out to the floor, and though it was crowded with slowly turning couples, Helen saw only Demetrios and his dark eyes, no longer laughing, but serious and intensely bright. Helen wanted to look away as he wrapped her close, but she stayed staring into his eyes, letting him see her uncertainty, more vulnerable than she'd ever felt in her life. But there was nothing mocking in his intense gaze.

"Just let me guide you," he said, and she did, stepping hesitantly with him, spinning when he turned her, his firm but gentle hands telling her which way to go.

The song ended, and they stood, Demetrios holding her close. His burning gaze traveled down to her lips, its warmth lingering on her face. She took a breath, shaky with nervousness and anticipation, and closed her eyes. Demetrios touched her face gently, sending warm shivers racing over her skin.

"Come," he whispered. "We need to move for the other dancers."

She opened her eyes, hurt and confused. He looked away, guided her off the floor. Did he not want to kiss her after all? Was he just trying to prove that he was always right, always in control? She followed him with her head down.

"Helen," he said when they sat. "Uh, Miss Botzaris, I should say."

She looked up and forced a smile.

"There's a problem with wearing costumes," he said softly. "Sometimes we let the costume wear us, make us do things we don't normally do. Things we might regret later." He reached out to brush a strand of hair from her forehead, and she leaned into his touch. He pulled his hand away. "I don't want to be a regret. I want to be a choice."

Helen's eyes widened. Were her dress and this place making her do things she would be ashamed of later? She liked Demetrios, didn't she? But he infuriated her at times. She wasn't sure if she wanted to slap him or kiss him, and it certainly wouldn't be right to do both. "I understand," she said.

He exhaled and nodded. "It's hot in here, don't you think? We could go to an ice cream shop if you'd like."

She nodded, and he escorted her out, where the fresh air brushed away the scents of the speakeasy and made her blush to think of her forward behavior.

Demetrios said little but led her back to the main thoroughfare, where an ice cream parlor attracted couples and teenagers. Helen hesitated to step inside, but in their American costumes, she and Demetrios attracted no unwanted attention. A few of the college boys even gave Helen appreciative stares that earned them a stern look from Demetrios. It felt unreal, to sit eating ice cream like every other American in the room. But did being American mean giving up being Greek? Headscarf or hat, yellow cotton or blue sequins: she could only wear one at a time.

Demetrios returned her home under the watchful eye of Mrs. Alberti with no more affection than a quick squeeze of the hand and left her head swirling with questions.

"How was your time with Demetrios last night?" Katherine asked quietly the next morning. Her belly was growing uncomfortably large, and she rested on the sofa with her feet up on pillows. Her voice sounded vulnerable.

"It was nice. Confusing."

"Confusing?"

"I just...don't know how I feel about Demetrios. Or how he feels about me."

"He always was hard to read. Georgios was so open, so passionate, like he was trying to make every moment count for two lifetimes." Her voice caught, and she was silent for a long moment. "Demetrios was the opposite. He often seemed bitter and so focused on his business, like it was all that mattered. I worry about you."

Helen was quiet for a moment. "You think he's playing games with me?"

"I don't know. Maybe." Katherine pushed herself up to meet Helen's hurt gaze. "I don't mean that someone couldn't love you, Helen —of course, they could—but Demetrios? Why Demetrios?"

Helen shrugged, stinging at the idea the Demetrios could be using her for some selfish end. Or that Katherine would think so. Why Demetrios? Warmth melted over her as she thought of the way he had held her and touched her, the way his eyes danced when he laughed. Was that something that could be faked?

"I have some errands to run today," Helen said quietly. "Do you need anything?"

"Helen, I didn't mean—"

"I know." She sighed, forcing away her hurt and managed a weak smile. "Do you need anything?"

Katherine sank back into the sofa. "No, thank you."

Helen took her hat and handbag and headed outside. Without thinking, she made her way toward Demetrios's shop. She didn't really need anything. Just clarity. Maybe she could find it there. Maybe she could see the truth in his expression in the daytime, undisguised by smoky music and low lights.

She entered the shop and had to blink several times to make sense of what she saw. Demetrios had reorganized everything. The men's goods sat apart from the women's goods, each neatly organized, and the rest of the dry goods were arranged in their places. It was still cramped, but a sense of order lay over everything. She smiled.

"You like it." Demetrios's low voice rumbled next to her ear.

She gave a start and smoothed her hair back to disguise her embarrassment. "It will make shopping much easier."

"It was an excellent idea," Demetrios said. "A stroke of genius on my part."

Helen's eyes narrowed, and Demetrios winked at her, the laughter back in his eyes.

She chuckled. "Indeed, it was genius."

He grinned. "I have something for you. It just came in."

Helen tilted her head and followed him to the bolts of fabric near the women's goods. He pulled out a smooth length of polished cotton in a blue-green so like the ocean she could almost hear the whisper of the waves.

"Oh!" She ran her fingers over the soft fabric. "How much?"

"I will give you enough to make a dress." When she looked up quickly, a protest on her lips, he added, "As payment for your decorating advice."

She struggled against her pride, then relented. "Thank you," she whispered. "It's beautiful. I often dream of Greece. Of the ocean. It will remind me of that."

"Is that all you dream of?" he asked quietly.

She looked up into his curious gaze. "I suppose," she lied.

"Everyone comes to America with dreams, you know. The question is, what happens to those dreams once they arrive and collide with reality?"

Helen had just wanted a place where she mattered to someone. Was that a dream? It seemed small, and yet at the same time so large that it had left a gaping hole that she wasn't sure she would ever fill.

"Don't try to deny it," Demetrios said, his low voice next to her ear, sending shivers through her and tightening her throat. "I saw it in your eyes as you sat on the train. I think that's why I couldn't stop myself from speaking to you. I wanted to remember how that felt again, just for a moment."

Helen pulled away, flustered by his honesty. "What did you dream of?"

"I thought I was going to come to America and get rich. Return home as a hero. My parents mortgaged their farm to pay the passage for Georgios and me. Imagine, sending a fifteen-year-old and a thirteen-year-old to a foreign land and hoping they would be your salvation!"

"You've done well here."

"Only by shedding all my dreams and taking reality by the horns. When I arrived, I had to pay a Greek labor agent for work. He arranged a mining job for me where I got paid less than the American men working beside me. When your face is coated in coal dust, it's hard to tell what nation you're from, but you could tell by looking at a man's paycheck. The labor agent took a portion of our checks and forced us to spend our earnings at his friends' shops, where they charged us far too much. He lived in the Hotel Utah and wore diamonds while his countrymen died in the mines. Being Greek was suffocating me." He smiled grimly. "I've never forgotten my duty. I send money home to my parents each month, but they will die and be buried, and I will never set eyes on them again."

"You couldn't go back to Greece?"

"Not now. I nearly starved myself to save enough to open my own store where I could charge fair prices and compete with the company stores, maybe drive them under. Being Greek is a burden in America, but at least I could lighten the load for myself and the other workers."

"That's a noble impulse."

"Don't paint me into too pretty a picture. My motivations were mostly selfish. I still thought I could catch some of the promised riches of America—and that those riches would give me security. But owning a store requires a lot of time and investment. Everything I make is reinvested or goes toward covering losses. Comfortable, but never wealthy. And I watch other Greeks come here, and I see the dreams fade in most of their eyes too."

"Most?"

"Yes. There are some that never seem to lose that hope." He

studied her face, and she tried not to blush under his scrutiny. "I wish I could understand it. I wish I could capture it again. It felt good to believe. It is life, to have a dream to believe in. Otherwise, we stop living and just...survive."

"You don't think you'll ever find something else to dream of?" It seemed too sad to Helen, to think of someone without any hope. And if he did not hope or dream, then he must have no room in his life for love. What was love but sharing hopes and dreams, pains and failures?

He shrugged. "I... I don't know."

"I have trouble believing that. You still laugh."

"Laugh or cry, I am just lining my gilded cage, pretty bird. But you... You don't have that same silly dreaminess in your eyes that I saw on the train, but there's still something burning there. I keep watching..." he smiled. "I guess I have found something to hope for. I hope that light never dies out."

He touched her hand, and she caught her breath at the rush of warmth that flooded through her.

"Mr. Nikolaides, sir!" The clerk gestured to a man standing in the doorway, shifting from foot to foot. The stranger's fair, freckled skin looked out of place in the Greek store.

Demetrios smiled ruefully and left Helen holding the blue-green fabric, her head in turmoil.

"Do you have any of that Pinkham's Lady's Tonic?" the nervous man asked. "I heard you might sell me some."

Demetrios's eyes narrowed, and he wrapped an arm around the man's shoulders. A friendly gesture, but tension tightened Demetrios's jaw. "Listen to me," he said, his voice low and menacing. "I don't need any of that kind of trouble here. I don't sell the stuff, and I want everyone to know it." He released the man with a bit of a shove.

Helen gave Demetrios a confused look as the other man hunched his shoulders and hurried out of the shop.

"Lady's Tonic?" she asked.

"Mrs. Pinkham's Vegetable Compound. It's mostly alcohol. Medicinal, you see, so it slips under the noses of the Prohibitionists, and moonshiners can use the bottles to hide more potent liquors. But the police are watching us Greeks. The KKK is too. They've attacked people they suspect of bootlegging. I can't afford any rumors about my shop."

Helen nodded automatically, her focus on the worry and frustration in Demetrios's eyes. She suspected it was about more than just protecting his investment. The pain of loss may have made him shield his heart, but she couldn't believe that he had really given up on hope for more from life.

Was that her concern, though? What did she hope for? As she sampled the opportunities America offered, she became increasingly uncertain of what she wanted from it.

Helen continued her routine, working day after day in the factory. The machines roared on, not caring about troubled hearts or frightening dreams of men in masks. She staggered into work one morning after another night where she couldn't fall into a peaceful sleep. Annie yawned as she took her place beside Helen. Helen yawned in sympathy, aching to go back to sleep.

"Sorry," Annie said, covered another yawn. "I have a colicky baby. If I didn't need this job …" She shrugged and smiled ruefully.

Helen nodded. The whistle blew, and the noise of the machines grumbling to life drowned out any possible conversation. The shuttle flew back and forth, and the shaft wound the fabric around and around, the never-ending threads always slithering forward. It was hypnotic, and Helen shook herself from a trance, trying to stay focused on her work.

A shrill shriek sounded over the roar of the machines. The whistle again?

Helen looked up to see Annie's face drawn in a terrified scream. Her skirt had caught on the shaft, steadily drawing her in. Annie struggled away from the machine, but a fragile human body was no match for the strength of steel and gears.

Grabbing Annie would do no good—the machine would tear the other girl from Helen's fingers. Instead, she snatched a pair of scissors and sliced the waist of Annie's skirt. The sound of it tearing was lost in the cranking of the factory, but Annie stumbled free. The machine slurped the skirt in, twisting it to shreds until it became so tangled it shuddered to a stop.

Helen dropped the scissors and stared in horror.

"What's going on here!" the foreman shouted into Helen's face.

Annie collapsed, shaking, and wrapped her arms around her exposed legs. Her face was as white as linen as she stared up at Helen with wide eyes.

"Her skirt!" Helen shouted. "It got caught. I cut it free."

She'd done it. The moment had been so fast and frightening, but she had kept her head and improvised. A machine could not have done the same.

The foreman's expression softened. He helped Annie back to her feet and led both women to his office.

"Are you harmed?" he asked Annie.

She stared at him, not seeming to understand.

"I said, are you harmed?" He gave her a little shake.

She gasped and shook her head.

"Okay. We'll find you something to make you decent again and get you back to work." He turned to Helen. "You saw it happen?"

"No, I only heard her scream." Helen shivered. She had only barely noticed the sound over the machines. Annie could have been mauled to death right next to her, with Helen completely unaware.

"And you cut her loose?"

"Yes."

"That's good, quick thinking."

"Thank you, sir."

"I'm not just passing out compliments. I want to make you a supervisor on this line."

"A supervisor, sir?"

"Yes. Overseeing the other girls—especially the new ones. Making sure their work is fast and good, and no more accidents. You'll get a small raise. Are you interested?"

Helen closed her mouth and nodded.

"Good. You'll start tomorrow."

Helen floated through the rest of the day, struggling to stay focused on her work. Annie came back to her machine, though her face was pinched and she didn't look at Helen. In shock. And she had to come back tomorrow with the knowledge of how close that machine had come to crushing her fragile life. Unless she found a job elsewhere, but so many of them were dangerous, especially for those whose English was too poor or whose skin was too dark to work elsewhere.

Well, Helen would help make sure the other girls were safe. Her chest swelled with a sense of purpose.

When she got home, she checked the money she had hidden under her mattress. Now, she would be able to add a little more each week. Already, she had enough to pay for her own little room, living under the same roof with friends. She had enough to send some to her parents, and soon she would be able to help them even more. Or return to Greece herself.

She stuffed the money back into its hiding place. What waited for her in Greece? She had to work hard here, it was true, but she had found a useful role. She worked long days, but her off hours were her own. She could save up enough...for what? A place of her own someday? Classes, so she could polish her English and get a better job? A dowry?

If she were to marry, her money would belong to her husband to do as he pleased with it. Being single was lonely at times, when she lay in bed at night, chilled by the draft from the window and wondering what it would be like to have someone to wrap his arms around her and keep her warm. If she belonged to someone, would he treat her like a possession or a precious gift? Being on her own might be the safest way to live. Yet as she curled up in the cold bed, she wondered if safety was worth the cost.

The factory looked different from the perspective of a supervisor. Helen wasn't in charge of much—the men oversaw most of the work—but her line of machines expanded her view of the world a little. Each girl moved like a part of the looms. The machines needed the girls to function properly, but at the same time, the girls were the weak link in the process. Every day, Helen watched to make sure they were staying awake, paying attention. Annie had quit her job a few days after her accident—hopefully moving on to something safer—but the thoughts of what could have happened to her haunted Helen, keeping her always on alert.

One night, Helen rode the streetcar home as usual, almost too tired to keep her head up. It was already dark, but as they passed Greek Town, she saw a crowd rushing and yelling something about fire.

"Stop!" Helen shouted to the conductor, but he ignored her.

When the streetcar slowed to turn, Helen jumped off. She fell and rolled but pushed herself back up and ran for Greek Town, thinking of all of her countrymen who might be in danger.

She stopped and stared when she reached the street where the crowd was gathered. A cross stood in the yard of one of the little Greek houses, with flames slithering up its base and along its arms. The angry red glare of the fire cast long, flickering shadows behind the stunned witnesses. The heat scalded Helen's face as the holy symbol crackled and blackened, smoke clouding the clear night sky.

Neighbors rushed forward with buckets and blankets. Someone kicked the base of the flaming cross, and it snapped like the breaking of bone, crashing onto the patchy lawn. Steam hissed as buckets of water sloshed on the fire, and men and women beat the flames with wet blankets and stomped on embers singeing the grass.

Helen stared in mute horror at the charred skeleton of the cross. A sob caught in her throat, and she swayed into the woman standing next to her: Agatha, with all hostility gone from her face. They shared a wide-eyed glance, and then Agatha caught Helen in her arms, and they cried into each other's shoulders.

Agatha pulled back, reaching for Alexander, who returned from stamping out the fire. Helen's whole body shook, and she tried to back away. A man with a soot-stained face stepped closer, and she gasped.

"Helen, it's me!" Demetrios said. "It's only me."

Helen stared at him, her hands shaking.

"Are you alright?" he asked.

She shook her head.

"Are you hurt?"

"No, but...why did they do this?"

His eyes darkened. "Because a Greek man dared to marry an American woman. They want our labor and our money, but not us, no matter how American we try to be. Well, they have us anyway." His expression softened. "Let's get you home."

Helen glanced over her shoulder. "It's not close."

"It's not that far. I'll walk with you. I want to make sure you're safe, and it will help me cool off."

She nodded. He paused and touched her chin. She started at his warm caress.

"I thought you said you weren't hurt," he said.

"I..." She touched her chin and found it sticky with blood. "I leapt off the streetcar when I saw the fire. I was afraid for everyone in Greek Town."

He shook his head and smiled, his teeth white against his sooty face. "You never cease to amaze."

She looked down, not sure how to react. Blisters marked his fingers.

She gently lifted his hand. "You burned yourself."

He stared at her hand touching his for a moment then closed his eyes and sighed. "It's nothing. Come along."

He gently tucked her arm under his and walked her back through the streets. His posture was tense, his gaze darting to every shadow.

"Do you think this is ever going to end?" she asked.

"When we let go of all of our ridiculous old customs and act like the Americans we are, they'll forget we were ever different," he said bitterly.

"You think we have to give up being Greek?"

"If we want to be American. It's fine to come here and earn some money to send back home, keep your head down, and return to

202

Greece. But those who want to stay in America have to become American. It's the only way we'll ever have safety or prosperity—by blending in."

She shook her head. "If you really believe that, then why haven't you become Protestant yet? Or Mormon?"

"Because they don't have the lineage. The authority. The Mormons at least make a claim to it, but the Orthodox Church traces its roots back—"

She chuckled.

"You're laughing at me?"

"I am. You're being ridiculous."

"Me? Ridiculous? How so?"

"You say we have to be more American, but you refuse to give up the most Greek thing about yourself." She lowered her voice. "Besides, I don't think we *can* stop being Greek. Other Americans aren't going to forget who we are, and neither should we."

A frown creased his forehead. "You may be right," he admitted quietly. "But I always hoped if I worked hard enough, I could leave behind 'dirty' and 'poor' and 'foreigner' and simply be judged on my own merits. Certainly, you agree that being Greek holds us back?"

Helen considered that. "There are some things I've learned to dislike about our culture. American women have more freedom—more opportunities. But I'm proud to be a Botzaris. Proud to be Greek."

He looked down. "I'm not sure what being Greek has ever gotten me, except being taken advantage of by mine owners and labor agents. But, working hard and being successful haven't bought me any peace either. I think it just makes these Klansmen hate me more."

They walked in silence for a block.

"Not everything about being Greek is bad," Helen said. "We are fighters, you know. And we have deep roots. We survive."

"Hmm," Demetrios said. They walked on, and he cleared his throat. "Would you consider being courted by an American? Or an Italian?"

"No, I don't think I would. I wouldn't want my children to lose their language or their religion."

"Then I suppose there's at least one good thing about being Greek."

She stared at him, but he looked straight ahead, a smile on his lips. She blushed and looked back down. Was he courting her, then? Her heart warmed at the idea. Perhaps it wouldn't be such a bad thing. He was a lunatic, but he could be a thoughtful one.

Mrs. Alberti opened the door for them, and Demetrios greeted the widow with a nod, which she returned. Demetrios squeezed Helen's hand gently, and his light touch sent pleasant goose bumps up her arm. She smiled a silly farewell at him, and he grinned, handsome even with his face stained in soot.

Mrs. Alberti pulled Helen into the house and looked her over. "You smell like smoke. You've been hurt. What happened out there?"

Helen's giddiness evaporated. "They burned a cross. I fell going to see what happened."

Mrs. Alberti kissed her cheek. "But you got back up, and that's what matters. Wash up. We have another day waiting for us tomorrow."

Helen sat in front of her mirror, trying out different hairstyles.

Katherine poked her head in the door, her eyes troubled. "You're going out with Demetrios again tonight?"

Helen took a deep breath and nodded. "I know he can be difficult sometimes, but—"

"Wait," Katherine said. "About that. I'm sorry."

Helen turned to face her friend. Katherine sat across from her on the bed.

"I think I've been jealous of Demetrios," Katherine said. "Georgios was. His little brother was more successful than him—opening his store while Georgios stayed at the mine. Demetrios offered him a place at the shop, but Georgios was afraid it couldn't support us, so he stayed at the mine." Katherine blinked, and tears rushed down her cheeks. "I think he was just being stubborn. Now he's gone. It wasn't Demetrios's fault, but I resented him."

Helen squeezed Katherine's hand. Katherine gave her a teary smile. "And now he's stealing you, and you've been like family to me."

"Oh, Katherine." Helen embraced her friend. "You're better than family to me. You don't make me wash your floors."

Katherine choked out a half-sob and then laughed. "Never. I do want you to be happy, and if Demetrios can offer that to you..."

"I don't know," Helen admitted as Katherine guided her back to the chair in front of the mirror. "I do like him. He's charming and attractive, and he treats me like... like a whole person. But he can be so stubborn, and he seems to want to turn his back on everything Greek."

Katherine nodded. "At least you have the opportunity to make a decision about him." She studied Helen's hair. "Too much curl. Where is Demetrios taking you tonight?"

Helen tried to flatten out her locks. "To a moving picture at the five-cent theater. It's called *The Thief of Baghdad.*"

Katherine groaned and curled up around her belly.

"What is it?" Helen asked.

Katherine gasped. "The baby. I think it's coming."

Helen stood, knocking over her chair. "Let's get you to your room."

Helen helped Katherine across the hall.

"Mrs. Alberti!" Helen called.

Helen guided Katherine to her bed and held her hand through another contraction. Mrs. Alberti and Maria ran into the room.

"It's the baby," Helen said.

Mrs. Alberti nodded. "Maria, go fetch the Greek midwife."

They sat with Katherine, trying to help her find a comfortable position until the midwife arrived. Helen nearly cried in relief at the sight of the old woman with a headscarf over her gray-streaked hair and years of experience etched in her wrinkled face.

But when the midwife felt Katherine's belly, a frown creased her forehead.

"What is it?" Katherine panted.

"The baby. I think it's turned the wrong way."

"What do we do?" Katherine glanced at all of them with frightened eyes.

"We pray. We do our best," the midwife said, but her voice was sad.

Katherine cried out at her next contraction, and the sound rang through Helen, filling her with terror.

A knock sounded on the front door, and one of the other girls called for Helen. Helen reluctantly tore herself from Katherine's side to dash downstairs.

Demetrios stood in the doorway with his hat in hand.

"Oh, Demetrios, I forgot!" Helen said.

Katherine cried out upstairs.

"What's going on?"

Helen hesitated. He didn't know about Katherine, and that was the way Katherine wanted it. But it was his brother's baby in danger. Did he have some right to know the child existed? Especially now, when the baby might not survive? Or would that just cause more pain for everyone?

Katherine cried out again.

"Is that Katherine? What happened?" he asked, taking a step forward.

"It's..." Helen took a deep breath. "Her baby is coming."

"Her... Do you mean she's carrying Georgios's child?"

Helen nodded, feeling like a double traitor at the mingled look of hurt and hope on Demetrios's face.

"She didn't want to be sent back to Greece," Helen said quietly.

"She thought I would want her to go? I want to see my brother's baby."

He took another step forward, and Helen reached out to stop him. "The labor isn't going well. The baby is turned the wrong way. They may not—" Her voice caught. "They may not make it."

Demetrios's face hardened. "I won't allow that to happen."

He dashed back outside. Helen stared after him for a moment then shut the door. Did he know a better midwife?

Another pained cry from Katherine sent Helen racing up to her friend's side. She didn't tell Katherine about Demetrios. They could worry about that later.

The midwife felt Katherine's belly when it tensed with another contraction, and she shook her head. "I do not think we can help the baby, but we can still save the mother."

A sob tightened Helen's chest as she realized what the midwife was suggesting.

"Maria, out!" Mrs. Alberti ordered.

Maria fled, her cheeks pale, and Mrs. Alberti followed her daughter.

Tears rolled down Katherine's cheeks, and sweat glossed her forehead. She tightened her grip on Helen. "Please, I don't want to lose my baby."

"Shh. You're not going to lose it," Helen said. Lied.

The midwife mixed up a drink for Katherine. "Take this. It will help you relax."

Katherine swatted it away. "Save my baby! It's all I have left!"

Another contraction wracked her body, and her belly tightened. They were coming closer together. The midwife shook her head sadly.

"No men!" Mrs. Alberti shouted from downstairs. "No men!"

"Out of the way," Demetrios's voice echoed up the stairwell.

Helen straightened. Did he have a plan to help Katherine? Helen met him in the bedroom doorway. A blond man with a black bag stood behind him, his face grim.

"What are you doing?" Helen asked, glancing between the men and Mrs. Alberti advancing on them like an unhooded executioner.

"I've brought a doctor."

Helen's shoulders sank. "We already have a midwife."

"She needs a doctor, not a midwife."

"No respectable woman wants a man to see her during childbirth," Helen whispered. "Especially an American man! She won't be able to relax or focus. The embarrassment—"

"Foolish woman! Hang the embarrassment and all your silly traditions!"

Helen stepped back, stinging as though he had slapped her. So, that was what he thought of her? Of being Greek? She shook her head and moved to slam the bedroom door on them.

"Wait!" The doctor stepped forward. "I've delivered breech babies before. Sometimes I can turn the infant. There is some risk to the mother, but I might be able to save them both."

The midwife scowled at him, but Katherine lifted her head. "Helen? I don't want to lose the baby."

"This man is a doctor. He can save your baby," Demetrios called over Helen's shoulder.

Katherine stared at him, her eyes glazed.

"He said it would risk Katherine's life," Helen said. "It's not worth it!"

"He'll save your baby, Katherine," Demetrios called as Helen pushed him away.

"Yes, please!" Katherine cried. "Save my baby!"

The doctor squeezed past them, taking off his jacket as he went. He ejected the midwife and slammed the door on all of them. Helen's throat tightened. Shut out.

She whirled on Demetrios.

"You can't promise her that her baby will live!"

"At least I gave them a chance! It's what she wanted."

"You may have killed her!"

He was just like the other men—always thinking he knew what was right, seeing women as something disposable. Helen narrowed her eyes. "You're not welcome here. I'm done with you."

Demetrios's hurt look quickly turned to anger. "Perfect."

He stormed down the stairs, past the wrathful glare of Mrs. Alberti.

Helen tried the door to Katherine's room, but it was locked. She wanted to slam her fists against it, break it down, but what would that accomplish? The worn wood of the door pushed back against her as she slid to the floor. Tears dripped down her face while she prayed. Her ear was pressed against the door, but all on the other side was silent. Like ancient ruins. Like a tomb.

The shrill cry of a baby broke the stillness, and Helen scrambled to her feet, leaning against the door. The handle clicked, and she nearly fell inside. The doctor swung the door open, cradling a squalling baby in one arm. Helen glanced past him. Katherine lay on the bloodied bed, her eyes closed, her face pale and still in its halo of dark hair.

"No!" The scream tore out of Helen. Pain and rage burned from deep in her stomach. She would kill Demetrios. She stumbled forward blindly.

"She's alive!" the doctor said. "I used chloroform to sedate her for the procedure. She'll wake soon."

Helen sobbed in gratitude and collapsed at her friend's bedside. The doctor handed her the baby. A boy. Perfect little hands and feet, wide eyes taking in the brightness of the world.

Helen rewrapped the baby and clutched it to her chest.

"What do we owe you?" she whispered.

"Demetrios paid me."

Helen mumbled a thank you. Demetrios's gamble had paid off, but the price he was willing to pay was too high. She could not bear his arrogance any longer. Yet at that thought, her heart cried out with a loneliness that she knew no cure for.

Helen made her way to work, keeping her head down. Little Georgios was growing quickly, but Katherine was exhausted from caring for him, and Helen wore herself out helping where she could. It kept her too tired to think about the news of KKK meetings and Greeks arrested for bootlegging. Almost too tired to think of Demetrios.

He watched her at church. She could feel his eyes following her, but he never moved to speak to her, and she would not speak to him, not even when Katherine did. The Greek community understood Kathrine's situation and welcomed her and her baby. Yet every time Helen held Georgios, she remembered that Demetrios had been willing to trade Katherine's life for his brother's baby. His American doctor had succeeded, but that did not mean that his American ways were always right.

She dozed off twice on the streetcar, jerking awake when it clanged to a stop. She avoided the eyes of the other streetcar passengers, afraid that she might see hate in their gazes. How could she know which of them went out at night with white hoods and terrorized the immigrant neighborhoods? They might harass her there in broad daylight, too, and she couldn't be sure anyone would stand up for her. America did not want her.

She got off the streetcar and walked a block before she became aware of yelling. Afraid of what she would find at the factory, she hurried forward, peering around the corner of a building. A group of men with signs stood in front of the entrance to the factory, shouting and shoving away anyone who approached. Another woman who worked on the looms walked up beside her and stared at the mob.

Helen glanced at her. "Are they the Klan?"

The woman gave her an odd look and shook her head. "I don't think so. It looks like a strike."

"A strike?" Helen looked back at the men and recognized some of their faces from the factory. They looked so different—no longer tired and sweat-drenched, but angry and determined. "What are they striking about?"

The other woman shrugged. "Safer working conditions or higher pay."

Helen nodded. It would be good to make the looms safer, and there would be fewer accidents if they didn't have to work such long hours or had more breaks.

"We get paid less than the men," Helen said.

"And today, we get paid nothing at all."

Helen gave a start. Of course. The men weren't going to allow the women to go into work either. No work meant no pay.

"What do we do?" Helen asked.

"Join the strike or go home. My husband's not going to be happy. We need the money."

The woman walked away. Helen watched the striking men a few more minutes then turned back. She could afford a few days without work, maybe. She had some savings. And Mrs. Alberti wasn't unkind; she would let Helen be late on the rent. But unless Helen was going to move back in with Alexander, she had to have income.

Yet the strike dragged on. After the first week, Helen looked for another job, but with the glut of workers, no one was hiring. The neat little roll of bills she had saved thinned. Soon, she would have to make a choice about what to do.

"I heard of a place hiring laundry workers," Katherine told her one morning as she rocked Georgios. "If you hurry, you might be able to get the job."

"Thank you!" Helen put on her hat and gloves and ran to the address Katherine gave her, instead of waiting for the streetcar. She arrived out of breath, taking just a moment to smooth her frizzled hair before stepping up to the counter.

"I heard you were hiring laundry workers," Helen said.

The man didn't even spare her a glance. "Position's filled."

"Oh." Helen's hope turned to ash in her mouth. "I see. Thank you."

Helen walked out, hardly seeing where she was going. Tears clouded her eyes, but she quickly wiped them away. She sat on a bench in a park and watched the children playing. What was she doing, crying over not being hired to do laundry?

It wasn't just the job, though. She liked being independent. Being able to choose. Yet for every step she took, something pushed her back two. Everywhere she looked, the promise of America seemed to be for someone else. Someone who spoke English better, without an accent. Someone who went to the right church, who had the right name, like Nelson or Smith. America, it seemed, was not for her, and she was running out of choices.

She could move back to Greek Town with Alexander and wash laundry for strangers, or she could go back to her village and work for family.

The roll of bills under her mattress might still be enough to provide her own dowry after paying for her passage back to Greece. The travel office was just around the corner. At least, she could find out what it would cost to go home.

She approached the counter, trying not to clutch her hands together like she was pleading.

"How can I help you, miss?" the man asked.

"How much are tickets to Greece?" She was proud that her English had improved enough to have this conversation, though she could never shake her accent.

The man checked his book. "The train ticket from Salt Lake City to New York City will cost sixty dollars, plus an extra ten if you want a berth to sleep in. That's changing trains in Denver and Chicago. The steamship passage is thirty dollars."

Helen tried not to gasp, but she felt like she'd been struck. Maybe he was trying to sell her first-class accommodations. "Is that for second-class rail and steerage on the ship?"

"Yes, miss."

"Thank you." Helen wandered away from the counter in a daze. Ninety dollars! Yiannis had paid so much just to bring her to Utah.

She found herself circling downtown, walking around the temple and the tabernacle, then up the hill to the Catholic church. The lush green lawn invited her to sit and look out over the city. How much money had she saved? Maybe forty dollars. Fifty dollars short, and that was if she left immediately and returned home with empty pockets. But what was she to do? If she stayed, her resources would dwindle until she had nothing left at all.

She stood and slowly walked toward the boarding house. It wasn't close, but even the small charge for the streetcar seemed like too much when she realized how dire her financial straits had become. How much could she earn if she took in some washing? Did she have anything she could sell?

She finally made her way back to Mrs. Alberti's.

"What's wrong?" Katherine asked when Helen collapsed onto the sofa.

"It's...I can't find a job. I'm not sure what to do. I'm not even sure if I should stay here in America."

"Oh," Katherine said softly, bouncing Georgios.

"Do you ever think about going back to Greece—on your own, not to live with Georgios's parents?"

"Sometimes. For now, I get the widow's stipend, but after that ends, I don't know." She met Helen's eyes. "But what's right for me isn't right for you. I'll miss you if you have to leave, but we can write, and maybe you can find a place for me if I come back too."

No more certain, Helen went upstairs and opened the bag she'd brought from Greece. She lifted out the jewelry she would have worn at her wedding. It was dull with dust, but she polished it until it shone again.

How long ago it seemed that she had arrived in Utah, thinking she was here to be a bride. It seemed silly now. What kind of life would she have had with Yiannis? It might have been a happy one, but she would have missed out on the adventure of working for herself, living on her own, befriending Katherine and the other girls at Mrs. Alberti's.

She packed the clothes and linens away. Her headscarf still looked pretty and fresh since she had not worn it for long. It would do nicely if she returned to Greece. She held up the jewelry and drew a deep breath. Now for the difficult part. She had to face Demetrios again.

Helen was certain her jewelry had value, but no one would appreciate it as much as another Greek, and she wasn't sure who else to go to. She might not get enough to pay for passage to Greece, but it would be enough to survive on, maybe enough to move somewhere where there were more jobs until she could save more. This was probably the last time she would have to deal with Demetrios. She didn't understand why her heart ached at the thought.

On the walk to his shop, she savored the transition from Little

Italy to Greek Town—the subtle shift in the colors decorating the houses, the clothes hanging out to dry, the scents of roasted lamb and baking bread. A few acquaintances in Greek Town greeted her, but she tried not to linger long enough to talk. If she was leaving, what was the point of making it harder?

She reached the door of Demetrios's shop and stopped to straighten her hair before pushing the door open. The little bell over the door sang its welcome. Demetrios looked up from his counter, surprise registering on his face before he hurried forward to greet Helen.

"I've been hoping to see you," he said. "Katherine is well?"

Helen flinched a little at the reminder. "She is."

"I know you're angry, but I would trust that doctor with my life. The life of my family too. I knew he could save them both."

His words twisted in Helen's chest. Of course, he trusted in the modern, American doctor, and Katherine was grateful that he had. Perhaps he had been right, but he didn't need the opportunity to gloat, especially not after he had called her foolish. She shook her head.

"I didn't come to talk about that."

He looked confused. "Then what can I do for you today?"

"I have a few things I need to sell," she said quietly, holding out the jewelry.

He lifted a necklace to study it in the light. "You mean you wish to pawn them? I can hold onto them for a month or two."

"I don't think I'll be back for them."

He looked up quickly, and she expected a barrage of questions or a lecture. Instead, his eyes looked pained. "What has happened, Helen?"

His gentle voice nearly broke her. "It's... I'm thinking of going back to Greece. I can't do this anymore. The Klansmen. The dirty looks on the street. And the strikes shutting down the factory. If I don't go now, I may be trapped."

He watched her intently. "It will get better, you know. Things turn dark, but the sun rises again." He hurried behind the counter and pulled out an English newspaper. "Look at this. The *Deseret News*. They condemn the Klansmen and their secret societies. And they're speaking for the Mormon church leaders too. A few angry men won't last long against that kind of social clout. Soon, everything will be peaceful again. You have to admit America isn't all bad."

"It's not, but neither is Greece." Helen studied the newspaper, picking out the many words that she knew. "I'm glad things are getting better, but I can't wait for it. How will I live? I can't go back to Alexander's again." She shuddered. "I won't. At least this way I have the freedom to pick my life's direction before I run out of choices." Her gaze pleaded with Demetrios, asking him to understand.

He cleared his throat and looked at the jewelry again. "I can give you sixty dollars for these. And I will hold them in pawn for you, in case you change your mind."

Helen was too stunned to object. She took the bills and almost walked into the street holding them out in her hand, until she had the presence of mind to stuff them into her shoe. Sixty dollars! She could live on that for quite a while longer, or she could leave tomorrow. Demetrios's generosity opened up a world of options for her, and she didn't know what to do with them.

She wanted to be home. But where was her home? She closed her eyes. Blue-green waters. Villages where sheep roamed in the streets and girls fetched water from wells. Where things were simple, and the sun shone in a way it didn't anywhere else. Just before she opened her eyes, she pictured a pair of dark brown eyes laughing, but she shook that image away.

Everywhere she looked in America, doors closed. The choices that had seemed almost ripe enough to pick withered before she could pluck them. She had no choice but to return to Greece before she ended up in poverty, with all of her choices gone.

Helen went to church the next Sunday wearing her headscarf. If she was going to return to Greece, she had to give up her American customs. The scarf didn't sit right on her short hair, though, and she missed the brim of her hat shading her eyes.

She paused on the street in front of the newly-completed Orthodox church, the white granite Corinthian columns gleaming bright and steadfast in the face of prejudice. Yet the cross-shaped building was made of red American brick, as if uncertain if it belonged in Greece or Utah. Or maybe it was comfortable being some of both.

Helen shook herself. She was happy for the Greeks in Salt Lake City, that they had such a church, but it didn't mean that her place was here.

As she waited for the service to start, she overheard two men arguing.

"Strikes only hurt us. We either go without being paid or work as scabs and everyone hates us."

"Ha! We have fought for freedom from the Ottoman Empire for centuries. Here, we fight to be treated fairly, and things are improving. But we do have to fight. We have to sacrifice."

The first speaker noticed Helen watching and gestured to her. "Miss Botzaris, you're out of work because of the strike. What do you think of that?"

She was too astonished at being a part of their argument to find her voice for her moment, but then she said, "The factory was dangerous. Too dangerous. It hurts to have no pay, but...yes, it is worth it if it makes the work safer for everyone."

"Ha!" the second man said. "You see, the proud Helen Botzaris, she knows how to fight."

Helen took her seat. Proud, was she? She was proud to be a Botzaris. Proud to be Greek. She was proud to have worked to support herself.

Was she too proud to admit when she had been wrong about America? About Demetrios?

Too proud to fight for what she really wanted?

The question worried her all through the service, whispering doubts in her ear as she tried to listen to the priest. When it was over, she scanned the crowd for Demetrios. She didn't really have anything to say to him.

He had called her foolish.

He had saved Katherine's baby.

He had infuriated her with his arrogance.

He had made her see things in a whole new way.

Helen caught a glimpse of him in the back of the church, but he was heading out the door, already gone.

She stood alone in the crowd, the buzz of conversation a hollow ringing in her head. This wasn't her world anymore. Or, was it Greece that she had left behind without fully stepping through the door into America?

She slipped outside and squinted through the dirty air of the city, memorizing the spires of the Mormon temple and the round dome of the capitol building imitating the splendors of ancient Greece. The sunlight in Greece was different—brighter and more golden—and she invited the memory of it to warm her, but the image was too watery and dim. Now, it was the light of Utah's sun that heated her skin.

Her feet guided her through Greek Town, and she tried to imagine saying goodbye as she walked. Outdoor ovens baked Greek food, while electric lights and running water indoors made life a luxury. Could she go back to hauling water and obeying her male relatives, no longer working for herself and her own dreams? What was it that had brought her to America?

The air was rich with the lingering scent of coffee and baking bread. Underneath it, the faint scent of something burning tickled her nose. Not like roasted coffee beans, but the strange, acrid stench of scorched wood and fabric.

A fire! And while everyone else was at church. She broke into a run, following the scent through Greek Town. To a street she knew.

To the front of Demetrios's store.

Smoke rolled up inside the shop windows. A fiery-red painted cross slashed across the front of the building, and the door hung loose on its hinges, glass scattered on the ground. Had Demetrios stumbled onto Klansmen in the midst of their vandalism?

"Demetrios!" Helen shouted. "Demetrios!"

She stepped inside. Smoke filled her nose and made her eyes water.

The shop was in disarray, the electric heater tipped onto a smoldering rug—the source of the smoke. In a few moments, it would burst into flame, and everything inside would be ash. She tore off her headscarf and ran out to drag it through the filthy water in the gutter. With the scarf over her mouth and nose, she raced back into the smoky building.

"Demetrios!" she screamed, her voice deadened by the scarf.

She tried to peer into the back office, but she couldn't see through the smoke. She pulled her scarf from her face and battered the smoking rug with the wet fabric. It hissed and sizzled, and more smoke billowed up from the floor. She hit the rug again and again, remembering the men who put out the flaming cross with their coats.

"Helen!" a muffled voice called.

She glanced up for a moment and saw Demetrios run into the shop, a handkerchief tied over his face. He thumped his damp jacket over the rug, and Helen swatted at smoking spots with her scarf. Shoulder-to-shoulder, they battered the smoldering rug as it threatened to burst into flame. Finally, the smoke thinned, and the sodden rug squelched underfoot. They both sat back, gasping for air.

"Outside," Helen said.

Demetrios nodded and took her hand. She squeezed it back and led the way outside. She took a lungful of clean air, but before she could enjoy it, Demetrios threw his arms around her, squeezing her breath out. Too stunned to pull away, she gave in and leaned into the comfort of his chest.

"Helen." He pulled away. "What were you thinking? You could have been killed."

"Me? I thought you were in there! I couldn't lose you!"

He stared at her, and the look in his eyes sent a warm flush over her cheeks.

"Do you mean that?" he asked quietly.

Did she? She had come to American looking for her home—a home worth fighting and sacrificing for—and it had seemed all of her dreams were turning to smoke and ash when she saw the fire.

Warmth started in her heart and spread down every limb. "Yes, Demetrios."

"Helen," he breathed, and he embraced her again. "Maybe you *are* a foolish woman." She pulled back, but he laughed and added, "and I am a foolish man. A foolish, stubborn man. Forgive me?"

She nodded and let herself melt into his arms.

"I was so afraid you were going to leave," he whispered.

"But you were the one who made it possible."

"I know. That's what made it all the worse. But I wanted you to choose. I wanted—I dared to *hope*—you would choose me."

She leaned back to look into his eyes, seeing there the reflection of his humor and his seriousness, and memories of warm conversations, dancing in the speakeasy, leaning on his arm when she was frightened. "I do."

He ran his fingers over her cheek, sending shivers through her core. She tilted her face up to him. He kissed her forehead, the tip of her nose, and then his lips found hers.

Helen pulled him closer to keep her knees from buckling, not caring that they were standing on the sidewalk and anyone could see them. They were in America, and he was a good Greek man.

Demetrios pulled away, his eyes laughing. "You know, I have some beautiful bridal jewelry in pawn, though it probably needs to be polished again now."

"You don't expect me to buy it back!" Helen said, laughing breathlessly.

He grinned down at her. "I'm willing to return it as a gift on our wedding day."

She smiled up at him, thoughts of their future together filling her with the warmth of hope and soothing the pain of her past fears and longings. "You have a deal."

"But I suppose we'll have to buy you a new headscarf," he said, twirling a strand of her loose hair around his finger, and nearly making her mind numb at the distraction.

"Never mind that," she murmured. "I prefer hats."

Epilogue

"They're coming!" Demetrios called up the stairs from the shop.

Helen and Katherine glanced at each other and quickly put away their paintbrushes. Decorating Katherine's new room would have to wait. Helen dashed across the hall to her and Demetrios's bedroom and pulled out her old headscarf—scorched in places but clean and beautiful to her, rich as it was with memories of Greece and America. She met Katherine and little Georgios in the hall. They trotted downstairs to wait by Helen's favorite display in the newly-restored shop: the items handstitched by local Greek and Italian women.

Demetrios took Helen's hand, running his thumb over her knuckles to give her pleasant goose bumps. "No hat today, Mrs. Nikolaides?"

"Today, I want them to know that I am Greek."

He nodded, and together with Katherine, they hurried a few blocks to where Greek Town intersected with Little Italy. A crowd of Greeks and Italians had already gathered, silent and somber as they lined the street. Demetrios helped them wriggle their way through to a spot next to Alexander and Agatha. Helen waved to Mrs. Alberti and Maria across the way, but then they all turned their attention to the slow parade of white-hooded men marching up the street.

The men's silent march sent chills racing over Helen to settle in an icy lump in her stomach. Katherine clutched baby Georgios close, and Demetrios tightened his grip on Helen's hand.

A quiet group gathered behind the marching men: Greek and Italian boys in their Sunday finest. The parade passed into the heart of the watching crowd, and a shout went up. The boys darted forward through the parade. As they did, they grabbed robes and hoods, pulling them up and knocking them off. The marchers stood unmasked in the center of the neighborhood.

The crowd of Greeks and Italians pointed and laughed.

"Look, it's old Mr. Magnusson. I guess we won't be shopping at his store again."

"Henry Bean! Anyone here work for Henry Bean? Don't bother going in to work for him tomorrow. We all quit!"

"It's George Townsend! And he likes to sneak down to Greek Town for a coffee. We won't serve him anymore."

The Italian band struck up a lively tune, drowning out the feeble attempts of some of the Klansmen to restore order. A few tomatoes flew as the men struggled to get their robes back on. They ran off, their heads covered, and the crowd broke up into circles of celebration.

"Do you think that's the end of it?" Helen asked.

"Maybe." Demetrios draped his arm around her waist, and she snuggled into his embrace, fitting perfectly against him. "We've taken away their power of fear, at least," he said. "Now they know we won't be chased off."

Helen glanced around the crowd. Katherine held Georgios and smiled as she spoke with Maria and some of the ladies from church. Alexander laughed with a group of Greek men, while Agatha watched her children dodge around the legs of the adults. The scent of basil wafted over them, making the autumn sunlight feel warmer. In the distance, streetcar bells clanged. Helen smiled up at Demetrios.

"No, we won't. This is where we belong."

Author's Note

Helen and Demetrios are fictional characters, but this novella is based on actual events in Utah in 1924.

In 1900, the US census listed only three Greeks in Utah. By 1910, there were several thousand Greek men drawn by the opportunities for work in the mines and railroads, but only a handful of Greek women. Many of the men had only come to America to earn money to support their parents or families back home in Greece, but some decided to stay and sent for "picture brides" to come to Utah and marry them after exchanging pictures (not always their own!). The women were willing to make the dangerous journey because Greece was struggling with the effects of economic depression and war, and without dowries, they could not find husbands in Greece.

The Greeks in Utah, as in the rest of America, faced prejudice because of their ethnicity, language, and religion. They were paid less than American-born workers and often worked in the most dangerous jobs. They had to pay bribes to wealthy Greek labor agents like Utah's Leonidas Skliris for these less-desirable jobs.

Though the KKK opposed Utah's dominant Church of Jesus Christ of Latter-day Saints (Latter-day Saints or Mormons), it still found a foothold in Utah for a time, even among some Latter-day Saints. The

KKK attacked Greeks and other immigrants, burning crosses on hillsides and in yards (such as the Greek man who married an Anglo American woman), and vandalizing businesses suspected of selling bootlegged liquor. Despite Utah's straight-laced reputation, it had its share of speakeasies and moonshiners during the 1920s.

The Castle Gate Mine disaster remains one of the top ten worst mine disasters in United States history, and the second-worst in Utah after the Scofield Mine disaster of 1900. Over 170 men died in a series of explosions in the Castle Gate Mine in March of 1924, including Greeks, Scots, Englishmen, Italians, Welshmen, Japanese, Austrians, Anglo-Americans, and African-Americans. The mine had recently laid off many of the single men due to a drop in demand for coal, so it was mostly married men with children who were killed. Unlike the Scofield Mine disaster, the widows and orphans of Castle Gate were awarded a small monthly stipend.

Factory work during this time was dangerous for all workers, and unions to protect workers' rights were discouraged in Utah. Despite this, there were occasional strikes—especially among miners—as workers sought better pay and safer working conditions.

Despite these hardships, the Greeks and other immigrants persisted. The first Greek church in Utah, built in Salt Lake City in 1905, became too small to serve the Orthodox community, so the Greeks bought land to begin the Holy Trinity Greek Orthodox Church in Salt Lake City in 1923, which still stands today. This church is the only remaining building from what was once a thriving Greek Town in Salt Lake City.

Though the descendants of these Utah Greek immigrants are now fairly assimilated into mainstream culture, they remain proud of their heritage and hold an annual Greek Festival in Salt Lake City.

To learn more about the Greek experience in Utah, I recommend the writings of Greek American historian and Utah native Helen Papanikolas, especially *An Amulet of Greek Earth* and *A Greek Odyssey in the American West*

Thank you to my critique partners in the Cache Valley chapter of the League of Utah Writers, UPSSEFW, and the Clandestines—you constantly push me to be a better writer. Thanks to Heather Maloney for beta reading. I also owe a great deal to the late Helen Papanikolas for her research and writing on the Greeks of Utah. And, as always, I couldn't do any of this without my wonderful family and all of their support.

About E.B. Wheeler

E.B. Wheeler attended BYU, majoring in history with an English minor, and earned graduate degrees in history and landscape architecture from Utah State University. She's the author of ten books, including Whitney Award finalist *Born to Treason*, as well as several award-winning short stories, magazine articles, and scripts for educational software programs. The League of Utah Writers named her the 2016 Writer of the Year. In addition to writing, she consults about historic preservation and teaches history at USU.

Other Books by E.B. Wheeler

British Historical Fiction:

The Haunting of Springett Hall

Born to Treason

The Royalist's Daughter

Wishwood

Moon Hollow

Utah Historical Fiction:

No Peace with the Dawn (with Jeffery Bateman)

Letters from the Homefront

The Bone Map

Blood in a Dry Town

Utah Women: Pioneers, Poets & Politicians (nonfiction)

www.ingramcontent.com/pod-product-compliance
Lightning Source LLC
Chambersburg PA
CBHW060429180626
46817CB00007B/2732